To all my devoted readers who made my dreams come true.
I love you with all my heart.

1

New Beginnings

My car tires crunch on the leaves as I round yet another curve on the one-lane road. The window of my twenty-five-year-old Mazda, which previously served its purpose as a family car, is rolled down to leave a gap. As I drive, picking up speed after the corner, the perilous wind finds its way inside, bringing the smell of wood and melancholy.

Bridgevale is a small town in Idaho. It has a population of fewer than one thousand people—nine hundred and seventy-three, to be precise—I looked it up last night. The town is known for its mountainous landscapes and secluded lakes. It'll be my home for the next three years.

I pull up to the immense house, releasing a heavy breath. It looks the same as in the pictures—a gray square building with a pitched roof. I've resigned myself to the fact my last-minute choice to attend university would result in a dull living situation, but now that I'm here, it doesn't look half bad.

It was my dad who persuaded me to get out of our town and start over. Easier said than done. But we both know that I will never stop blaming myself for the accident if I continue to stay at home.

I do my best to block out the raw and agonizing memories, but I still find myself silently crying into my pillow every now and then, more often than not. The last two years of my life have been an onerous blur of events.

I've applied to universities in advance, however, I wasn't sure if I'd be attending. It wasn't until a week ago that I've finally agreed with my dad about getting out of the house.

Given that classes start on Monday, I couldn't get a dorm on campus with such short notice. I also can't afford to rent a place on my own. I looked at ads on the university's Facebook page and found this place right away.

Walking up to the door, I hope this will be a much-needed fresh start. A new beginning—as lousy as that sounds.

Now that I'm in front of it, the house stretches wider, taller. I knock on the wooden, olive green door. I don't take my bags, in case this is the wrong house, but I'm sure it isn't.

A petite girl wearing a bright yellow sundress and cream ballet flats answers the door, I recognize her immediately as Olivia. We've been texting for a few days, and I stalked her Facebook profile before agreeing to this. I'm secretly praying this isn't some sort of sorority house.

"You're Carlotta, right?" she asks with a smile. I shudder at the sound of my full name. It's not that I dislike it—it's that the only person who had ever used it, is now dead. So, I guess you could say I prefer not to hear it. I sent Olivia a photo of my driver's license, and since she's never used my name over messages, I haven't been able to correct her yet.

"Calla." I force a smile, so I don't seem rude.

"Cool. Call me Liv," she says, her curls bouncing on her shoulders with every word. "Do you need help with your bags?"

"Yeah, sure. Thanks," I say. From what Liv has already mentioned about the house through text messages, I know to find my bedroom upstairs, across the hall from hers. Luckily, the room is already furnished with the basics—a bed, a desk, etc. Courtesy of the landlord. I brought my books and clothes to last me the first year.

"Zach!" Liv calls, and a blond boy appears behind her. He's half a foot taller than her and has the physical build of a basketball player. His brown eyes sparkle brighter from the warm color of autumn encompassing us.

He plants a kiss on Liv's cheek, and she giggles. "This is my boyfriend Zach," she introduces. He beams at me. "Zach, this our new housemate, Calla. Be nice."

He rolls his eyes at her warning. "I am *always* nice. Who do you take me for?" he jokes. "It's nice to meet you, Calla." He extends his hand like a gentleman.

I take it, and he gives me a light, friendly squeeze before returning his attention to Liv.

Zach wraps his arm around her waist, and she leans into him. My mind drifts to Nate. Nate, who broke up with me a few months ago in anticipation of a carefree, single life at the same university I've only *just* decided to attend. I don't condemn him, but there's still a part of me that wishes things were different.

Nate is one of the few people who was there for me after the accident. Despite what he said about wanting to enjoy university, the accident played a substantial part in why we broke up.

I pushed everyone away. I wanted to be alone, all the time, like isolating myself would somehow rehabilitate me. In reality, I was punishing myself, but that made me want to isolate myself more.

Carrying in a box from the car, I allow my eyes to wander. Inside, the vast space swallows me up, at least I don't have to worry about the house being too small. The floors are wooden and dark gray under my boots—I hope this place has heating.

At first glance, the place summarizes what I imagined a college house to look like. It's shabby and full of hard edges. The only compromise to comfort is the old shaggy rug, which fills the living room and has seen better days. By the stairs, a green plant rests in a large pot. How has it survived this long?

"Is it just you two? The ad said three housemates?" I ask. A hint of vanilla and citrus brushes against my skin when Liv stands next to me.

"There's Ace as well. He won't be here until Monday, though," Liv informs. "He usually keeps to himself. His room is down here." She gestures, pointing to the door in the corner, away from everything.

"Anyways, I'm so glad you're here! I was worried about living with just boys." She shudders, scrunching her nose in disgust.

After they help me carry my stuff to my room, I receive a key and a brief explanation of the house rules. There's a bathroom across the hall from my room, which I'll be sharing with them. Ace has his own bathroom in his room.

I can also bring anyone over so long as it isn't a guy from their rival, Ashworth University. Apparently, there's been a feud between them since anyone can remember. I agree with the terms, needless to say, I'm not interested in bringing guys here or anywhere.

Liv leaves to let me settle in and reminds me to let her know if I need anything. She glides out of my room, her gentle curls bouncing behind her.

My room is bigger than I expected and makes me glad I found

this place. My housemates seem normal and might even make good friends.

I unpack my clothes, hanging mostly everything in the closet and setting the rest in the small dresser by the pale green wall. I stack my books on the ground near the desk and sigh. Biting my nails, I realize I have no idea what university is going to be like.

I glance out the window. Why would anyone choose to rent this to students? This is more of a vacation house. It's hidden in a secluded area, away from the university share houses, and it took me longer than anticipated to find the street that leads here.

The view from my room is magical. I've always appreciated fall—that's one of the few things in my life that still hasn't changed. The air is crisp, just how I like it, and the trees are on fire with color. I smile at the inferno near my window, remembering how my mom always scolded me for bringing leaves into the house.

I would do anything to hear her voice again—to see her. My mother had always put everyone else before herself. She was kind-hearted, and passionate for a breath of life. She didn't deserve what happened to her, and it was all my fault.

My eyes stare out the window, not really looking at anything in particular; however, a lake in the distance captures my attention. It peers at me with tranquility and invitation—the stillness of it forming a glass mirror with golden orange hues of the scenery around.

I make a mental note to take a walk in that direction during the week. I might even bring my journal and write. Even though it used to be my favorite thing to do, I haven't written anything in two years—perhaps a new beginning will mend that.

I decide to call my dad to let him know I arrived and that no, I don't want him to get one of his many cop friends to check up on me. That's the last thing I need.

I dial his number, and he picks up on the first ring.

"Hey, Cals, I was getting worried. Did you get there okay?" he asks.

"Yeah, sorry. I was just unpacking," I say, sitting on the pink blanket on my bed.

"How is it? Do they seem nice? You know, if you don't like it, I can give you more money to get your own place," he frets. He means well, but we both know he already struggles with the bills. There's no way he'd be able to afford it.

"It's good. They're nice," I assure him.

"Don't just say that, Cals. If I find out there's some funny business going on, I will bring a whole damn SWAT team," my dad barks, and I sigh, knowing it isn't a joke.

Even though he's the one who encouraged me to pursue my dreams, a sense of guilt gnaws at me for leaving him all alone in that house.

My heart has always been set on becoming a journalist, on writing stories and building a voice for those who don't have one. Perhaps, no matter how cliché it sounds, I want to believe that I can change the world in a way that no one else can.

After reassuring my dad that I'm okay and there's no need for him to check up on me, I finally end the call. I'm surprised he didn't lecture me on boys and parties, he must be relieved I'm finally out of that house.

Lying back on my bed, I turn to gaze toward the lake, the mountains, the quiescence of time.

Eventually, I drift off to sleep. The first day of university will probably be an absolute disaster—from the possible run-in with Nate and not knowing many people, to being in a foreign place. I need all the rest I can get.

2

First Day

My alarm goes off on Monday, triggering my panic. I attempt to talk myself out of this feeling—*everyone goes to university, everyone is new at some point, you're going to be okay*—but the uneasiness lingers as I get ready.

I'm apprehensive that everyone will already know each other. Most of them attended the same high school, half an hour away. I'm just someone who moved two hours from my hometown because I couldn't get into any other university, thanks to pitiable grades and a lack of attendance. But also, in hopes of escaping trauma.

The scalding water runs down my back as I stand under the shower, mindlessly staring at the chipped tiles on the wall—mentally preparing myself for the day ahead.

I put a little extra effort into my appearance for the first time in a long time, wearing my best pair of high-waisted jeans and a cream-colored sweater with baggy sleeves. I leave my straight hair loose and un-styled, dabbing a little concealer under my eyes. One last glance in the mirror, and I'm good to go.

Liv and Zach offer me a ride to class, but I decline. I have a meeting with the chancellor in the afternoon, and I don't want to make them wait for me, so I follow them in my car instead. The campus isn't far, only a five-minute drive.

Trailing the narrow road, my eyes wander to the trees that radiate hues of yellow, orange, and red. They're positioned close to each other, and the thick branches extend at the top toward each side, delivering the feeling of driving through a tunnel with surrounding flames.

We arrive at the campus a little early, and they show me around. Zach is a sophomore, so he takes the lead as a tour guide. Surprisingly, the campus is bigger than it seemed in the photos. One massive building is a soft ambiance of red brick, divided into different sections for each department, and to the right side, the dorms are located.

Zach leads us across the field, where football is played throughout the year. Bridgevale University is famous for its athletic scholarships, hence the main hallway in the building is dedicated to trophies and medallions.

A boy with light brown hair calls to Zach, running toward us. "Hey, man, didn't I tell you to wait for me?" He grins.

His gaze flickers to me, and his smile grows wider. As if on cue, Liv gestures toward me. "This is our new housemate, Calla. Don't try anything funny," she warns him. I'm thankful for Liv, I've barely spent any time with her, and already, she seems like someone I would get along with, or *used* to get along with.

The brown-haired boy capes his arm around my shoulder like we know each other already. "Theo," he introduces himself cockily.

"Hey! I said no funny business," Liv cries, swatting his arm away from me. I emit a small laugh.

Theo scrunches his face into a pout, he's kind of cute. He

reminds me of a grizzly bear—he's even built like one, tall with broad shoulders, a footballer's body. I bet he plays too.

To my surprise, Theo is in two of my first lectures, and I find myself relaxing now that I know someone. It's comforting getting to know a group of friends for the first time in a long time. They all seem to adopt and welcome me into their group with open arms. From what I can gather, they all went to the same high school—but Zach is a year older. There's also Ace, who I haven't encountered yet, but I'm sure he'll be just as welcoming.

Theo and I head toward our first class and fall into small talk. "I live down the road, in the frat house. The best way to experience university life." He grins.

"I guessed as much. The t-shirt gives it away." I examine it. The black t-shirt states: *warning, may contain alcohol.*

"You don't like it?" he asks, feigning to seem shocked.

"It suits you."

The class has less than thirty people, not surprising for a town with a small population. All the students are scattered across the room, away from each other. Theo heads for the empty spot at the front, and I trail him.

"What are you majoring in?" I ask Theo during our lecture.

"Engineering," he answers proudly. I widen my eyes, I wasn't expecting that answer from the goofy attitude.

"Smart and pretty." I wink, and his grin spills with pride.

"I'm here on a football scholarship, but the school forced me to take this English Sociology class for extra credit—it was the only way they'd accept me into the program, since I didn't get the best grades in high school," he explains.

His eyes dart back to the professor before facing me again. "So, what brings you here?"

"The only university that accepted my stupid ass," I joke, hoping I didn't offend him. Theo cocks his head to the side, and my need to explain rises. "School wasn't on my mind for the last couple of years..."

It's not that I'm unintelligent and witless—I was the top student in my class—*was* being the key word here. I *was* doing great before the universe decided to ruin me. After that, I stopped trying.

I don't want to bring out the sob story about the accident. And I appreciate when Theo nods and doesn't press me for further information.

There's a forty-minute break before my next class, and Theo insists we meet up with Zach and Liv. I'm hesitant because they are all so close—I don't want to intrude in their friendship group.

"It's fine. Don't you want to hang with the cool kids?" he asks and throws his arm over my shoulder, leading me out of the classroom.

We arrive at a cafe down the road from the university. The building is painted navy blue with a matching wooden bench to the right. A clear sign hangs from the pitched roof: *Cosmos Café*. I like that this town is small, it saves me a whole lot of gas money.

Liv spots us and waves us over toward the corner where they're located. She sits next to Zach, and there's a blond guy in a multi-colored button-up shirt across from them that I don't recognize.

Theo walks up and slaps the blondie playfully across the back of the head. The blondie turns around, and as soon as he realizes who it is, his mouth turns up into a wry smile. He's out of the booth in one swift motion and attempting to tackle Theo in the middle of the café. I stare at them with wide eyes. I glance around the café, but no one else is paying attention to their childish behavior. Liv and Zach entirely ignore them. This must be their usual conduct between each other.

"I see you found yourself a girl. Finally, Theodore." Blondie runs a hand through his messed-up hair. I'm about to object, but he flashes me a toothy grin.

"I'm kidding," he says. "The day Theo gets a girlfriend, we'll all be doomed. I'm Josh, by the way."

"Speak for yourself, Evans," Theo grumbles, not impressed by Josh's comment, and slides into the seat next to me.

How does Liv deal with all the testosterone in the air? She must be used to it by now. "How long have you guys known each other?" I ask.

"Since before we knew how to walk. We all grew up in Wallace," Zach tells me.

"Are you coming to the party on Friday night?" Theo interrupts, looking up at me.

Me? Party? I don't think so.

"Of course she's coming," Liv answers, and I glance around the café uncomfortably.

"Uh, I don't really do parties," I say quietly. They stare at me like I said the sky is falling.

"C'mon, it'll be fun," Liv presses.

"You have to come. It's the first party of the season," Josh joins in. "Everyone is going to be there."

The fact that everyone is going to be at the party doesn't make it sound appealing. They're all looking at me, waiting for me to agree, and there's no way I can get out of this one.

"I guess I can come for a little bit?" It comes out as a question.

"Great! I'm so excited!" Liv exclaims, and I force a smile.

✦

I wait out the front of the chancellor's office. Since I accepted the university offer so late, the chancellor requires to go over a few things. I'm uncertain what they are, but I assume it will be the standard—a brief welcome, and perhaps a discussion about any future goals or what I plan to achieve with my time here.

Yelling originates from the office, and my head snaps up. Who can possibly be yelling at the chancellor on the first day of the semester?

I try not to eavesdrop, but it's hard with all the bellowing and swearing. I can't decipher what they are talking about, but whatever it is, it seems heated and not university-related. Something about a competition and bigoted terms.

"You are so fucking fortunate that I'm in a good mood," the voice growls. Goosebumps crawl up my arms—if that's the good mood, then I wouldn't wish to hear him in a bad mood, whoever it is.

There's silence for a moment, followed by a loud thump, like a fist striking a wooden desk. I gulp loudly, and my heart beats faster. Maybe I ought to come back later.

I stand to leave, but at the same time, the door flies open. Something hard collides with my body, and I stumble back, spilling my coffee. My bag slips from my shoulder and tumbles onto the floor.

"Why the fuck are you in the way?" a voice growls.

"Sorry," I manage to squeeze out in a small voice. This is one of the things I wanted to avoid on my first day. I don't look at him, afraid to meet his glare—instead, I eye his shirt, ensuring no coffee spilled on him. But it's hard to tell, since it's midnight black.

He sighs and bends down to pick up my bag. "Here." His voice is rough, with pique still present. He shoves my bag into my hands, and my eyes scan the tattoos that cover his arms. There are different images scattered across his skin, yet they also manage to tie in together.

I keep my head down, avoiding eye contact with him, but I sense his eyes piercing into me. Why is he still standing here?

Don't look. Don't look.

I foolishly look up at him.

His eyes instantly attract my attention, intimidating and intense. They are the most cavernous I've ever seen, a mix of blue, gray and green.

He meets my gaze, and when our eyes lock, there's a flicker of recognition, perhaps a hint of admission too. Either way, something in them transforms and shifts his demeanor.

"Are you done staring?" he snaps. I drop my eyes to the ground in embarrassment. Apparently, it didn't shift his demeanor too much.

"Next time, watch where you're fucking going," he snarls and turns on his heel, not offering me a second glance.

"Asshole," I call, loud enough for him to hear. He doesn't turn around.

I'm left dumbfounded and outraged. That's precisely the kind of person I don't want to deal with, a bad boy with a bad attitude. I make a mental note to stay away from him, that should prove to be effortless. I head into the chancellor's office in a foul mood.

The chancellor is a man in his low thirties, this surprises me, as I expected him to be older. He folds his hands, and his eyes, drooped down on his face, scan the file that rests on top of the desk.

"Calla Maven, is it?" His voice is raspy, and he clears his throat.

I nod.

"Mr. Howley. Take a seat." He motions to the empty chair in front of his desk, coughing into his hand. I take the seat. "I see that you accepted our offer late. Were you considering other options?"

"I had my mind on other matters," I answer carefully, aiming not to get myself in deep waters where the truth is required. The last thing I want to talk about is the events that led me in this direction.

"Hmph," he emits, scrutinizing the file like he's expecting for words to appear or for me to say something. I don't.

"I looked over your file and noticed that you're interested in a journalism major. We have some great programs that could boost you into that career, and we have partners all over the country—including New York, if that's something you would be interested in."

It's always been a dream of mine to live in a big city and experience the world. My mom pushed me toward my goals, reminding me that there's nothing I couldn't achieve. *If you yearn for it and work for it, there's no reason why you won't fulfill every dream.* The words echo in my head, reminding me of the power they once held.

"That would be something I'd be interested in."

The chancellor nods, his dull brown hair catching the sun through the window—with some grays already present. He continues, "However, I have also noticed that your grades from your last year at high school have dropped tremendously. I want to give you a chance. Therefore, I have taken it upon myself to enroll you in English Sociology. It's a class for students who may not have had the best grades—to gain extra credit."

In the class I had with Theo this morning, I recall him mentioning that he was required to take it if he wanted to keep his football scholarship.

"Of course," I say. If this university can allow me to work in one of the world's biggest cities, then I'm prepared to study my ass off.

"Great. I would suggest taking up some volunteer work at the university, perhaps something relatively similar to your major, such as writing a column in the school newspaper a few times a month," the chancellor continues.

I haven't written anything in a long time, let alone shared my work with the whole school. But my mom's words continue to repeat themselves over and over—I doubt many people read the university newspaper. "Sure."

For the remainder of the appointment, Mr. Howley discusses the different departments here and subtly gives directions to the school therapist's office. He provides me with an email for the person who deals with the newspaper, instructing me to send an article about what I feel is appropriate when I'm ready and they will consider it.

On my way back to the house, I contemplate if I made the right decision coming here—to this university, to this town. Perhaps a gap year wouldn't have been so bad. I could have enrolled in programs to gain extra credit, and that would've boosted my GPA. Yet, I sincerely doubt I would have done that. Instead, I would've made up an excuse and continued to mope. I made the right choice, I hope.

"How was the rest of your day?" Liv beams at me as I amble inside the house. She sits on the kitchen counter, popping grapes into her mouth—living the dream.

I roll my eyes and sigh.

"What happened?" she probes. The earlier incident outside the chancellor's office still weighs snugly in my chest.

"Ugh," I groan. "Some wannabe bad boy, asshole—" I begin, but Liv's attention isn't on me anymore. I stop mid-sentence and slowly turn to follow Liv's gaze.

The wannabe bad boy, asshole, is standing in front of me. His glare bores into mine.

"Ace," Liv greets him.

3

Ace

Ace towers over me. "The fuck is *she* doing here?" he growls. I lift my head to meet his contemptuous stare and once again, I'm drawn to his beautiful eyes. The rest of his face is firmly defined. His eyebrows are furrowed, his full lips are drawn into a line, and a dark stubble contours his jaw.

Even though he's fully clothed, his muscles ripple across every part of his body. Most guys here participate in sports, hence their toned bodies—such a shame that the looks in before me went to waste on an asshole.

"Ace, I told you we would be getting a housemate. You were fine with it," Liv reminds him in a calming tone.

"Not her," he says. His eyes don't leave mine—flames dance in them, the anger transparently present with no hint of mercy.

"Excuse me?" I ask. I can't comprehend what I did for him to detest me so much. Sure, today's incident was unpleasant, but I barely said anything to him, apart from calling him an asshole. In my defense, I had every right, since he was behaving like one.

"Calm down, you're acting like a child," Liv says unpretentiously. She turns her body to face him, swinging her legs around the counter.

"She needs to go," he declares slowly. His hands ball up into fists at his side. I should be afraid of him, and I am, only a little. He's intimidating, especially when his jaw is ticking like that. He fascinates me with the amount of anger he holds. Who spit in his breakfast today?

"Um, I can go pack my bags," I state. That's obviously the only solution—coming here was a bad idea. I'm using this complication as an escape route, but I doubt anyone in my position would have a different outlook.

"Oh no, definitely not. You're not going," Liv tells me, but she keeps her eyes on Ace. They stare at each other for a few moments, and surprisingly, Ace is the first to break eye contact.

He storms to his room and slams the door so vigorously that I jump from the impact. Seconds later, troubling sounds derive from his direction. I stare at the closed door, not understanding what happened. Is he breaking things? That guy has some serious anger issues, but Liv acts like everything is fine, chewing her grape with pleasure. I assume this isn't the first or second time this has happened.

"I'm so sorry, I didn't know he would act like this. He's not usually *this* bad," Liv tries to reassure me.

"I might have pissed him off by bumping into him in the chancellor's office," I admit, even though I know it wasn't my fault.

"Oh," she says and furrows her eyebrows. "Did Ace talk to De—I mean, the chancellor?" she corrects herself.

"Uh, more like yelled," I admit, and she nods.

There's silence between us as her eyes don't leave Ace's door like she's considering going in there and putting some sense into him herself.

"What's going on?" Zach staggers down the stairs, stretching his arms over his head and stifling a yawn. His hair is tousled and swiped to the side, his eyes bloodshot.

"Ace is here…and he's in one of his moods," Liv replies as if that explains everything. "Can you go make sure he doesn't damage any walls? Otherwise, he'll be paying to fix them."

Zach sighs and glances in the direction of Ace's room. He gives Liv another look, but she urges him to go. He closes his eyes for a moment and rolls his neck from shoulder to shoulder. He then proceeds to shuffle to the door as if it's a chore and closes it behind him.

"Sorry, you must want to run for the hills after this," Liv says.

I do, but I consider my other housing options. The dorms are full—I can go online and see if there's anything else available.

"I can leave if it's a problem," I tell her. I don't want to be where I'm not wanted.

"No, you're not leaving because of him. I like you, and so does everyone else," Liv says. Except for Ace, but I keep my mouth shut.

"Ace is just Ace," she tells me as if reading my mind. I don't know what that means. I nod slowly and take the stairs to my room. There are no destructive noises anymore, so I assume Zach tamed the wild animal.

I shut my bedroom door and lay on my bed. Reaching for my laptop, I search for other accommodation around here. There isn't much, unless I want to live at an actual sorority house.

I refuse to give up after a little hiccup gets in the way. But Ace doesn't seem like a minor hiccup, he's a damn downpour, and I'm uncertain if I'll be able to survive near someone like that. I plan to keep my distance. It may prove to be strenuous since we'll be living under the same roof—although not impossible.

Staring at the ceiling, my chest is heavy with exasperation. For all I know, this may be the first obstacle the universe is throwing at me, something I'm required to overcome.

Prevailing over the asshole.

My classes commence a little later today. When I wake up, the house is empty—thank God for that. Slipping my feet into my fluffy bunny slippers, I head toward the bathroom, turning the shower on and allowing the water to heat up before stepping inside.

When it nears nine o'clock, I grab my laptop and two textbooks from my room and head downstairs toward my car.

"Hey, Calla, over here!" Theo calls once I arrive at class. I turn in his direction only to discover the beautiful-eyed monster glaring at me. I may not have thought this through. Of course, Theo is friends with Ace. It makes sense since they're all one group.

Theo motions me to come and sit next to him, and I weigh the options in my head. If I sit next to Theo, Ace will most likely be furious. If I don't, I will have to sit alone. I don't have many friends here, and I'm not about to lose the only friends I've made because of some jerk who thinks he's entitled.

I make my way over to Theo, clutching my bag to my chest. My nails dig into my palms. "Hey." I slide into the seat.

"Have you met Ace?" Theo asks me, turning toward him. "Of course, you two met, you're living together," he realizes.

Ace doesn't pay attention to me anymore. Instead, his focus is the pencil that he's twirling between his rough fingers. I'm unsure if that's better or worse—what's his problem? He's been overly hostile, rude, and destructive since the moment we've met, for absolutely no reason—his behavior is unsettling, to say the least.

After class, Theo informs me everyone is going to the café again this afternoon. A subtle invitation into their group. Will *he* be there? My eyes shift to Ace over Theo's shoulder, but he doesn't react. He's still ignoring my existence.

"Okay, I'll meet you there," I tell Theo. He sends me a boyish grin, showing a full row of pearly whites.

After parking my car across the road from the café, I cross the quiet street. I'm reminded that I should get a job for after class and weekend work. The guilt of my dad paying for everything is gnawing at me from every direction.

When I reach the large, blue door, my eyes shift to the flyer on the window, and my breath hitches in my throat. It's as though the universe knows I require a reason to stay.

Tugging the flyer off the door, I head inside. Liv notices me immediately and begins to wave me down, the bangles on her wrist clanking together. I motion to her with one finger, saying 'one second,' and shuffle to the counter.

A curvy blond girl with pink bangs approaches me and withdraws her notepad. "What can I get you, babe?"

She twirls the pen on the ends of her hair—she seems around my age, and I gather she attends Bridgevale University too.

I place the flyer on the counter in front of her. "You're hiring." It isn't a question, but the uncertainty in my voice hints for a confirmation.

"I'll get my uncle," she says and looks over me. A smile forms on her painted pink lips. She walks toward the back of the shop, and before she disappears behind the small green door, she turns back to me. "I'm Mia."

"Calla," I reply, echoing her smile.

I fiddle with my fingers as I wait for her uncle, picking at the dead skin. I glance over my shoulder at the group, and Theo catches my eye, flashing me a comforting smile. His expression quickly turns quizzical. Before I can silently explain the situation to him, my attention snaps back at the sound of footsteps approaching.

The man in front of me is nothing like I expected. His long shabby hair and beard fill most of his face, but his dark blue eyes, blue enough that they seem as though they belong in the deepest part of the ocean, take the stage. I can't pinpoint an age bracket for him. A part of him looks young enough to fit into university, and the other part, seems old enough to be my dad.

"You're looking for a job, aye?" he asks and runs his tongue over his front teeth, resulting in a sucking noise. His voice is filled with a thick Australian accent. What brought him here?

"Yes." I nod in agreement.

"Perfect, you're hired," he says and staggers back behind the green door without turning around. I stand frozen in place, perplexed by the 'interview.'

Mia delivers a sympathetic smile. "I'm sorry, I should have warned you before getting him. He doesn't say much and goes off his 'vibes,' as he likes to call them. I guess you ticked the box."

"Oh," is all I manage to say.

"When can you start?" she asks me.

"Tomorrow. I have class until two, but I can make it by two-thirty?" I take into account how long it will take me to drive home and change after class.

"That's no problem. I'll see you tomorrow. We can talk about the rest then." Mia smiles. I take that as my cue to leave—there are already a few people waiting to be served behind me.

As I walk toward the group, I can't help but notice how… simple it was to get a job, how easy it is to fall into a group of friends—everything is lining up for some unexplainable reason. The only contradiction is Ace.

Theo and Josh are quarreling over who gets the last slice of pizza. "It's mine. You already had your half," Josh argues.

"But you don't even want it, man. You just said you're full," Theo reasons, reaching for the slice.

Josh smacks his hand away. "I changed my mind."

The more time I spend with them, the more I understand how they communicate with one another. They act like brothers, but there's no resemblance whatsoever—I assume they have known each other for a long time, more than the rest of the group.

"Did you just get a job?" Liv raises an eyebrow at me as I slump next to Theo. It's the only space that's available in the booth. She's holding a small pocket mirror and fixing her rosy lips with a cosmetic pencil.

"Uh, yeah, but the boss seems a little strange," I admit, and she laughs like that's already a known fact.

"Yeah, he is," she agrees and leans into Zach subconsciously. He kisses her on the cheek and whispers something in her ear. I turn away to give them a little privacy. Theo and Josh are still arguing, unaware of my presence.

My eyes travel across the table and land on Ace. He's already looking at me. He doesn't bother concealing it or glancing away, his eyes are lined in dark shadows. I hold his gaze in a challenge. His threatening behavior radiates an enigmatic ambiance, and it intrigues me.

"I didn't see you there." Theo beams as he turns to face me, throwing his brawny arm over my shoulder in a friendly gesture, at the same time interrupting the eye contact between Ace and me.

"Hey." I smile back at him.

"You're still coming to the party?" Josh pops his head over Theo's shoulder, a smile that would usually tug at every heartstring on show.

"Do I have a choice?" I sigh, hoping to get out of it. I have some schoolwork to catch up on and an article to write.

"Definitely not," Liv joins in.

4

Unfortunate Incidents

A few days have passed without another dreadful incident. I've settled in at my new accommodation and acquainted myself with my class schedule. Every day the group meets at the café to catch up and fill each other in on their days. I find myself joining them when I can, in between classes and work.

Stepping onto the foam mat after a steamy shower, I still myself as the sound of my phone ringing echoes through the house. It's coming from downstairs, where I must have left it after arriving home from my classes this afternoon.

The only person who reaches me on my number is my dad. Since arriving here on Friday, I haven't called him. He must be getting ready to get into his patrol car and drive here himself. I'm excited to tell him that I've found a job, and everything is falling into place. I'm making friends, and the classes are engrossing—maybe it wasn't such an awful idea to come here after all.

The house is empty. Liv texted me earlier in the day to notify me she and Zach went out to a movie and won't be home till late. Wrapping a towel around my body, I rush downstairs to answer my phone.

Clutching the stair handrail, I round the corner into the kitchen and collide with something hard. *Someone* hard.

My head throbs, and I'm convinced I can see stars for a few seconds. The towel that I held onto for dear life has now fallen at my ankles as I struggle to come back to my senses. When I do, I find myself in a situation that I'd rather be unconscious for.

I'm naked—absolutely and utterly naked—except for my fluffy bunny slippers and staring into a pair of amused eyes.

Ace.

To make matters worse, Ace is shirtless himself. I'm unable to move fast enough, reaching for the towel that I dropped, I cover myself. It doesn't change the reality of this situation. He's already seen me naked. It can't possibly get any worse than this.

My eyes trail down his body, I can't seem to control myself. He must've had a shower in his bathroom as well. His hair is damp, and droplets cling to his chest.

I don't have to see myself to know that my face has turned a shade of crimson. My mouth opens, but nothing comes out. I'm embarrassed to the point of going mute. This is just splendid!

"I thought I told you to watch where you're going," Ace snaps. I'm not sure why I act surprised. He's rude every time we have the pleasure of interacting.

The shadow of the cloudy afternoon peeking through the kitchen window creates his eyes to appear darker, enraged. I get the indication this must be his usual demeanor, some people are just bad-tempered.

"What's your problem?" I snap back at him, my own anger taking over. "What have I done for you to resent me?"

His face softens a little, but that could be my imagination. "Just stay out of my way," he warns and strides away from me, slamming his bedroom door behind him.

I groan in frustration. It's like drawing blood from a stone.

Climbing the creaking wooden stairs back to my room, I press my dad's contact. "Hey, sorry I missed your call," I say once he picks up.

"Hey, Cals. I'm just ringing to make sure you're okay. I can't help but worry," my dad says through the phone.

"It's okay, Dad." I understand his uneasiness.

He's the last parent I have left, and I'm his only child. We survived the most challenging time together, but perhaps the trauma left our relationship hindered in more ways than one. We don't talk about the accident. We barely talk about *her*.

"I'm doing fine. I've met some friends, and I might be doing some articles for the university's newspaper," I tell him. If my dad understands that I'm progressing, then he'll stop worrying about me so much.

"Oh," he says, surprised. "That's great! I'm proud of you for giving this a chance, kiddo." After a few seconds, he adds, "Your mom would be too."

My mom was an English teacher, passionate about the world. Although, at times, I wonder if she had been too invested in idealism. She was continuously lost in the presence of words, the consumption of them seeping through pages and pages of her journals. I have yet to bring myself to read her journals, which reside in my childhood home's attic.

There were times when I sat in my room, staring at them—unable to go past the cover. I'm afraid that I would finally lose every part of my mom if I did read them. I'm not prepared for that.

"How are you doing, Dad? Is everything okay back home? Are

the bills paid?"

My dad tends to leave things forgotten when he gets too overwhelmed with them. We don't particularly struggle financially, but we also don't have spare money, especially with only one income and my college tuition that my dad's paying for. I took out a student loan, but my dad insisted on paying for some of the degree—claiming he's been putting money away for it ever since I was five.

"Don't worry about that, I'll manage. You don't need to look after me. Focus on your studies. Start over, make friends…live a little," he says, but I'm not convinced. There's not much I can do except take his word for it.

A few days pass. I attend my classes and work three shifts at the café—I haven't run into Mia's uncle, Brody, since the 'interview.' Essentially, Mia takes care of the front end of the café and Brody does the back-end while also working on a "project." Unfortunately, Mia gave me no clarification on what that project entails. Nevertheless, it's refreshing to busy myself with tasks and get into the routine of being a university student.

Friday afternoon rolls around, and everyone is diverted by the conversation of the first party of the semester.

"Come, sit. I'll do your makeup." Liv ushers me to a chair near her dressing table—not granting me a chance to decline. Makeup brushes are strewn on the table with every eyeshadow color imaginable.

"Have you ever been to one of these?" I ask as Liv twirls one of the brushes on my closed eyelid.

I've been to house parties before, in my sophomore and senior years. It was something that everyone was doing, and being one of the popular girls in school, it was almost a given that I had to attend.

Liv laughs. "Not a frat party, but I've been to plenty of house parties. You'll be fine. Drink, have fun," she reassures me. There's an uneasy presentiment that this will be a disaster.

Liv doesn't let me glance in the mirror until she completes the "masterpiece," as she calls it. I gasp when she hands me a mirror. "Wow."

"I know, I'm good." She laughs again. I'm unable to stop looking at the girl in the mirror. Me.

I haven't worn makeup in a long time, and even then, it didn't look *this* good. Liv didn't go overboard—my eyeshadow is light, but my dark circles are covered. My appearance is vibrant, with my light freckles covered, my hazel eyes are the focal point.

Staring at myself in the mirror, I'm reminded of how I resemble my mother. I've taken after her looks, but my dad's personality—cool and calm even when thrown into questionable situations.

"Thank you," I say to Liv.

She shrugs like it's no big deal. "Now, do you have something to wear? A dress, preferably?" She raises her eyebrows.

"I'm sure I can find something." I head for my room before Liv tries to dress me in her significantly over-the-top clothing. It does wonders for her body, but I'm a little more self-conscious and aim to be under the radar.

I pick out a black dress and wear a white turtle neck underneath. It's chilly outside, and I'm not freezing my ass off for the sake of this party. Pairing the dress with white sneakers, I look myself over in the full-length mirror by my closet. The dress hugs my curves nicely, and I remove the scrunchie from my chocolate-brown hair, allowing it to fall loosely down my back.

Downstairs, Liv has two shot glasses lined up. She slides one toward me, and I open my mouth to decline. Liv pouts before I have the chance to say anything. "Come on, please."

Start over.

Make friends.

Live a little.

My dad's words echo through me. He gave me a whole speech to encourage me to come here. I'm almost positive this isn't what he had in mind, but I must start somewhere.

Surprising myself, I reach for the shot glass and throw my head back while pouring the contents down my throat. My instant reaction is to cough and gag, but I hold back the urge, and eventually, the lingering taste of alcohol fades.

"By the way, that's not my first choice of an outfit…but on you, it looks amazing," Liv says after taking her shot and scrunching her face. The boys are already at the party, so it's just Liv and me.

It's only a fifteen-minute walk to the frat house through the fields of trees, along the narrow pathway that lacks any sort of lighting. The air is crisp and clean with the imprint of a woodsy fragrance. Leaves crunch underneath our feet, and we move closer together at the sound of any noise.

Once we get closer and onto the road, I hear the music's blaring—this must be why the locals don't live this close to the university.

People are gathered around the front lawn. Some are talking to their friends, laughing. Others are already throwing up—I guess they started drinking early. I turn away from them before I feel sick.

Liv takes my hand in hers and pulls me toward the front door. She greets a few people, and they greet her back. We don't stop until we're inside and she's pouring us drinks into two red cups. Bobbing her head to the music, which has the capability to pierce one's eardrums too close to the speaker, she hands me the cup as her eyes scan the place.

I do the same and spot Josh in a bright yellow t-shirt—next to him are Theo and Zach. I yell over the music to Liv, nodding toward them. "There they are!"

Liv takes my hand, and we push past a group of guys in the middle of what's meant to be a living room. It's now transformed into an area for beer pong. A hand slides around my waist. I turn, coming face-to-face with an older guy. A dark yellow stain covers the top half of his shirt, and he reeks like off-beer.

Swaying from side to side, he clings to me for support and smirks. "How about a kiss, baby?"

I grimace. Has that ever worked for him before? "How about a broken nose, jerk?" I retort, and he drops his hold on me.

Liv and I make it to the group without another incident. Theo takes a few steps to embrace me in one of his bear hugs, but Josh beats him to it.

"I'm glad you made it." Josh grins. Theo glares at him and shakes his head.

"Didn't really have a choice," I joke and look at Liv. She's already by Zach's side, ensuring the girls around them know that he's taken—I don't blame her, they seem to linger.

"That's not what I want to hear. Tell me you came for me," Josh jokes back. He's already had a bit to drink, the alcohol on his breath is overpowering.

Theo stands to the side, talking to a girl with pigtails. His eyebrows are furrowed, and he scratches the side of his head. He notices me looking at him, and his expression changes, the sides of his mouth turning up at the corners.

I unconsciously scan the room for Ace so I can stay away from him, as per his request. A few days have passed since the towel *incident,* and I've done my best to avoid him. The more it crosses my mind, the more embarrassed I become.

Ace, the asshole who despises me, witnessed me naked, and in return, I confronted him. It wasn't exactly an ideal situation.

We've been at the party for less than an hour, and I already want to leave.

"Hey, what's up with Ace? Is he always so…moody?" I ask Liv. We're upstairs in Theo's bedroom. Liv didn't want to use the abhorrent bathroom downstairs, and I can't say I blame her, it reeks like vomit. Theo said she could use the one in his room, and Liv dragged me upstairs with her. My eyes roam the space and land on the medallions and trophies on his dresser.

"No, not usually. At least not anymore." Liv fixes her hair. She's already tipsy from a few drinks and even more talkative.

"Any more?" I sit on Theo's bed while I wait for Liv to fix her bobby pins.

"Yeah, he went through *something* a couple of years ago, but he's better now."

"He doesn't seem to like me," I admit. It's not that he doesn't like me. He hates me.

"Ace takes time to warm up to people. I'm sure he'll come around soon," she reassures me, but I'm not convinced.

What's he like with other people? I can't imagine him being anything but a rude asshole. He has friends, that *must* count for something. I push the thought of Ace out of my mind—I'm okay with acting like he doesn't exist.

Liv slides the last bobby pin in her hair to hold the side pieces in place and retrieves a makeup kit from her bag. My mouth gapes open, how that even fits in her bag is beyond me. She spends another fifteen minutes touching up her already-flawless face.

"Do you need anything?" she asks me.

I shake my head. My makeup is subtle, and I don't see the point of adding more to deal with drunken, horny university guys. Once Liv is finished, we walk back downstairs. I grip onto her, afraid that she might fall down the stairs if I don't.

"I'll be right back," I say.

She nods and walks toward the back of the room. I head to the kitchen, pushing through the crowded house. Whoever is going to clean this mess tomorrow has my sympathy. Cups are tossed everywhere—vomit covers the counter, floor, and even the walls. I hold my breath as I empty my cup down the kitchen sink.

It's my third drink, and I don't know how I got through the first two, but Liv insisted. My head spins. I don't like the way alcohol makes me feel—out of balance with my mind.

I fill the cup with water and drink that instead, attempting to rid the way my body tingles all over. I refill the cup before turning around and coming face-to-face with the one person I didn't expect to find here.

Nate. My ex-boyfriend.

His caramel locks curl over his forehead just like I remember, and his gaze is set on me in bewilderment. A feeling of nostalgia washes over me, he's exactly like I remember him, except drunk. Very drunk.

"Calla," he drawls my name like he doesn't believe he's seeing me.

"Hey," I say, aware that this must be a shock to him. At least I knew Nate would be going to this university, but I left him blind-sided. I decided to attend almost too late and barely told anyone.

I also don't owe Nate anything. He left me.

"I missed you so much." He comes closer. I take a step back and stare at him in disbelief. I remind myself that this is only the alcohol talking and doesn't genuinely mean what he's saying. At least I don't think he does.

"You look so good. Did you change your hair?" Nate examines me. I didn't change my hair. It's the first time I look put together in a long while. We both know it. I'm getting my life back on track, *without you*, I want to say, but hold my tongue.

Nate was the popular guy in high school—tall, handsome, and the football team captain. I was the cheer captain. It was inevitable that we would end up together. Isn't that how it goes, the football captain and the cheerleader?

Nate was my first everything. I thought I loved him. Now, I'm not so sure that was the case. We were young and only dated for three months before my mother died. Everything changed after that.

"Nate," I warn him, but he's too drunk. His eyes are bloodshot, giving the impression that he either started drinking early or decided to add other stuff into the mixture. He leans into me, and I push him back. "Stop."

"Don't be like that. You never looked this good when we were together, especially after..." Nate begins.

Anger bubbles inside of me. He knows precisely how to get a reaction out of me. My fist retracts, and I squeeze my eyes shut. Once I power through, it collides with something, Nate's face, I hope. When I open my eyes, to my disbelief, Nate's face is entirely intact. He dodged my punch, and he's grinning from ear to ear.

My eyes dart to the left of Nate, and I lock eyes with the person I intended to avoid tonight. He's holding his bleeding nose.

5

Flip of a Switch

The cup full of water that I was holding spilled over my dress when I threw the punch. Something that I've never done before. How did Ace get here? Was he eavesdropping, or just happened to be in the wrong place at the wrong time?

"I-I'm sorry, that was an accident," I gasp.

Ace lifts a hand to his nose and wipes the blood from it using the back of the sleeve. A devious smile grows on his face when he examines me.

I do a double-take. Is Ace smiling? But maybe *smile* isn't the right word to describe it. A soft curve is planted on his full lips, and the shadow of a small dimple marks his cheek. On anyone else, it wouldn't be classified as a smile, perhaps a scowl at best. However, it's the first time I've seen Ace look less than pissed.

It's only now, when I come out of shock that I realize my hand is throbbing. Nate shifts toward me. I hold out my other hand to stop him. "You! Don't you dare touch me," I seethe.

"Come on, Cals! You can't blame me for that." He's amused with his pathetic, crooked smile that I used to be dumbfounded by.

Ignoring him, I examine my hand. It's red and swollen, and I can almost go as far as to say something is broken. I bite the inside of my cheek to get the pain off my hand. The prickle of tears builds in my eyes, but I push them back.

"That looks bad." Ace looks at my hand.

No shit, Sherlock.

He opens the freezer and rummages behind all the forgotten alcohol bottles that people placed here at the start of the night. He retrieves an ice pack and wraps a tea towel around it before taking a few strides toward me.

"I'm sorry." He takes my hand in his, slowly placing the tea towel on it. I wince under his touch. It's warm and sends a strange tingling sensation through me. Taking the tea towel with the ice pack from him using my other hand, I break our contact.

I snicker, looking up at him. "You're apologizing when I'm the one who punched you?"

He stares at me like he's looking through my soul. His eyes are as penetrating as the first time I saw them, and I have to drop my gaze to the ground to avoid beguilement.

"I guess I am," he says, almost to himself.

"Are you feeling okay?" I'm confused by the change in his demeanor. He was nothing but rude and arrogant every other time. Now, I punch him and suddenly he's…nice? Another side effect of the personality disorder, maybe?

"Did I hit you too hard?"

He laughs, actually laughs. The hearty sound delivers goosebumps up my arms, and I'm left completely stunned. I conclude that I've given him a concussion. There's no other explanation for his behavior.

"You need to get that checked out," he says. I'm too busy

wondering what happened to the Ace, whom I met at the start of the week. Does he have a twin? "Let me take you."

"Hmm?" My eyes shoot up to him.

"Let me take you to the hospital," he repeats.

"Uh, I don't think that's necessary." I attempt to flex my fingers to prove that I'm fine, but pain shoots through them.

Ace watches me, tilting his head to the side when I meet his eyes.

"I guess I should, but you don't have to take me," I say, even though I won't be able to get myself to a hospital unless I walk.

"Come on." He motions me to follow him. I'm still wary about the sudden change in his attitude.

I trail behind him, amazed at how people seem to make way—they are either afraid of him or have great respect. I go with the former.

Ace walks toward Zach and Theo. They stand behind the beer pong table, waiting for their turn. Someone from their team shoots the ping-pong ball inside one of the red cups, and they erupt in cheers.

"Where are your keys? I need to borrow your car." Ace looks at Zach.

Oh, no. I can't let him drive. I can't be a passenger in a car at night. It triggers flashbacks of the *accident.* I rack my brain for an excuse, anything.

Zach pulls the keys from his pocket without hesitation and hands them to Ace. "Is everything okay?" He glances from me to Ace. From my pulsating hand to Ace's nose, which still has a little blood on it. "You must've really pissed her off this time, man."

"I think she broke her hand. I'm going to take her to a hospital to get it looked at," Ace replies. Zach raises his eyebrows. "This time, it wasn't my fault," Ace adds and sets the keys in his hoodie pocket, along with his hands.

Theo looks cautiously at my hand. "Do you want me to come with you?"

I'm about to decline his offer—I don't want to ruin his night, and from his occasional swaying, I can tell he's had a lot to drink, but Ace answers for me. "No."

Ace reaches the front door and glances back, expecting me to follow him. I walk toward him but then pause, coming to my senses. First of all, I have no reason to trust him to drive me anywhere, and secondly, there's the issue of me being in the passenger seat at night.

"Why should I trust you? I punched you, and you're offering to take me to the hospital. How do I know this is not part of your revenge plan?"

Ace shrugs. "You don't." He turns and continues toward the car.

"Should you be driving? Haven't you been drinking?" I ask when I catch up to him.

"No. I haven't been drinking." Ace's single stride is twice the length of mine, and I speed-walk to compensate.

"I still don't think you should be driving. I may have given you a concussion. We both should get checked out," I say.

He scoffs. "I've been hit harder than that."

I don't doubt it. With this attitude, I'm sure there have been countless times when someone had the urge to swing him a right hook.

Being in the law upholding profession, my dad insisted that I know how to throw a punch. "For self-defense," he assured me when I tried to tell him that throwing fists wasn't something on my to-do-list.

So, one day, we spent hours perfecting my technique in the

garage. "Keep your knees bent… Move your hips and torso." But most importantly, "Keep your thumb outside of your fist."

He failed to mention that punching someone with a significant amount of force was likely to damage me more than my opponent. This is apparent, at least in my current case. Ace's face is built from iron. I'm also tipsy, which may be why I decided closing my eyes would be the right decision.

Ace opens the passenger door to Zach's white Subaru and waits for me to climb in.

"I guess chivalry isn't dead," I remark, glancing from him to the door. His face doesn't change. Instead, he walks toward the driver's side.

"Wait," I call out. "I'll drive." I hold my hand out for the keys.

Ace stares at it like I have grown a third one. "Not a chance."

"Ace…" I begin, not knowing how to explain my dilemma. "Uh, I-I can't be a passenger in a car at night."

It sounds crazy, and I try to avoid situations like this. I expect Ace to laugh or look at me like I'm insane. I brace myself for him to ask questions, and my mind begins to construct lies.

"Okay, but I can't let you drive with one hand." He comes closer. We stand inches away from each other, his hand leans on the car door.

"Where's your motorcycle?" I ask.

He motions across the street. "But you're actually crazy if you think I'm letting you anywhere near the handlebars of my bike in your state. With *one* working hand and *drunk*," he emphasizes.

I look up at him—his broody eyes are set on me with curiosity. I'm not drunk, perhaps tipsy, but there's no point in arguing with him. "You drive," I state.

"Motorcycles are okay?" He raises his eyebrows in question.

"Anything is okay, just not a car at night," I specify.

He nods and, again, doesn't ask why. We set off in the direction of his motorcycle, toward the end of the street.

"I'm sorry again. The punch—it wasn't meant for you." Guilt consumes me. Admittedly, I may have fantasized about punching him since the first time I met him, but I never imagined I'd go through with it.

"Nate, wasn't it?" he asks.

"Hmm?"

"The punch, it was meant for Nate?"

"You know him?" I turn to look at Ace. This is the last thing I imagined happening tonight, having a normal conversation with him.

"No, I overheard you say his name."

"Oh, right…"

We walk in silence through the street, and the sound of the music fades with each step. My hand throbs, and I hold it up to my chest. I didn't think my night would result in this situation.

"Since you didn't even hit the person you intended to, I assume punching is one of your weakest points," Ace says.

I narrow my eyes. "Since you took it with grace, I assume you're used to getting hit."

Ace comes to a halt in front of his motorcycle, which is midnight black, and a helmet rests on top of the seat. No wonder he parked so far away.

He smirks, the shadow of his dimple showing under the street lamp. He sets the helmet on my head, and the breeze transmits the smell of his aftershave toward me. I inhale sharply.

He climbs onto the bike smoothly, and I follow suit, swinging my leg over while hovering my working hand over Ace's shoulder for support. He watches me with amusement and perhaps a little bit of uncertainty. I can't tell.

The motorcycle roars to life, and I wrap one of my hands around Ace's waist for support, feeling nothing but muscle. Instead of the gesture feeling peculiar and uneasy, it's okay.

Luckily, my hand isn't too bad, just a hairline fracture on my knuckle. Ace waits for me while the doctor sees me.

"You must've hit something hard," the doctor states. He tapes my hand and tells me it will heal within three weeks but to limit using it.

"Can you take me to the house? I don't feel like going back to the party," I ask Ace when we're walking toward his motorcycle again.

"Sure."

The only sound is the engine of the motorcycle along the isolated road back to the house. I clutch to Ace with one hand while glancing up to the sky. There's a narrow opening where the stars glimmer through the tops of the vast, bushy trees. I allow my head to fall back and the cool breeze to sweep against my skin, nipping at my nose.

My hair blows behind me, and I inhale deeply. For once, I allow myself to accept that maybe this is where I'm destined to be—new town, new friends, a new beginning.

It's not long until we're in the driveway, and Ace cuts the engine, climbing off. He walks with me inside the empty house and flicks the light switch, illuminating the space. Is he going back to the party?

I move toward the fridge and grab a bottle of water. Then, I reach up to the cupboard above, where Liv informed me the painkillers are kept. My hand is throbbing, and so is my head from the loud music at the party. My fingers brush the small box, but I can't quite reach it even when I stand on my tiptoes.

When footsteps move toward me, my body stills. Ace leans over me, his body heat dancing with mine. I suck in a deep breath—

citrus with an overdose of oakmoss reveals a rugged trail of mystery and captivation. I don't dare move.

His fingers brush mine insouciantly, and he pulls down the box for me. I turn to face him, and he hands it to me. I feel the need to thank him for this and for tonight, even though I don't know why he bothered with me. I'm hoping that at least we'll be civil from now on.

"Thanks for, uh, taking me to the hospital, even though you shouldn't have. I mean, I'm the one who punched you." I press my lips together.

"Calla." My name rolls off his tongue, and he takes a step closer to me. My eyes travel to his lips. They tug up at the corners, revealing a faint smile. He's about to say something, but his phone ringing interrupts. Withdrawing it from his pocket, he glances at the caller ID. Theo.

He answers, placing the phone to his ear. The silence in the house allows me to discern parts of what Theo is saying. I catch the words *Ashworth University*, *crashing the party,* and *you need to get here now*.

"I'm coming," Ace says into the phone.

6

Mars and Jupiter

On Saturday, I spend the day catching up on classwork, which consists of assigned textbook readings. For the better half of the afternoon, there's nothing left to do. I open a blank word document on my laptop and hover my fingers on the keyboard in an attempt to commence writing an article. Instead, I discover myself with an empty mind and nothing itching to get out.

The house is vacant, and there are no signs of life. The only sound is the wind humming outside my window, which is slightly ajar, rustling the life out of the elderly trees. After a few moments of staring at the blank screen, waiting for something, any sort of inkling, I snap the laptop shut and groan in frustration. I reach for one of the books that I brought with me, *Little Women*—it was my mom's favorite. I open it to the first page.

The following day brings another shift at the café, and even though I slept less than four hours last night, I'm glad to be occupied with something. The sleep issue is not ideal, but better than having complete insomnia.

The first couple of months after the accident, I struggled to get any sleep—each time I closed my eyes, recollections of the accident scene pervaded me. I woke with hot flashes and ear-piercing screaming. Finally, my dad forced me to see a therapist on his already-suffering wage.

"Hey!" Mia greets me once I arrive at work. Her beady blue eyes scan my appearance before she places the frozen strawberries in the blender, she adds banana and some cinnamon powder.

"Hey." I watch her make the order. She pours the smoothie into a glass and slides it over to me, her pink fingernails already scanning the next order.

"Table eight," she tells me nonchalantly. I'm already on the clock. The thing about Mia is, I don't know whether she likes me or she's just acting friendly.

I grab the smoothie and head over to the booth. The caramel locks force me to stop in my tracks, and I practically turn around. Nate sits in booth number eight. I take a measured step back, hoping to escape. Instead, his head snaps up, leaving me with no choice other than to head toward his table.

"I'm sorry about Friday night. I was drunk," he says when I set the smoothie in front of him. "I was surprised to see you, and, uh…I don't know why I said what I did," he rambles, looking up at me apologetically. His familiar eyes sparkle, and I fold my hands against my chest.

"How did you know I would be here?" I didn't see him come here before, so this clearly isn't his usual spot to grab some casual lunch by himself.

"I didn't." He smiles guiltily and adds, "Nice surprise, isn't it?"

"Sure." I roll my eyes and turn on my heel, heading for the counter.

Nate's fingers softly wrap around my wrist, and I turn back to look at him. “I miss you,” he says. The words don’t spark anything inside me like I thought they might have. Instead, I’m annoyed that he might be expecting me to say it back.

“Nate, I’m working.” I tug my hand away from him, walking away. He wanted to be single for university—I guess now he regrets the decision. It’s not that I’m petty, but when your ex-boyfriend says he misses you after breaking up with you to be single for university, it makes you feel a certain way—almost gratified.

Mia glances from me to Nate and then back at me again, waiting for an explanation. “Is that your boyfriend?”

“Ex,” I reply.

She arches an eyebrow. “He’s cute.”

I shrug. Is it weird that I don’t care that Mia is attracted to him?

Brody rushes past us. He mutters a phrase underneath his breath about Mars doing something weird with Jupiter, struggling to get his arms through the brown jacket. It’s the first time I see him since the ‘interview.’ I watch him quizzically. I’ve never seen someone more fascinating than him, he’s one big conundrum.

“He’s obsessed with horoscopes,” Mia explains when she detects me watching Brody cross the road through the burgundy shades of the café window.

I revert my eyes to her, but Mia doesn’t seem to care that I was observing Brody. The last thing I need is for her to think I’m checking her uncle out.

“Horoscopes?” I ask.

“Yeah, anything superstitious, really. He’s into all that stuff,” Mia clarifies in a way that implies she’s not a great believer in whatever Brody is a part of.

“And you’re not?” I ask.

Mia glances at me as if not expecting me to ask her that. “I’m not sure. Before living with Brody, I wasn't into any of that stuff, but now… I don't know."

I read my horoscope sometimes, but I don't take it seriously. They're written in a way to fit everyone into their theory. *Some important decisions are going to come your way.* One person could say a critical decision is what to have for dinner, while another person has to decide whether they should take their mother off life support. Notice the vagueness?

After I finish work, I enter the house and discover board games sprawled across the living room floor. Liv and Zach huddle together as a team, discussing something about the game. Theo and Josh are bickering—what a surprise. Ace is on his phone. This looks like the usual interaction between them, as I recognize the way their group works.

No one notices I walked inside except for Ace. His head snaps up, and our eyes lock for an elongated moment. The unexpected eye contact sends a shudder up my arms, and he tilts his head to the side as if perceiving the change of atmosphere before dropping his gaze back to his phone.

So, we aren't talking again? I haven't seen him since Friday night. Why did I think it would be different after the incident? I mean, I punched him, and he took me to the hospital, we got along. Why *wouldn't* it be different after that?

"Hey," Liv greets me when I go for the stairs after taking a water bottle out of the fridge. "Want to join us?"

"Yeah, you can be on my team. Theo is dragging me down," Josh jokes, and Theo shoves his shoulder.

"Don't start. You're the one who rolled a two!" Theo interjects, and I laugh.

I glance from the group, which is filled with laughter and

banter, toward the stairs leading me to my room. I've become accustomed to segregation. Perhaps it's time to break the vicious cycle of estrangement. I step toward the group.

Theo scoots over and motions for me to sit next to him. Josh does the same. I roll my eyes at their internal competition and assess the situation at hand. If I sit next to Theo, I'll have to also sit next to Ace. The last thing I want is to endure his bizarre mood swings. Choosing Josh, I provide Theo with an apologetic shrug. He furrows his eyebrows and drops his head to the board game.

"Were you out last night?" I ask Liv, even though I know they were out and didn't get back till late. I remember the emptiness of the house and the strange feeling of…being left out? It's not like they owe me anything, I just met them, but I thought… *What? What did I think—that they were going to invite me to everything?*

"Yeah, we were at the club," Liv informs me. Ace throws a warning look to Liv, but she continues, "You can come next Saturday—"

At this, Ace cuts her off. "No. She can't."

My mouth gapes open. Undoubtedly, Ace is back to his usual charming self. I can't say I've missed it. Liv shoots him an irritated glance, a promise that she'll confront him, but not in front of me. Frustration courses through my veins. Why am I this bothered that Ace doesn't like me? I've never been one to seek approval for my character or actions.

Zach sets up the classic game of Scrabble, and we begin to assemble words. Occasionally, an argument erupts between Josh and Theo about a word's legitimacy and results in Liv retrieving a dictionary.

"Come on, have a drink with us," Josh begs me. I'm about to decline for the third time. He's very persistent, but I'm unable to drink alcohol again this weekend.

"She doesn't want one," Ace snaps. All eyes go to him, and I notice he isn't drinking either. He doesn't meet my inquisitive gaze, and I'm confused by his contradicting actions.

"Actually, Josh, I think I might have what you are," I say, glancing at Josh with a wide smile. He's holding a glass with what seems to be a fruity soda, but there's no doubt in my mind about how much alcohol it contains. I observe Ace staring at me out of the corner of my eye, and his jaw strains in…aggravation?

The next morning, I descend the stairs after my shower to discover Ace in the kitchen with his back to me. Great. I assumed waking up earlier would allow me to avoid this exact situation—avoid *him*. The fact that he's shirtless doesn't help. The morning sun glimmers on the ridges of his muscular back, and I'm unable to look away. I snicker as the scene unfolds in front of me.

This is the very last thing I expected to see—Ace flipping pancakes by the window. I didn't take him for a pancake guy. I have the urge to kick myself for finding him even the slightest bit attractive, but the feeling comes to an end when he turns and opens his mouth.

"Done staring?" Ace asks, arching an eyebrow with every amount of arrogance possible.

My cheeks flush a shade darker, but I keep my eyes on him, not bothering to look away or give him the satisfaction of my embarrassment now that I've been caught red-handed.

"Do you have a personality disorder?" I question, catching him off-guard. At this, he raises both eyebrows, and his full lips coil at the corners in amusement.

"No. I don't, Calla," he answers as if it were a common question. His eyes don't strain away, anticipating my reaction.

"What did I do for you to hate me then?" That's the only other explanation for him to act like this toward me. There's a long pause before he decides to answer. The words that flow out of his mouth next make me reconsider asking him.

"For me to hate you, I'd need to feel something—and frankly, I feel nothing for you."

Asshole. I wasn't prepared for that, and I resist the urge to punch him again—my hand is still swathed in a bandage from Friday night. "That seems blatantly untrue, considering your reaction to learning that I was staying here. You know, you shouldn't lie to yourself."

Ace scoffs, his eyes never leaving mine. "That's ironic coming from you…" He strides toward me, and I suck in a breath. "Have you admitted to yourself that you find me impulsively attractive?"

When I don't reply, he smirks. "I'll take that as a no."

He's unbearable—I can't deal with him. "Wow, can we just pretend for one moment that you're not an arrogant asshole?"

"But I'm only getting started," he says, testing my patience.

"Ugh, I think *I* actually hate you!" I've never met someone more infuriating than him.

"Good. You'd be stupid not to." The assertiveness that spills from that sentence astonishes me, and yet, I can't seem to pinpoint what it is about him that seems to keep me on edge.

"Pancakes?" He places the warm plate in front of me, which is topped with whipped cream.

I glower at the pancakes and then back at him, dumbfounded once again by how he seems to change his mood from one extreme to the other. It's exhausting to know where I stand with him.

In the heat of the moment, I grab the stupid pancake with the whipped cream and splatter it on his smug face. I don't stick around to see his reaction—grabbing my bag from the chair, I storm outside.

The mild exercise calms me as I march to campus through the shortcut that Liv showed me. Unfortunately, my day is already cursed from the bitter morning run-in with the asshole I live with. I only hope that it gets better from here, but it doesn't.

I stride into my first class right as it begins, eager to see Theo—he never fails to brighten my mood. That thought is short-lived, and the smile that I managed to preserve on my face disintegrates into thin air when I notice Ace next to Theo. Damn his motorcycle.

Glancing toward the back of the room, I consider taking one of the empty seats there, but I don't want to provide Ace that satisfaction. So instead, I push my shoulders back and head toward them.

"Hey, Theo!" I say and then turn to Ace. "Hi, Ace. I hope you enjoyed your pancakes this morning." I force a wide smile.

He narrows his eyes at me, and I sink in the chair next to Theo, but not before noticing the outline of a smile fighting to emerge on Ace's full mouth.

The professor discusses our assessment piece. "This year's assignment will focus on the current social issues. You will work with a partner, and both of you will choose different topics which you must synthesize to form a well-drawn analysis on how these issues overlap." He paces from one end of the room to the other while speaking. "Perhaps you would like to draw from your personal experiences. In fact, as this is a team-building assignment, I would encourage all of you to get to know your partners and conceivably share why this topic is important to you."

I can already detect that this assignment is going to be challenging. I'm not willing to share my personal life or thoughts with a stranger.

"Open your devices and head to the assessment tab, where you'll find an extensive list of issues to choose from. After choosing, you'll automatically link with your partner based on which topic you have both picked."

My eyes scan through the list of issues, they're all broad. My eyes land on one—*divorce rates and their impact on children.* My parents were happily married, so this would be an ideal topic to cover without getting personal with someone. As soon as I click it, Ace's name pops up with the issue that he chose—*the effects of alcohol abuse and how it impacts families.*

This can't be happening, out of all the people in this class, we chose matching topics. After this morning, the last thing I want to do is to spend time with Ace. It will drive me to the point of total insanity. On top of that, the issue that Ace picked hits a little too close to home.

"Who did you get?" Theo asks, peering over from his laptop. "Ace Blackwell," he reads from my screen. "Hey, Ace! You and Calla are partners," Theo says, elbowing him lightly to get his attention.

I don't have to look up at Ace to know what his expression is like. We're both not thrilled about this. I spend the rest of the day consumed by the thought of spending time with Ace. I consider speaking to the professor about changing topics, but Ace has already done that. I noticed that he stayed back after class, and I assume it didn't go well.

I persuade myself that, perhaps, this might not be too bad. I'm intrigued to get to know Ace Blackwell, to find out why he is the way he is—angry at the world, bad-tempered, and an outright asshole. Is it worth risking my vulnerability to find out his?

✦

I'm grateful when Nate doesn't come into the café while I'm working today and surprised when Mia says, "There's this thing on Thursday night, drinks and music by the lake. Lots of people from the campus are going. Wanna come?"

It's the first time she has talked to me like a friend and not a co-worker. "Sure," I agree. It will be refreshing to get out of the house and spend some time with Mia outside of work.

When I arrive home, Ace is talking on the phone through his door. His voice is soft and filled with something that I didn't think he was capable of…warmth? I'm unsure who he's talking to, and before I question what the hell I'm doing, I raise my hand and knock.

"I'll call you back, yeah?" he says into the phone.

The lock clicks, and the wooden door swings open. Ace's face is inches from mine. Before I'm able to stop myself, my eyes drift down his chest, lingering on the ink that covers his entire body. Doesn't he own a freaking shirt?

"Can I help you, or didn't you get enough of a show this morning?"

Taking my attention off him, I grind my teeth. How can one be so full of themselves? I look past him to get a glimpse of his room, mostly because I don't want to look anywhere in his direction and give him the wrong idea. I'm not interested in him, but one can certainly appreciate his looks. My eyes land on a bookshelf, and my eyebrows furrow in confusion. Ace reads? I doubt that—it's probably just for show.

"Do you think you can be civil for this assignment?" I bring my eyes back to his.

"Hmm." He leans against the doorframe, and his broad shoulders almost occupy the entire space. "Like friends?" he says, primarily to himself, weighing his options.

I roll my eyes at his egotism. "Yes." I'm irritated again.

"One would think that your actions this morning were extremely unfriendly," he reflects with a hint of amusement. Ah, he's mad about the pancakes.

"You deserved it."

"It wasn't enough when your fist collided with me on Friday night, no?"

"That…was an accident," I retort.

Ace tilts his head to the side and raises one of his dark eyebrows. *Was it?* "You know this assignment requires getting to know each other."

"I heard the instructions."

"Well, in that case…" He steps closer. "You asked for it. By the end of this assignment, I will learn everything there is to know about you. Your flaws, everything that makes you tick—all your sensitive little buttons. How does that sound?"

Is he hoping that I will back down? I don't.

"Asshole," I mutter.

"Goodnight, Calla." He shuts the door in my face. I groan in frustration, and I swear a small chuckle derives from the other side.

7

Playing with Fire

Being friends with Ace is like playing with fire, hoping that I don't get burned. For the most part, we have kept out of each other's way.

I still haven't written anything for the university newspaper, and I question why I'm even pursuing this career if I can't write a single article. It's like the part of me that had previously been able to come up with ideas is buried, unable to come up for air.

I don't have to work today, and I'm back at the house earlier than usual. I recall Liv telling me that she and Zach won't be home till later, and I'm left in the house alone. After reading a book and watching a movie on my laptop, I head downstairs to get some water.

From the kitchen, I notice Ace's door is open—it's never open. And I wasn't aware he was home. So I use this opportunity to hastily grab one of my notebooks from upstairs and stand in his doorway, clearing my throat.

"What?" he arches his eyebrows but doesn't look up from the laptop.

"The assignment? I thought we could go over a few things now," I say.

I look around his room—it's much bigger than mine, and his king-sized bed fits comfortably in the middle. There are no windows, but a large glass sliding door, slightly ajar, leads to the back patio, where a small wooden table has auburn leaves strewn on top. The sun is almost set behind the mountains miles away, and the breeze sweeps through, carrying the promise of colder days.

"I'm busy."

Of course he is, but the assignment isn't going to write itself. Ignoring him, I pad over to the edge of his bed, laying my notebook out. I sit as far away from him as I can, crossing my legs. His mouth twitches. Is he holding back a smile?

I lift my pen, twirling it around my fingers. "Are you always such an asshole when you first meet someone?"

He closes his laptop, providing me with all his undivided attention. It's deep and, in a way, discomforting. As a result, I lean back, and if I move a little more, I'll end up on the floor.

"Hmm?" I prompt under his gaze when he doesn't answer, because the tautness is getting too much. Why is he staring at me like that?

"Only when it works them up so much." He smirks, finding humor in my discomfort. I open the notebook and pretend to write something in it. Ace raises an eyebrow in question.

"Why does it bother you if I don't like you?" he asks, leaning forward, and I pause. "But it's not just me, is it? Why does it bother you if *someone* doesn't like you?"

My bottom lip grazes my teeth, and I consider the question. Ace is right, partially. It does bother me if someone doesn't like me, but it bothers me more that it's him. I'm not going to tell him that.

"Do you read?" I glance toward the large bookshelf, getting the conversation off myself.

"Mostly autobiographies. Some classics." He understands what I'm trying to do but doesn't mention it. I realize he tends to do that. He didn't question me about the passenger-seat-at-night issue, and now, he isn't insistent on answers.

"Why did you pick this topic for the assignment?" I ask, crossing into a boundary that may be personal. His face twists into a grimness that I haven't seen him display before, something between sorrow and rage.

"It's a vast issue in society, something that needs to be talked about more often," he says but doesn't expand.

So, we're going to beat around the bush for this assignment. Both of us are unwilling to discuss the personal connections that we may have with the issues at hand or answer any question that perhaps hits too close to home. I stare at the blank page on the notepad.

He sighs. "I've witnessed the way alcohol abuse can tear families apart."

Is this what Liv was talking about at the party? *He went through something a couple of years ago.*

My dad and I have also experienced firsthand the vile consequences of alcohol. "We don't have to talk about it," I say.

"It's kind of the whole point of the assignment."

Precisely what I tried to avoid by picking an issue that didn't hold any personal sentiment. "Okay," I mutter and motion for him to continue his story.

He narrows his eyes at me like he expects me to be the one to tell him something, and when I don't, he opens his laptop back up. "Research it is."

I retrieve my laptop from upstairs, and we both begin working on the assignment. Ace researches the sources, and I make notes of them, combining the information.

The more I spend time with him, the more I wonder if we have simply got off on the wrong foot. Perhaps it's easier to hate the idea of someone but more difficult to hate them when they're right in front of you.

Ace provides me his full attention, occasionally plugging the silence in the room with questions that are easy to answer and don't put a heaviness on either of us, but they also have nothing to do with the assignment.

"I can't believe you don't know who the Arctic Monkeys are. They are the most superior band of all time," he says. It's refreshing to see this part of him, less of the asshole and more of the ardent side.

I roll my eyes and press my lips together. "I suppose you're going to tell me that you also like Nickelback."

He shakes his head in disbelief and reveals a crooked grin. "I'm not going to be shamed for my music choice by someone who probably listens to Hannah Montana." I refrain from asking him what's wrong with that. I'm confident he'll find plenty of issues with it, and I won't be able to live it down.

My arm supports my weight on the bed, and I leave my legs dangling off the side. When I glimpse back at Ace, it seems as though he's moved closer. The faint contact when our hands brush causes my mouth to dry. I clear my throat, eyeing the notes I scribbled in my notebook, not at all interested in them.

"Almost half of the marriages in the United States end in divorce," Ace reads from a website. "One would think it's like taking a gamble."

"But wouldn't you want to take that gamble with the person you love?"

He sneers. "There are other ways to show someone you love them."

"So, you don't believe in marriage?" I prompt.

I'm not sure if I believe in it myself. I'd like to think I do, since my parents were happily married for more than fifteen years, but at the end of the day, it's a meaningless concept. However, I certainly wouldn't be opposed to it if I met the right person, far, far in the future.

"Did I say that?"

"You're certainly implying it."

"My father was unfaithful to my mom through their whole marriage. I'm allowed to have doubts about the process," he asserts.

Ace sighs silently as if he didn't mean to reveal that fragment of his past. Another piece of the puzzle assembles and renders Ace that much less hateable. I don't say anything, not knowing what the right thing to say is in this situation.

I change the subject. Something that I've become accustomed to doing when anyone asks me questions about myself. "If you could live anywhere in the world, where would it be?"

Ace closes his laptop. "Norway. It's quiet, the scenery is remarkable, it's cold. And let's not forget the Northern Lights," he says, gazing into the distance. We both like the cold, interesting.

"Since we've moved onto philosophical questions, what superpower would you want to have?" Ace asks me.

I raise my eyebrows at the purposeless question. But I know Ace is doing precisely the same thing I am. Keeping far away from the problematic questions—ones that we're not ready, or ever will be, to share with each other.

"To bend time. Pause, rewind, fast-forward," I answer.

A smirk plays on Ace's mouth, and he presses his lips together.

"What? Don't tell me you would choose flying or reading minds or something equally unnecessary." I roll my eyes.

"No, I'd choose the same as you."

My eyes widen a fraction. "Why?"

"With time manipulation, there'll be no missed opportunities, no mistakes that I can't fix. I'd be able to relive the best moments in my life and skip the worst, if there are any."

I stare outside, toward the back patio. I can't see anything through the darkness. What time is it? How long have we sat in his room? It feels like minutes.

My eyes fall to the time on his watch. "It's past eleven? Sorry, I didn't mean to keep you up this late." I forget that people actually sleep. That's not a luxury I have.

"It's okay. I don't sleep much anyway."

"Hmm?"

"My mind has a way of being dark and twisted when vulnerable," he mutters under his breath. Did he mean to say that out loud?

"You mean, you have nightmares?" I'm barely aware of my voice. I know what it's like to close your eyes and have your mind satiate with sinister thoughts—internal darkness that pushes you toward irrationality.

Are we both still holding on to something that we should let go of? *What's your secret, Ace?*

"I guess." His voice is barely a whisper. It brushes delicately against my skin. How did we get so close? And why don't I have the urge to move away? Is it because I'm beginning to see similarities between us with each spoken word?

I glance up at Ace through my lashes while holding my breath. His eyes are primarily gray, with a hint of green and blue electricity. After naïvely being hypnotized by them, my attention trails down to his sensuous mouth, which curls at the corners into a devilish smirk. My heart hastens—it's thumping against my chest.

We both know if one of us moves forward, our lips will connect. I can't comprehend my thought process and why I suddenly want that to happen. Perhaps it's fatigue and irrationality mixed with the unknown. Tomorrow, Ace will return to being an asshole, and I'll be the one to get burned—don't play with fire.

I feel nothing for you.

Using my hand, I push myself off the bed, breaking the moment—keeping myself sane. "I should probably go to my room anyway. I'll see you tomorrow."

"Afraid you're falling in love with me already?" he jokes, lightening the mood.

I scoff. "In your dreams, Blackwell."

He grins. It's such a rare but heartwarming sight. "Goodnight, Calla."

✦ ✦ ✦

Stepping inside Mia's house, I'm unable to take everything in at once. I don't expect this. It's like walking inside someone's mind—definitely Brody's.

The spiral staircase toward the right catches my attention, it's painted chalky white with a wooden rail. The rest of the space is decorated with plants, so many plants, and a bright, patterned rug occupies most of the living space.

"I'll just quickly get changed. Do you need anything?" Mia asks.

I look down at what I'm wearing—black leggings, an oversized t-shirt, and boots, the same clothes that I wore to work. I didn't bring anything to change into, and I don't plan on dressing up for this event. It's something to take my mind off everything else. To spend time with ordinary people, doing normal university things.

"I'm good. Take your time."

I'm drawn toward the large bookcase stretching across the back wall. It's filled with hundreds of books. I detect most of them are dated from the scuffed edges and faded colors. I trail my fingers over the spines and scan the titles—they all seem to be spiritual, and I understand what Mia means about Brody.

I draw one book out and glance at it.

"Page twenty-four," a gruff voice speaks behind me, and I turn to discover Brody. A light-colored shirt loosely hangs off him, and his vision is directly focused on the book in my hands.

"Hmm?" I ask, but I'm already flipping through the pages.

"First line, page twenty-four," he repeats.

"The stars will burn in flames," I read out loud and look at him for an explanation. He doesn't provide one, like I'm supposed to know what that means, and shuffles toward a small room, shutting the door behind him. Okay then, that was bizarre.

The gathering is on the other side of the lake, across from where I'm living. It doesn't take us long to walk there from Mia's house. "Have you always lived with Brody?" I ask as I rub my hands together to warm them.

"Only for the last few months," she tells me and adds, "My parents kicked me out for, um... *rebelling*." She snickers. "By rebelling, I mean cutting my own bangs and dyeing them pink."

"Oh, where are you from?"

"Utah," she answers, granting me a look that should explain everything. Unfortunately, the only thing I know about Utah is that it's fantastic for skiing.

There are a few people at the bonfire tonight. My eyes adjust to the malicious light of the flame, and a stocky figure jogs toward me. "I didn't know you were going to come." Theo collides into my body, embracing me. "I should've asked you. Fuck, sorry! I didn't think this was, um, something that you'd want to come to," he rambles.

"It's okay." I hug him back. He smells like washing detergent mixed with smoke from the fire.

Over the last couple of weeks, I learned that Theo is overly affectionate with *everyone,* and knowing that makes me more comfortable. Not that I wasn't comfortable around him before, but the last thing I want to discover is that he has some sort of crush on me.

"Mia," I say as a way of explanation as to why I'm here. I turn to motion to her, but she isn't there. I glance around, she seems to have disappeared into thin air.

Josh is by the bonfire, and he waves me over. My eyes dart to his side—toward Ace and another girl. He doesn't even bother to look at me, and I don't anticipate anything more from him. Just because we spent time together the other day doesn't mean we're going to be best buddies. It's only for the assignment.

Perching my butt on the wooden log between Josh and Theo, I recognize some of the people from a few of my classes and some from Theo's frat house.

"Here." Mia appears behind me and places a cup into my hand.

I crane my neck to glance at her, and her pink bangs dangle in my face. "Thanks," I say. I bring the cup to my nose and instantly regret it. The smell of alcohol overpowers any mixer she's placed in there.

Someone brought a speaker and is blasting Blink 182 songs. Couples are making out around us, and once again, for some uncertain reason, my mind drifts to Nate. I immediately compel my mind to rid the thoughts.

There are marshmallows, which people are toasting on the fire—a fire hazard on sticks. Drunk teenagers and an open flame don't sound like the best combination, and I don't want to be stuck in the middle of it all when something terrible happens.

Josh is telling me something, and I'm looking at him, his mouth is moving, but I can't concentrate on his voice among everyone else around us. However, I can hear the conversation beside Josh, the one with Ace and a dark-haired girl I don't recognize.

"Let's go back to your house," she offers.

"Maybe later," Ace replies.

"I'll make it worth your while." Her hand travels up his leg.

I turn away and focus on the music, subconsciously taking a sip from the cup Mia given me and pulling a disgusted face as the bitter taste of alcohol meets my tastebuds.

"I'll be right back," I say, standing, becoming a little nauseous. I notice from my peripheral vision that Ace's head snaps up, and he shakes the girl's hand off his thigh.

"Are you okay?" Mia questions silently with her lips. She's fallen into conversation with Theo. I nod and head toward the deck on the lake, farther from everyone.

I relish my own company—most of the time, I prefer it. But I don't like being alone for long enough that the wicked thoughts take over. I never used to be like this. I was an extrovert before. Before and after my mom's death—I use those words to depict the timeframe in my life. Everything was better *before*.

The air on the pier is cooler, purer. I inhale a deep breath, leaning against one of the wooden pillars, and stare into the distance. I often find myself disconnected from my own body, or perhaps disconnected from the world may be a better phrase.

I can't help but question the purpose of everything. The meaning of our existence or why I'm here at exactly this interval. The universe is endless, truly limitless, and even time is an illusion—in reality, it doesn't even exist. I've read somewhere that clocks run faster at mountain peaks than they do at sea level. So, essentially time is not constant, it's merely a deception assumed by our inaccurate observation.

What's the point of living? Is it a way to pass time that doesn't even exist? And maybe, inherently, nothing matters in the grand scheme of things.

When I used to see my therapist, she called it "nihilism," and a way for me to overcome it, is to avoid yielding to it. She impelled me to find at least a small amount of meaning each day.

"Why is someone as gorgeous as you all alone?"

The voice startles me and plucks me out of my thoughts. I turn to find a tall figure standing before me. A faint red light flickers between his lips from a cigarette.

"Uh." I don't know what to say and look toward the group, considering how loud I would have to yell for help if he turns out to be a creep.

"I'm Logan." He flashes me a smile. I'm able to only partially decipher his features. His chestnut-brown hair is short and slicked back, and a crooked nose rests above his thin lips.

"Calla," I reply, and our eyes meet. An uncomfortable feeling springs through me. "Do you go to university here?" I attempt to make small talk. I don't want company, but I'm unsure how to evacuate this situation without being rude.

"Not exactly," he says, and before I can ask him what that means, my eyes widen. In the distance, Ace strides toward us. I glance from Logan to Ace, my brows furrowing in confusion. Is he lost?

Ace stops at my side and laces his fingers through mine. What is he doing? I'm frozen. I've completely forgotten how to move. His calloused thumb brushes against the back of my hand, and the warmth from our contact spreads through me.

"What are you doing here, Logan?" Ace's tone is low and laced with irritation.

Logan shoves one hand in his pocket and takes a deliberately unhurried draw from his cigarette while assessing the contact between Ace and me.

"Relax. I was just leaving." Logan flicks his cigarette into the lake, and I hear the faint sizzle from it extinguishing. "See you around, Calla." He offers me a wink, and Ace's grip tightens around mine.

I cover my grimace with a forced smile. Something about Logan seems off, but I can't quite place my finger on it.

Ace and I stand in utter silence with our hands still intertwined. I wait until Logan's silhouette is a small shadow in the distance before breaking our contact and placing a considerable amount of space between us. "What the hell was that?"

"What was what?" Ace shrugs, acting as though he has no idea what I'm talking about. Is he serious?

He steps toward me, and my pulse quickens. Why does he do this to me?

I take a step back, overlooking the fact that I'm already close to the edge of the deck. It all happens too quickly for me to grasp. One minute, I'm glaring at Ace, prepared to confront him about the stunt that he pulled, and the next, I'm engulfed by ice-cold water.

Oh my God. This can't be happening right now.

When I surface for air, Ace's face is filled with legitimate concern. He kneels near the edge, offering me his hand. I deliberate pulling him in with me, but I doubt he'll fall for that trick. So instead, I set both of my hands on the deck and hoist myself up.

I'm soaked, cold, and downright pissed off.

Ace's lips are pressed together, and his chest shakes vaguely. Is the asshole suppressing a laugh? This is all his fault. If he didn't come here endeavoring to act as a knight in shining armor, this wouldn't have happened. I'd still be dry and toasty—instead, I'm shivering while the cool breeze grazes against me.

"Shut up," I warn, finally climbing out of the water.

"I didn't say anything." Ace raises his hands in defense, his grin as wide as the Cheshire cat.

"I don't care. Shut up."

He grasps the back of his hoodie and slides it over his head, passing it to me. "Here." Of course, there's no shirt underneath his hoodie, what a shocking surprise.

I'm about to decline his offer, I don't need him to save the day, but another breeze forces me to reconsider. I grasp the hoodie with trembling hands.

"Take your shirt off," he orders.

"What?" I clench my teeth together to stop them chattering from the cold.

"Calla, it's drenched." He looks down at the considerable puddle beneath my feet to prove his point. "You'll still be cold."

Why does he care? I glance toward the crackling fire in the distance, where there's laughing and loud music, and then back at Ace. There's no chance I'm taking my shirt off in front of him—I'd rather have pneumonia or whatever consequences come with this.

"Here," Ace says, standing in front of me, so no one will be able to see me get changed. He turns with his back to me.

He doesn't give me a chance to decline, and I'm sort of grateful.

My stubborn self would have suffered to prove a point. I remove my wet t-shirt, dropping it gently on the ground, it makes a *splat* when it hits the wooden platform. I hold my breath, nervous about making any sort of noise.

When I pull his hoodie over my head, the intense smell of Ace fills my lungs, propelling goosebumps up my arms. I blame it on the cold. I recall that I'm still angry at Ace. I'm mad because his mood swings give me whiplash—he says he doesn't feel anything for me, but then he does this? What game is he playing?

"What are you doing here? I was speaking to Logan," I say. I don't care for Logan, and I'm glad he's gone. He was giving me the creeps, but that's not the point.

"He isn't a decent person," Ace conveys.

What a hypocrite. "And what? I suppose you are?"

Ace turns to me with a solemn expression. He closes his eyes for a moment, and when they open, for the first time, there's something soft about them. The way he's looking at me right now is different from all the other times.

"I didn't say that, and to put it bluntly, I'm worse. Really, Calla. It'd be best if you stayed away from me."

I'm at a loss for words. He's the one who waltzed over here to save the day, and he's telling me to stay away?

He's utterly mad.

8

The Illegal Hobby

On a gloomy Saturday afternoon, I'm in the kitchen engrossed in a book when Liv stumbles through the front door carrying a box. Leaving the book facedown on the counter, I turn to face her.

Liv sighs, resting the box on a chair. "Do you know there isn't a single fabric store in this town? I had to drive all the way to the city!" She slumps her elbows on the counter and yawns.

"A fabric store?"

"I took the task of designing the cheer squad outfits for the next semester. Have you seen them? They are atrocious. I mean, who puts a vomit green with an orange?" She shudders. "We're fortunate that the university colors have changed since then, but the uniforms haven't been revamped since the seventies."

This doesn't surprise me. Liv strikes me as the type of person to do this sort of thing, hence why she's doing a designer's degree. "Have you always wanted to be a designer?"

She beams at my question. "Ever since I was young. I think my mom knew as soon as I cut into her wedding dress at the age of five. She was furious, but it had those hideous sleeves on it, and I think my five-year-old self knew that it was a tragedy that required fixing." She laughs, and I join her.

"Hey, are you busy tonight?" She glances from me to the book that I set on the counter upside down. "I guess not… Wanna come with us to the club? Theo and Josh are coming too," Liv invites me.

My thoughts wander to Ace, recalling his reaction the last time Liv invited me to come to the club with them. I hope he isn't going to be there. "I'll get ready."

I take a shower and get changed. I'm still in my room when the sound of bickering originates from downstairs, a sign that Josh and Theo must be here. I grab a jacket and check my appearance in the mirror before rushing down the stairs.

Zach drives us there, parking his Subaru on the road before we get out and make our way down the narrow alleyway. The sound of the streets on either side bounce from one cobbled wall to the other. The faint glow of the sunset peeks from a distance, highlighting the emptiness.

We walk lazily toward our destination as if we have been here a hundred times before. Finally, we make a turn to our right, which leads to a set of descending stairs and reveals a metal door at the bottom. Zach holds it open for everyone.

I'm not sure what Liv meant by the *club,* but a possibly-illegal underground fighting club isn't what I had in mind.

There are so many people here, enough to make me hunch my shoulders to avoid bumping into them. We push past, forcing our way toward the back. Only a few people are our age, the rest are much older. Some have drinks in their hands, and I scrunch my nose at the overpowering smell of cigarettes.

"I thought I told you not to bring her." Ace storms toward us.

Oh, no. Where did he come from?

"Ace, relax. She's fine," Theo says, throwing an arm around me in defense. Ace's eyes darken, and they shoot from me to Theo, irritation spills abundantly from his body.

"Fuck! I can't do this with her here."

I'm so drained from this situation between us. One day he's fine with me, I can even say that we've been getting along, and the next, he makes it an issue.

"Why don't you leave, then?" I don't understand what he's talking about, and frankly, don't give a shit anymore.

He laughs, but it doesn't reach his eyes. Instead, they are hard and narrow. "I can't fucking leave. It's my fight, Calla."

Great! I've completely embarrassed myself. Why didn't anyone tell me this? I glance at Liv in question, and she shrugs innocently in a way that says, *I thought you knew.*

"Everything about this is illegal," I remark.

Ace's eyes travel to Liv and then Theo as if silently communicating that he told them so. He's pissed off, it's clear from the way he towers over us with distinct male dominance, but when isn't he?

If my dad knew that I was here, participating in illegal activity... he wouldn't be impressed. I can picture him ordering a whole SWAT team to shut this place down.

Ace's name is called from the stage, and he turns to me. "Just stay out of trouble." For a second, his voice softens. When our eyes meet, I wipe the sweat from the palms of my hands on my jeans. Ace is looking at me like he knows all my secrets. I don't know anything about him, except that he's a lawbreaking asshole—that sums it up.

"You brought her here. Make sure she doesn't leave your sight," Ace orders Theo before striding away. Why does Ace care what happens to me all of a sudden? But this isn't the first time he's done this.

"Alright, alright," a familiar voice booms through the place, and the loud voices surrounding us dim. The only sounds left are the breathing and occasional whispers of the crowd. "You all know the deal, so let's start off by introducing our first competitor." My eyes scan the crowd for the source of the voice.

I can't believe what I'm seeing—it's the university chancellor, Mr. Howley. This gets better and better. I turn to Theo. "That's the school—" I begin.

"Shh." He glances around, checking no one overheard me. "His name is Dean, and I don't think he wants everyone knowing his day job."

I wonder why.

Ace's opponent steps into the ring, and my stomach sinks. The man is twice the age of Ace, and he towers over Ace by a mile. I don't know why, but I'm suddenly anxious, and my heartbeat quickens. Does Ace have a death wish?

I glance at Liv, then Zach, they're talking amongst themselves and making jokes. I can't say that I like Ace, but I didn't assume that his best friends would want to see him end up in a hospital. Or worse, much worse.

When the fight commences, it's clear that age and size don't have anything to do with skill. Ace is in his element. His opponent attempts to throw punches, but Ace dodges every single one of them. Ace jumps on the balls of his feet, challenging his opponent—wearing him out.

I'm unable to peel my eyes away from Ace. The way his body strains, exposing all his abdominal muscles, is almost sinful. Well, I guess I figured out what he does to keep fit. Ace's eyes land on mine through the crowd. It's as if he senses me checking him out, and his mouth screws up into a cunning smirk. He claims my gaze for an elongated moment.

The crowd grows restless, catcalling, and shouting. Ace notices this, and he finally throws his first punch, forcing his opponent to stumble back into the despair of the ropes. Unfortunately, he doesn't have the time to recuperate before Ace follows through with another blow and then another. It's clear who the crowd favorite is when the words of encouragement spill, bellowing at Ace. "Finish him!"

I have the urge to look away. The opponent's blood is splattered on the floor and smeared over his face. Ace's hands are covered in it too. Nevertheless, it's as though someone is holding my eyes open and compelling me to watch. Ace doesn't stop until Dean, who I assume is the referee, hauls him off the slumped body.

The crowd erupts into cheers, and I'm pushed and shoved in every direction. I turn to search for Theo or anyone to grab onto. Shit. There are hundreds of people here, and I rise on my tiptoes, scanning the crowd for my friends with no luck.

"I had a feeling I'd see you here," a voice to my right rumbles. I spin to find Logan leaning against the wall, hands in the pockets of his jeans. I'm able to make out his features better now that we are under a reasonable amount of light, instead of the shadows.

"Your boyfriend is quite the fighter," he observes with a feral grin.

"Ace is *not* my boyfriend." Far from it.

"No?"

I shake my head and purse my lips together. Again, the same feeling as last time washes over me, instructing me to get the hell away from him.

"What's the deal with you two anyway?" I dare to ask. Ace wasn't thrilled to see Logan at the bonfire.

Logan chuckles. "Ace and I share…history. Perhaps this isn't the best place for me to tell you about it. Let's get out of here?" He stands upright and moves closer to me.

My breathing accelerates as my hands shake, and my eyes scan the place for the group. Logan doesn't look like the type to take no for an answer, so I quickly race through ideas in my head.

He takes another step forward, smirking in a challenge, and I retreat into something warm and hard. A hand glides around my waist and pulls me closer. I don't have to turn around to know it's Ace. Everything about him is familiar, although it shouldn't be.

"Logan, get the fuck away from her."

"We're just talking." Logan shrugs and looks from Ace to me. I don't dare to glance back at Ace, but I know the way his jaw is ticking in wrath.

"Next time, don't even look at her," Ace instructs. He turns away and pulls me with him before Logan has the opportunity to reply. I'm appreciative of Ace—who knows what would've happened in that situation, but I'm also irritated. What if I actually wanted to talk to Logan? Who does Ace think he is? We need to have a serious conversation about his contradictory behavior.

I shrug him off and spot Theo and Josh heading toward us, along with the others. We push past the crowd toward the back door and climb the stairs to meet the night's fresh air. I inhale deeply and relax my shoulders for the first time since entering this building.

Ace's motorcycle is parked across the road. How did I miss it when we arrived here? That thought is immediately erased when a much bigger dilemma hits me. It's dark, and I didn't drive here. I can't be a passenger in the car when it's dark.

What was I thinking earlier when I agreed to come? Oh, that's right, I wasn't thinking. I must have been too caught up in Liv's invitation.

I glance at the car, and I notice out of the corner of my eye that Ace is observing me, he knows I screwed up. He raises an eyebrow at me and pauses, waiting for me to come up with an excuse. I can ask the group if I can drive, but that would prompt more questions than I'm ready for.

"Hey, Liv," I say, and everyone turns at the sound of my voice. I clear my throat. "I don't think I'm feeling too well. I might walk to the house. You know, the fresh air will make me feel better, I think," I babble, not grasping what nonsense is spilling from my mouth. All I know is I can't get in that car. Ace's lips twitch into a smile.

"Are you insane?" Theo says, chuckling. "It will take you hours, and we're not going to let you walk at night by yourself."

I clearly didn't think this through.

Ace is in the middle of the road, between the car and his motorcycle. Luckily, it's a quiet street. "Calla is coming with me," Ace says casually. My mouth gapes open along with everyone else's.

Not long ago, he didn't want me here, and now he's offering to help me. I didn't ask for his aid, and frankly, I'm over his behavior. "I'm not coming with you, Ace," I say, and he stares at me like I told him the world is ending.

"You are," he states in a definite tone.

"I'll walk," I say to everyone, but mostly Ace. I throw an apologetic glance at the group and set off in the direction that I assume we came from. Everyone is still too stunned about Ace's offer to follow me.

After a few minutes of walking, I retrieve my phone and type the address into Google Maps. Two and a half hours. Can this day get any better? This is the exact reason why I don't do everyday things that people my age do. However, I would argue at this moment that going to an underground fighting arena isn't a regular thing.

It isn't long before the sound of a motorcycle approaches behind me. Here we go. Here comes the whirlwind of mood swings. "Get on the bike, Calla," Ace commands as he pulls up next to me.

"No." I maintain my eyes ahead and continue walking. Ace struggles to keep up with me and balance on his bike at such a slow pace.

"Are you always this stubborn? I'm trying to help you. Just get on the bike." He dismounts his bike and walks it next to me. I roll my eyes at the irony.

"Why do you care what I do?" I ask, not anticipating an answer.

"We're friends," he states.

I have the urge to laugh, because we certainly aren't friends. I don't even know what it means to be friends with Ace. Since we've met, he's been nothing but disrespectful to me, speaking about me like I'm not there, communicating only when it accommodates him, and ordering me. "I'll walk."

"Fuck, Calla. I thought you wanted to be friends?" Ace runs his hand through his hair in frustration. He has to be kidding me, he's behaving like I'm the one providing him with mixed signals.

I halt and face him, narrowing my eyes. "Are you sure you don't have a personality disorder? I can't keep up with you! One minute you feel nothing for me, and the next, you act like a possessive boyfriend. Then you tell me to stay away from you! Now, you want to be friends?!" I'm almost yelling in the middle of the road. I may appear psychotic to innocent bystanders, but I can't keep up with him.

He kicks the side stand of his motorcycle more forcefully than necessary and crosses his arms. "I'm trying to save you from disappointment."

"What's that supposed to mean?"

He exhales deeply and shakes his head, unable to provide an answer. I don't care anymore. "Whatever."

I turn on my heel to walk away, but his fingers curl around my wrist, pulling me toward him. My feet topple over each other, and I stumble into his chest. Ace encircles his arm around my waist to stabilize me, I hold my breath as my cheeks burn.

The corners of his mouth arch as if he knows what he's doing to me. It's an unusual feeling, one that I've never felt before, especially not with Nate.

With Nate, it was innocent. Our relationship was built on friendship and familiarity more than anything else. We had sex because it was something everyone else was doing, and when I tell you my first and only time was horrible, I'm not exaggerating.

Nate claimed to have slept with lots of girls before me, but I think that was only his ego talking. He skipped foreplay and went straight for the big bang. The pain was unbearable, and Scooby-Doo, which played in the background on the large plasma TV, wasn't helping me relax. To make matters worse, Nate's poodle was attempting to hump his leg the whole time.

Fortunately, it took less than five minutes for Nate to finish, and I didn't have the urge to try it again since. Thinking back on it now, I'm surprised that we proceeded to date for another month after that unfortunate event.

I peek up at Ace through my lashes, he's already watching me. For a second, and *only* for a second, my gaze trails to his lips, and I envision what it would be like to welcome them against my own. *Snap out of it!* Ace is not someone I should be getting tangled up with for many reasons.

"Let's start over. As friends?" he says.

There's that word again, and I still don't know what it signifies. I deflect my attention from his mouth, striving to better understand what the word *friends* means to him.

He sure doesn't act like this with Liv or any of his other deemed friends. "You'll have to elaborate on that. I'm struggling to keep up with you."

Ace pauses for a moment with his arm still around me, and he scans my expression for clarification.

"You want to be friends…like you and Liv?" I prompt.

He closes his eyes briefly and shakes his head, which makes me even more confused. I attempt to turn away from him—there's only a certain amount of Ace I can handle in one day, and that limit has already lapsed.

Ace gently positions his hand on my jaw, turning me to meet his gaze again. "Like you and me." I'm still confused about what that means, but the way he says it causes me feel *something*, something that I shouldn't. Am I reading too much into this? Is this another one of his games?

"Is this just another act, Ace? Because if it is, then I don't want to be a part of it. I'm exhausted with the way your moods abruptly change."

"I'm sorry," he says. I stare at him, perplexed at the words that emit from his mouth. I never expected an apology, even though I damn well know his actions merited one.

"An apology? Wow, who would have thought we would come so far?"

He shakes his head with amusement. "Now, get on the bike."

I shoot him a look of disapproval, and he adds, "*Please* get on the bike, Calla."

9

The Game

Ace disappears for the remainder of the weekend. He drove me home on Saturday night after the club, and I haven't seen him since. I spend the weekend with Liv, helping her start on the cheer squad uniforms.

There's a lot I don't know about her. She grew up competing for the spotlight amongst her four younger siblings. Her parents divorced when she was only five years old, and although she says she doesn't remember it much, her countenance tells a different story.

On Monday, after classes, I arrive home to find a pink sticky note on my door with a CD taped underneath. **My favorite is track 3**. There's no doubt in my mind that the note is from Ace. I peel it off and take the CD in my hands. The only place I can listen to it is in my car. Ace is either very observant or simply assumed that I have a CD player, which no one does these days.

I go downstairs to thank him for it, maybe even listen to the CD in his room, where he's bound to have a CD player. However, I find the house empty. Instead, I grab a pen from my room and a sticky note from my stationery. **Why autobiographies?** All of his books are some kind of autobiography. I could never quite get into one myself. I stick to fiction.

The following day, I find his reply stuck to my door. **Everyone who writes them finds the good out of every seemingly dire situation**—an interesting way of perceiving things.

Ace and I communicate through sticky notes for the remainder of the week. I don't ask where he disappears to or why he's barely in class, our assignment isn't due for another three weeks, so we have time.

We open up more than we would have in person. The distance between us serves as a safety barrier that we can lean against. Yet, neither of us pushes too far, afraid to spiral down into the unspoken shadows and ultimately destroy the pathway we have built.

The university football team—which Theo is a part of—has their first season game on Thursday night. Theo suggested I come with Liv and Zach to watch. It's only a fifteen-minute walk to the fields from our house, and it's "sure to be a rowdy game," as Theo had put it.

I walk downstairs to meet Liv and Zach once I get ready, only to notice that Ace is leaning on the open-door frame. He wears black jeans and a dark t-shirt that match his persona exceptionally well. In some ways, he's an enigma that's impossible to solve, and yet, I notice a part of myself when I look at him. A piece that's bitter at the world and striving to push everyone away who tries to help.

Pausing on the stairs, I allow myself to watch Ace as he stares out into the distance. His tattooed arms are folded over his chest, closing himself off.

The wooden stairs creak beneath my feet, and his head turns in my direction. His eyes roam me once—twice. I force myself to not quiver underneath his mysterious gaze.

"I suppose that's better than your pink slippers." He gives me a knowing smile, showing his prominent dimples off.

Oh God, the towel incident from two weeks ago. He decides to bring that up now?

Heat charges to my cheeks. "I don't know what you're talking about."

"Don't you?" he prompts, taking a few steps in my direction. I'm still on the stairs, watching him inquisitively. One would think Ace's tall and strapping figure weighs him down. However, his movements are anything but that. On the contrary, they are oddly graceful.

I shake my head in response, maintaining my eyes on him. A playful smirk dances on his enthralling mouth, and I put my foot out to take another step toward him. Unfortunately, I misjudge the distance of the stairs and stumble forward, grabbing the wooden stair rail.

Once I stabilize myself, my eyes land on Ace. He's on his knees at the bottom of the stairs, ready to catch me. "What were you going to do?" I ask, furrowing my eyebrows.

"Soften the blow, so I could make a joke about you falling for me." He grins.

I roll my eyes. "That's unfortunate."

Ace opens his mouth to say something, but he's interrupted.

"Ready?" Liv says from the top of the stairs. She looks from me to Ace, and her jaw drops as she raises her eyebrows in question.

"Waiting on you two," Ace answers, standing up. Liv and Zach descend the stairs, and we set off toward the university campus.

The night sky is covered with a blanket of clouds that float above us at a rapid speed. Occasionally, there's an opening where a group of stars peeks through, fighting for air, but the shadows that follow swallow them up again. The atmosphere is muggy with the promise of rain later on.

Ace and I end up walking behind Liv and Zach. They're grossly in love, and it shows. Their arms are draped over each other, and Zach says something that earns a burst of laughter from Liv. Occasionally, his lips brush her temple, and I notice how Zach pulls her closer to him.

"How did they meet?" I ask Ace.

Liv overhears me and turns around, her smile widening. "It was love at first sight. Isn't that so, babe?" She tugs on Zach's arm.

"There's no such thing," Ace interrupts.

I disagree. My dad fell in love with Mom when he first saw her. He's told me the story over a hundred times.

It was one of his first shifts on the job. He got called to deal with a public nuisance matter. My mother was twenty-four, freshly single, and drunk—stripping in the middle of a busy highway. She didn't remember how she got there. Instead of arresting her, my dad dropped her home in his patrol car with the lights on simply because she requested it. He didn't even question it, he was too consumed by her. They were inseparable after that.

"What would you know? You've never had a girlfriend, Ace," Liv says and turns back to Zach.

I raise my eyebrows. "You've never had a girlfriend?"

"It's not a big deal." He shrugs.

It kind of is. I've had numerous boyfriends from first grade up until the last. None of them had been serious, but that's not the point. "Is there a reason?"

"I've never met someone who's been able to keep my attention for long enough. I don't think it's fair to stick around purely for the sake of it." Ace shoves his hands in his pockets.

"That's an awfully cocky thing to say," I note, glancing at him for elaboration. We pass a street lamp, and the warm yellow ambiance forces Ace's eyes to appear softer.

He raises his eyebrows. "Do you want me to lie and tell you that the reason I've never had a girlfriend is because I'm a conceited asshole?"

A suppress a smile. "That certainly would be more believable."

Ace chuckles and shakes his head. The hearty sound sends a burst of electricity through me. I'm still trying to get used to him being anything but an asshole, so when he laughs like that, it seizes me by surprise.

I swear, from the moment I punched him at the party, he's had a whole mood revamp. I'm still confused by it, but I'm not going to bother questioning it anymore. I like this side of him.

"Thank you for the CD, by the way. You were right—Arctic Monkeys are pretty good."

Ace glances at me and offers me a look that says *I told you so.* "What's your favorite song?"

"Ah, I think it would have to be *505*."

"One of my favorites too," he says. Our arms brush unintentionally, and the hairs on the back of my neck rise.

"Have you traveled?" I ask.

"A bit. My father..." His tone sharpens. "Travelled for work a lot. Sometimes he'd take my mom and me with him, it didn't happen very often. But I visited Canada and England when I was younger," he explains as we continue walking.

"And then my mom's parents lived in Spain, so we visited them every now and then. Until my Abuela—grandmother—passed and my mom moved my Avô into a nursing home here. He's passed away since too."

"I'm sorry." I'm surprised that Ace chose to reveal that much information about himself, about his family.

"It was a long time ago." Ace brushes it off. "I wasn't extremely close to them."

"So, you have a bit of Spanish in you?"

"Only on my Abuela's side. My Avô was Brazilian."

I make an effort to look him up and down. "I can see it." It explains his skin's beautiful light brown complexion and the striking dark hair.

I stare at my feet as we cross the road, heading toward the campus.

"Your favorite movie?" Ace starts up another conversation.

"I can't pick one," I say. There are too many great films. I've watched them all through the days I locked myself in my room.

"Name a few," Ace suggests.

"*The Time Traveler's Wife*—but the book is so much better—*La La Land*, *Eternal Sunshine of the Spotless Mind*..."

Ace laughs.

"What?"

"I don't get it. What's the point of erasing their memories if they were going to come back together again?" He looks at me for further clarification.

The movie follows a couple who embark on a journey to erase themselves from each other's memories after an awful breakup.

"It shows that despite their best efforts to forget each other, and despite each other's flaws and failures, they're still willing to give it another chance. People can't be modified by ignorance or renunciation," I explain, mindlessly moving my hands around.

He shakes his head. "If you observed the ending, it shows that they end up in the same position over and over again. They find each other, fall in love, break up, and then erase each other over and over. I don't see why they would waste their time."

"Yes, they may eventually break up, but they don't care. It's about their time together. You've never had a girlfriend, and it shows." I roll my eyes.

Ace shoves his hands deeper into his pockets. He shakes his head again, a smirk emerging on his broad mouth.

I'm surprised to see the red university buildings in the distance already. The walk went quicker than I anticipated. We make our way to the fields at the back of the campus. The football guys are divided into four groups. Each group is doing warm-up drills that have been assigned to them.

Theo spots us and confirms the coach isn't watching before jogging toward us with a grin. His already athletic figure is emphasized by the protective layer of clothing clinging to his shoulders and legs.

"Hey, guys! Get ready for a dirty game. The guys from Ashworth have already started fights with two of our guys. We're not going to be holding back," he says, anticipation peering through his voice. Theo is jumping from foot to foot in the same spot, keeping his body warm.

Oh, Ashworth University. The rivals.

"I hope not. I came tonight to see blood spilled," a voice speaks from behind us. I twist my body around to find Josh standing with his arms crossed. When did he get here?

The coach, that's in no shape to play himself, blows the whistle that dangles off his chest. "Theo Medeiros! Get over here, now!"

"Oops, sorry, guys. Have to go!" Theo says and jogs off toward his teammates.

We find our seats in the grandstand, away from everyone else. Once the game starts, Josh calls out encouraging words to Theo.

"Come on! You got this, Theodore."

My gaze darts to Ace, but his attention isn't on the game anymore. His body is rigid, and he's gripping the seat with his hands so brutally that his knuckles have gone white. His forearm veins are present, swelling due to the tension. My eyes continue to travel up the leanness of his body, which is stiff on the bench, finally landing on his face.

Ace's mouth is set into a forbidden line. His jaw is clenched so powerfully that my own teeth begin to ache. "Hey, you okay?" I ask, following his gaze.

A blacked-out vintage Chevrolet has pulled up in the parking lot across the road. The streetlamps that surround the area are bright, so I can discern the details. There aren't many cars there, only the ones from Ashworth University, most students from ours came here on foot.

The driver's side door of the Chevrolet swings open, and an eerily familiar figure climbs out. I squint, peering over Ace's shoulder. The guy turns, giving me a clear view of his face. Logan. He sticks his chest out further and stands taller. Another person gets out of the passenger seat. I don't recognize him.

"Stay here," Ace snarls. He stands and storms toward Logan. His hands are clenched into fists at his side, and I hope a fight isn't about to break out in the parking lot. From the way Ace is striding toward Logan, the chances of a peaceful confrontation seem awfully limited.

The hurricane of Ace blows to Logan's car, and a heated argument erupts between them. I can't distinguish what they are saying, but Ace's rage is burning off him. Logan, on the other hand, is inclined against the side of his car.

Ace slams the hood of the car with his hand. "Get the fuck

out of here!"

I'm so consumed by the scene unfolding in front of me I barely notice Zach and Josh are already halfway there. Liv escapes her seat to follow, and I find myself doing the same. We jog down the stairs and through groups of game-watchers to catch up to them.

We get closer, and a feral smirk appears on Logan's mouth when his attention lands on us. "Hey, what's going on here?" Zach asks. No one listens to him.

"Logan, you have three seconds to leave," Ace seethes, inches away from his face. I've seen Ace angry before—all the times that we ran into each other when we first met. But this is different. The colossal fury is building through his shaking body. I'm terrified of what might happen if the situation isn't diffused. Fast.

Logan doesn't move. His smirk doesn't falter as he speaks. "Or what?"

As soon as the words leave his mouth, Ace grabs Logan by the collar. Everything happens too fast for me to comprehend. Logan's friend, the one that came with him, is instantly at Ace's side. Josh and Zach are there, too, preparing for a fight to break out.

Zach places a hand on Ace's shoulder. "Let it go, man. Come on, let's get out of here."

Ace ignores him. Instead, he shoves Logan with a colossal amount of force into the open driver's side door. Logan staggers back, but regains his balance without delay. He's not backing down.

"You don't want to see what will happen," Ace corners him.

Logan shakes his head, an animalistic expression crosses his face. A vicious sneer.

He knows he's outnumbered, but he clearly doesn't seem to care. He's either foolish or knows something that we don't. "One wrong move, Ace, and everyone here will know your secret. Do you think your friends will accept you after knowing what you've done?"

Ace glowers at Logan with absolute hatred. His eyes flicker toward us, from Zach to Josh, and then linger the longest on me. There's a glimmer of culpability through the rage and animosity which gushes through him. Ace turns on his heel and storms off in the opposite direction.

I have the urge to follow him, to ensure he's okay. Yet, I'm unable to move my feet, they are fixed to the ground.

"Good decision," Logan calls after him, brushing his shirt with his hand as if this was merely a misunderstanding.

"I'm going to make sure he doesn't do anything irrational. Stay here, watch the game," Zach says to us and chases after Ace.

Liv nods in understanding, and when I don't make a move, she tugs on my arm. My feet move, shuffling in front of one another. As we walk back toward the fields, my own hands are shaking uncontrollably.

We stay for the remainder of the game, but the mood has drastically fallen. No one speaks of the incident. The words that Logan said replay in my mind over and over. Logan holds something over Ace that not even his best friends know. What could possibly be so awful?

✦

Ace maintains his distance from me after the game and once again disappears over the weekend. No one says anything, and Zach becomes more distant than usual. I focus on my university work and finally type up an article for the newspaper. After reading over it more than a hundred times, I delete it.

Nate hasn't come into the café since the day after the party, so

I assumed, as one would, that he received the message. But that doesn't seem to be the case, because when I turn around, he's right in front of me.

"Want to go see a movie?" he asks as I move past him with a tray of coffee cups. I set the tray on the bench behind the counter and place the cups in the sink.

"Nate, I'm working," I say, throwing mango bits in the blender for a smoothie order.

Mia is off today, so I'm working with Brody. He seems normal... well, more normal than usual. Maybe Mars isn't doing something uncanny with Jupiter anymore. Brody doesn't communicate much, and perhaps that would be awkward for some, but a sense of calm washes over me in his presence.

"I'll wait." Nate takes a seat on the barstool near the counter.

"Nate, what are you doing? We broke up," I ask, not wanting to cause a scene.

"I miss you," he says. I roll my eyes. "Seriously, Calla, I do. I miss being able to talk to you, and you know... just hang out like we used to. It's different here. I haven't made many friends, and..."

He looks genuinely upset, and I kind of feel sorry for him. "Fine, we can go see a movie. But don't get any ideas. This doesn't mean that we're getting back together," I make myself clear. Apart from the minor incident called losing my virginity, which put me off sex for the rest of my life, we had pleasant times together.

Brody eyes Nate now and then. "Is that your boyfriend?" Brody finally asks me.

"No, ex," I reply.

"Hmm," he hums, but I can sense there's something else on his mind—unless I'm imagining things. Liv and Zach walk into the cafe when there are twenty minutes left of my shift, with Ace following suit. His gleaming eyes search for me, and when he finds what he's looking for, a crooked grin emerges on his mouth.

Even after a week, I'm still not accustomed to this side of him. A switch has flipped, and he's suddenly pleasant. This is only toward me, his behavior toward others hasn't changed, making me feel… *What? What does that make you feel, Calla? Warm and fuzzy? Snap out of it, because it probably isn't going to last.* Although my conscience is right, I can't help but notice the good in him, and I want to spend time with him. As friends, of course.

Over the week, I've discovered that he's an old soul at heart. Apart from Arctic Monkeys, the CD that he gave me had other rock music on it. Some nights I stay in my car listening to it. His favorite color is black. I told him it's not a color. Still, he was adamant that it could be whatever he wanted it to be, I didn't bother arguing.

Ace's gaze shifts from me to Nate, who's sitting in front of me. Nate is clueless as he scrolls through his Facebook feed, patiently waiting for me. I'm about to clock off when Ace approaches us and towers above me. "Do you want a ride back home?" Ace questions without acknowledging Nate.

Zach and Liv leave the café. They open the door wide enough for a breeze to glide its way inside, and the smell of Ace's aftershave lingers in the air, musky with a hint of sweetness.

Nate's head snaps up at Ace's words, and he rises from the seat. He stretches his body out to appear taller. "There is no need, dude. I'll take her."

"Why bother when I'm going there anyway?" Ace smirks, his eyes not leaving mine. He doesn't even send a glance in Nate's direction.

Out of the corner of my sight, Nate shoots me a look. I tear my eyes away from Ace. "He's my housemate," I explain to Nate, unsure why I even need to.

"Calla and I are going to the movies," Nate presses, his eyes darkening with irritation, and he steps closer to me.

"Well, that's funny, because I clearly remember Calla and I making plans to work on our assignment tonight." Ace raises his eyebrow. "Must have double booked yourself there, Calla." A boyish grin crosses his face.

What? I don't remember making any plans with him tonight. I glance at Ace, puzzled. I'm uncertain if he genuinely believes that we have something planned, or is this one of his games?

"We can work on it tomorrow?"

"No…tonight, Calla." My name rolls off his tongue like honey, with a hint of a sharp edge.

I rack my brain for any recollection of making plans with Ace. Eventually, beginning to doubt my memory, I glance back at Nate. "Maybe another time," I say. Before I have the time to spit out an apology, Ace wraps his arm around my waist. He tugs me smoothly toward the door.

"What was that?" I cross my arms once we're outside. My eyes dart through the window toward Nate, who's still standing where I left him. I'm not exactly sure what Ace just pulled, and I'm not in the slightest bit impressed. Why does he think he can do that? Logan, now Nate.

"What was what?" he asks nonchalantly, attempting to put the bike helmet on me. I stop him and place my hand on his solid chest. I attempt to push him away from me, but he doesn't move, so I end up taking a step back. This results in Ace furrowing his eyebrows.

"We didn't make plans." I wait for an explanation.

"Didn't we? Hmm…" He pauses for a moment and cocks his head. His eyes sparkle. "Well, do you want to work on the assignment tonight, since you don't have any other plans?" A smile crosses his face.

"Ace—" I begin, still requiring an explanation for his behavior. I haven't spoken to him since the game. The memory of the pure vehemence of anger is still vivid in my mind.

"Perfect," Ace says, not allowing me to finish. Instead, he sets the helmet over my head.

Ugh! What is wrong with him!?

He hops onto the motorcycle and watches me, waiting for me to get behind him. I roll my eyes and swing my leg over the side. I don't have the energy to argue with him, and it's either walk home or this. Plus, I can't escape the lively feeling embracing my body at the thought of spending more time with Ace.

I place my hands loosely around his waist. He stiffens, his stomach becoming rock-hard underneath my faint touch.

I keep my hands freely around him the whole way home, avoiding grasping tighter when we round the corners. My eyes remain open, even when they water in the breeze. We pass the shadows of the trees at a swift speed. We're barely going fifty miles per hour, but liberty encompasses us. My soul feels limitless and untamed. Is this why Ace prefers motorcycles?

Back at the house, I walk toward the stairs with Ace behind me. "Where are you going?"

"I'll just quickly change and grab my notepad," I say and continue heading up.

"Notepad?"

I turn and motion with my hand. "The assignment? I thought you wanted to do the assignment, Ace. Isn't that why I'm not at the movies with Nate?"

His face tenses up at the mention of Nate, but he covers it with a smile. "Yeah, the assignment… I'll be in my room, so…come when you're ready."

He's acting strange.

In my room, I change into a long white t-shirt and some pajama shorts. I run a brush through my hair and clean my teeth before grabbing my notepad, heading downstairs.

Ace is lounging against the headboard of his bed. He's changed into light gray sweatpants, and, you guessed it, he's shirtless. I glance around his room to his bookshelf, toward the door that leads outside—anywhere but him, but I find my gaze drifting toward him. It's hard not to when someone looks like *that*.

Ace skims a hand through his hair, and his muscles contract with every movement. He looks at me and runs his tongue over his bottom lip, knowing *exactly* what he's doing. I bite the inside of my cheek.

Oh my God. Stop standing there and staring at him!

I ensure to sit as far as I can from him and bring my knees up, leaning my notebook against them. His eyes scan me, and his lips twitch into a smile. Finally, he looks away and picks up the TV remote. "Do you want to watch a movie instead?"

My eyes widen, and I'm lost for words. "Are you kidding me? What about the assignment?" Ace bends over to the other side of the bed, where his books lie on the ground, and pulls out a paper, handing it to me.

"What is this?" I ask as my eyes linger over it. "Is this the assignment? You wrote the whole assignment by yourself?"

"Feel free to change things as you see fit. I emailed you a copy as well. Since I haven't been around, I assumed it's not fair to expect you to do it alone. Plus, you're stubborn and unwilling to talk about how the issues at hand affect you, so I took it upon myself."

When I'm too stunned to reply, he nudges me with his elbow.

"Don't look so pleased. Now we have time to watch a movie." He grins, turning on the TV.

He scrolls through the options before choosing a horror movie. He then proceeds to get up and turn the lights off. I stare at him, dumbfounded. Ace continues to surprise me in every way, and I'm curious to read what he's written for the assignment.

He shuffles down the bed, getting comfortable. I do the same, my arm brushing against his. Goosebumps accompany the faint contact between us. I don't dare glance up at him—my eyes are glued to the screen even though I'm too distracted to pay attention.

"Are you always needing to take control of everything?" I ask, finally meeting his curious stare.

"Are you mad that I wrote the assignment? I didn't think you would mind," Ace replies, tilting his head quizzically while assessing me with those charismatic eyes of his.

I shrug. "I'm not mad about the assignment. Thank you for writing it. However, I've come to realize it's a pattern with you. The constant pull toward requiring to take everything into your own hands," I explain, striving to get a better understanding of his furtive thoughts, even though it may be something he won't want to answer.

His actions prove to be on the same wavelength as mine, we both feel secure when in charge. Yet, his are heightened. I've come to realize, his moods are the driving force for the events that follow. I may be wrong, although I doubt it. "I'm just curious," I add.

"It's a sense of stability. I'm not sure why you may be surprised. I know for a fact we're not so different, since both of us want power of the most fundamental element. Time."

I refrain from telling him that perhaps, time doesn't exist. It's not the point, and Ace is right. With time manipulation, there would be endless possibilities and different outcomes, and I would be at the helm of them, able to alter any situation as I see fit.

Tearing my gaze away from his, I don't move for the next hour as I reflect on our conversation. My body becomes rigid, and pins and needles form in my leg. I wiggle back into the headboard, unable to sit still. My t-shirt rides up, and so do my shorts, exposing the rest of my upper thigh.

Ace's eyes are on me—I can feel them. The lingering makes my throat dry. I struggle not to flinch away or show him that he affects me in a way that I can't possibly begin to describe.

Eventually, I build up the courage to face him—to meet the dark, alluring stare that ignites a wildfire inside of me. I want him to touch me, so I can experience the spark that often follows our contact. My eyes trail down to his tempting lips, which part marginally. How would they feel against my own? The wildfire flares with need.

Oh my…what am I thinking?

"Is there a problem?" I ask, my voice softer than intended. Ace's eyes snap away from mine. He mumbles something I can't quite catch under his breath. His jaw tenses, and he exhales deeply, shaking his head.

"I'm going for a shower," he states, storming toward his bathroom. I'm a bit taken aback by his suddenness. I continue watching the movie before turning the lights on. Ten minutes later, Ace finally returns.

He sits next to me. His shoulder is cool against my own. "Cold shower?"

"Hmm? Uh…yeah, the hot water is broken," he replies, not looking at me.

It wasn't the last time I checked.

10

Solace

I descend the stairs. "Is there a certain plumber that you guys use?" I ask Liv. Our shower is leaking, and the water pressure feels like someone's peeing on you. It'll take me at least two hours to wash my hair.

"Already called him. He won't be here until Tuesday," she informs me, and my eyes widen. It's Friday. "We'll have to use the one in Ace's room," she adds.

"His hot water is broken." Seems like we'll be having cold showers for a while.

"It was fine half an hour ago?" She spreads butter on her toast.

Oh.

Liv and I've been spending a lot more time together. It's effortless to fall into a routine of familiarity. A routine where my life is reaching some normalcy, no more inclination to isolate myself.

I retrieve a tray of strawberries from the fridge and close the door, turning around. *Oh, God.* Ace stands in front of me…directly in front of me. How did he get here, swiftly and out of no-where?

"Good morning," he says. The husky voice draws my eyes up

to his perfect mouth. I wonder how many girls he's kissed and what it did to them to feel his lips against theirs. I want him to—

Stop. I ought to bring these amatory thoughts to an end, especially when Ace observes me with a mindful eye. It's as though he knows my precise thought process.

I peer up through my lashes, meeting his penetrating eyes. My cheeks burn. "Good morning, Ace," I say, but it surfaces as barely a whisper. My lips are dry, so I run my tongue over them.

Ace coughs, clearing his throat. I use this moment to take a step back, away from him. There's too much tension between us. Why does he have to stand so close to me? He picks his shirt up off the bench and puts it on, promptly marching out the door without another word.

"You and Ace, huh?" Liv places the butter knife in the dishwasher.

"Hmm?" I quickly glance over to her, and she arches her eyebrows in accusation. "No, no, we're just, uh, getting along—like friends," I ramble, retrieving a glass of water.

"Friends? I don't recall myself looking like that at my friends."

I groan, taking a sip.

"I wasn't talking about you, but now that you mention it…" She sits on the stool across from me. She places her elbows on the counter and her head in her hands. "Are you and Ace…you know?" She wiggles her eyebrows. "Fucking?"

I spit my water, almost choking on it.

"Liv!" I shoot her a wide-eyed look, grabbing a wash cloth to wipe the mess.

"I'll take that as a no." She chuckles while taking a bite of her toast.

"Definitely a no," I agree, but I gulp loudly, unable to get the idea out of my head.

Fridays are usually long-drawn-out. I only have one lecture and no work. I don't particularly enjoy not having anything to do. My mind demands to be occupied. If I let it roam freely, I discover it tugging me toward the past that I can't change, no matter how hard I yearn to.

Earlier in the week, Theo asked me to help him study. In order to keep his scholarship and continue playing for the football team, he's required to get marks above average, something he's currently struggling to achieve, especially with the classes that require math.

Since my mom was a school teacher, she kept me ahead in my classes and taught me more than was needed. So, it's no problem to help Theo study, even though we don't share the same class.

"What's the story between you and Josh?" I question, and Theo raises an eyebrow. "You know, since you two are always bickering like old women." Our textbooks are spread out on his bed and on the floor. We've been studying for the last couple of hours.

He laughs, the sound bouncing off the walls. "Josh's dad is my dad," he says, and I form an 'o' with my mouth. I guessed they were close, but I didn't realize how close.

"Josh is my half-brother. We have the same dad. He cheated on Josh's mom," he explains. "It's really messed up."

How hasn't this come up in conversation earlier? But I guess everyone assumed that I already knew. "Somehow, messed-up things seem to generate something good with them too," I say. The universe has a funny way of bringing people together.

Theo nods, almost to himself. "You're right."

"Have you always wanted to be an engineer?" I ask.

"It was the only subject that interested me in school. I liked to build things and understand how they work. The only issue that's holding me back is the math side to it," he explains.

Theo jumps on the bed, and I emit a small squeal. He tickles me, and I can't breathe. I'm laughing and telling him to stop, but he doesn't oblige.

"What's that noise?" I ask in between laughter and catching my breath. The muffled sound of house-party music etches its way through the walls.

"The beginning of a frat party," Theo says sheepishly, supporting his weight on his elbows.

"Oh. No, I'm not staying for that." I quickly sit up.

Theo pouts and sets his hand on his chest, over his heart. "Come on, please. Liv will be here, and that weird girl is coming too, I think," Theo informs me.

I cock my eyebrow. "Mia?" Theo nods, and I roll my eyes. "She's not weird."

"She is a little," Theo says, I narrow my eyes at him. Mia isn't weird, people are quick to criticize.

"I don't know. I'm not really into parties or drinking," I say, and he delivers another pleading look. "Fine, I guess I can stay for a little."

Shortly, the music is blaring, and people begin showing up. Theo drags me downstairs and fills a red cup with water, passing it to me. "Thanks," I laugh, accepting it.

"I'll be right back," Theo tells me, walking toward the back door. I stand in the kitchen, shifting my weight from one foot to another, scanning the room for anyone I may recognize.

I stroll outside once the music gets rowdier, hoping to escape this place before Theo notices I'm gone.

My eyes immediately land on Ace. He's leaning against a tree with the same girl from the bonfire and a few other people I'm not acquainted with. The girl's hand lingers up Ace's arm, and she giggles too much when he speaks. An unusual feeling pierces my chest.

Turning on my heel, I step back inside, but not before I notice Ace's head snap in my direction. My heart races in my chest, and I have no urge to acknowledge that observing them together makes me feel a certain way when, frankly, I shouldn't care.

Pushing past a few people, I stand in the hallway, seeking to soothe my breathing. More people are inside now, and the atmosphere strains in on me. I lean my shoulder against the wall, letting the coolness seep through the thin material of my shirt.

A calloused hand snakes around my waist, and I know it's Ace. Spinning around, I face him. His touch is uninviting, cold—especially after he's been touching someone else. I shake his hand off and cross my arms over my chest.

Ace sighs and turns around, about to walk away. I'm bewildered. It's like he wanted to say something but changed his mind. What was the point of him following me inside?

"You're unbelievable," I say, taking a step after him. He turns around abruptly, causing me to take a step back.

His eyes darken—an eclipse of irritation. It's the same expression he carried when we first met. "What's unbelievable is that you expect something different," he says, bracing his hands on the wall, either side of my head. He leans even closer toward me.

His breath brushes against my lips. "I'm not a good person. I will disappoint you." But it's as though his words are merely a distraction. All I can think about is how stable he makes me feel and how envious I was when I saw him with someone else.

"You say that, but you're also the one who came after me," I tell him. "If that's true, then why don't *you* stay away?"

"Do you think it's that easy? You drive me fucking insane." He sighs, running a hand through his dark, windswept hair.

"I know the feeling," I say sarcastically, but he doesn't smile. I bite my lip, almost drawing blood.

"Do you have any idea what you do to me? What that does to me?" He stares at my mouth. I'm perplexed. He can't be implying what I think he is.

"You can't say things like that to me," I state, even though ember emits in me when he does.

"Why?" he asks, and I can see a smirk arising, but I can't be a hundred percent sure.

"Because...because you were just with another girl." *Because we're just friends. Because your mood swings are not something I can deal with on a daily basis.*

"Do you want me to stop being around other girls?"

"No, I just..." I don't know what to say, I'm lost for words. What do I want?

"Come with me."

"Where?" I question, but Ace doesn't reply. He grasps my hand, and I foolishly follow him. The house is packed, and we are forced to shove past everyone. Well, *I* have to—people make way for Ace.

I shove past a guy with a bald cut, and he licks his lips. Gross. Within a second, my hand slips out of Ace's, and the bald guy is groping me. "Where you off to, sexy?" he whispers in my ear, and I resist the urge to throw up.

My knee collides with his crotch, and he stumbles over in pain. "Feisty," he says before reaching for me again. I don't have time to blink before Ace stands between the guy and me. Ace sizes him up, and a dangerous smile crosses his face.

"Don't," I warn Ace, resting my hand on his arm. Ace doesn't look at me, he's still glaring at the guy who's not backing down from a fight, daring him to make the first move.

I tighten my grip on Ace's arm, which finally seems to get his attention. His eyes are shadows in the night, craving a fight, but they mollify when he realizes it's me. He's angry—he's always angry. I'm unsure at what, maybe the whole damn world.

Ace seizes my hand and gently pushes my body in front of him. His resplendently muscular chest faintly touches my back, and even though I'm in front, he's in control.

"Ace, what was that? I can take care of myself. You don't need to come to my defense all the time." I spin around when we're finally outside, away from everyone.

"Don't start, Calla." He tugs on his hair, not looking at me.

"Don't start? Don't start what?" I ask, annoyed. He's the one who was about to instigate a brawl in the middle of a party, and he's ordering *me* not to start.

"Hungry?" he asks, neglecting my question entirely. I narrow my eyes. I'm about to tell him no, but my stomach grumbles in response instead. *Traitor.*

"We'll get something to eat." He takes my hand again, the gesture becoming overly comfortable. I can get used to this, and that terrifies the shit out of me. "Is this okay?" he asks, glancing at our hands. I give him a small nod, it's more than okay.

Ace is hot-tempered and impulsive. He gets under my skin more than anyone else has. He's messy and full of hard edges, yet there's something about him that keeps me coming back for more. Conceivably, it might be the fact that I see so much of myself in him.

It seems as though we're both trying to find a place in this world. Perhaps, we're hoping for something that doesn't exist—a sense of belonging, or maybe something to tell us we're on the right path.

We stroll through the empty park fields in no rush to get to our destination. I sneak glimpses at Ace, at the dark stubble piercing his skin around his mouth. At the way his chest heaves with every breath. His eyes flicker toward me now and then, as though he's attempting to figure something out.

"Ace?"

"Yeah?"

"Why do you think you're a bad person?" I ask. His fingers tighten around mine, and I sense this is not a question he wishes to answer. There's a significant pause, and I assume he's not going to respond.

"I've done immoral things. Things that I can't bring myself to even talk about. To anyone," he finally says. His mouth sets into a grim line, and he stares into the distance. My mind wanders back to what Logan said at the game.

"Haven't we all?" I finally ask.

The silence drowns us in its ubiquity, and I can virtually hear both of our hearts racing in unison. "No, Calla. Not like this." He halts, turning to face me. His eyes have too much grief and rage. Toward whom? Himself?

Ace opens his mouth like he wants to say something, but then he closes it, struggling to talk about his past. I understand. I understand what it's like not to want to talk about harrowing events. I know what it's like to blame yourself, because if it weren't for me, my mother would still be alive.

I don't have time to consider what I'm doing before reaching out and tracing his cheekbones with my fingers. His skin burns under my fingers, and when his eyes meet mine, they are full of immoral promises. "Ace, we all do bad things. But not all bad things make us bad people. Redemption is possible."

He doesn't say anything for a moment. The silence between us speaks a thousand words. "And sometimes the worst things that we do lead us to the best things that happen to us," I add, recalling the conversation with Theo.

Ace reaches for my hand, the one that's still on his cheek. He links his fingers through it, drawing it to his tender lips.

Breathe, I remind myself, *you need air to live.* The mellow brush of his mouth against my fingers sends a tremble through me. It's gone as quickly as it comes, and I'm left speculating if it was even real or a part of my imagination.

Ace chooses a small pizza shop and holds open the door for me. The ambiance of the interior, its mouth-watering aroma of wood-fire pizza, further clarifies that I'm famished. Although, I'm unsure if the food will fully satisfy me. Perhaps, I'm hungry for the sentiment of Ace's company.

He places his hand on my lower back when I walk past him, the touch delivering warmth throughout me. There aren't many people inside, and he leads me to a seat near the window, which overlooks the deserted street.

"Do you like fighting?" I ask after we order food. I bite my straw and look up at Ace.

He laughs, but it doesn't reach his eyes. Instead, it functions as a barrier between his true emotions. "Not the way I do it," he answers, and I'm not sure what he means.

"But you do it almost every weekend," I say, trying to understand him, trying to get to know him, because something keeps yanking us together like a rubber band. We pull away and then are launched back.

"I need the money," he says. I realize he must make a lot from one fight. I recall how many people were betting with multiple hundred-dollar bills at his last one. But why does he need that much money?

It's like he knows I'm going to ask, because he steers the conversation in a different direction. "Majoring in journalism?"

"How did you know?" I ask, and he shrugs like it's obvious.

"Do you read other books? You know, apart from autobiographies?" I ask. I'm unsure why I continue to bring it up. Maybe it's because you know a person much better if you know what they read and why.

"If you only read what everyone else does, you can only think what everyone else is thinking," he says, but it doesn't answer my question. Why does he have to be like this? Vague with his answers, almost discarding my questions, but nevertheless, still providing a pitiful response.

"Why journalism?" Ace asks me.

I shrug. "It's freeing. I can travel the whole world and live internally through my own words in hopes of making a difference along the way."

"Would it be odd if I said that I expected that answer?"

"In what way?" I ask.

Ace smiles. "I get a sense that you're not the one to stay in one place for too long."

I tilt my head, studying him. He appears to understand an awful lot about me. Am I that easy to decipher?

"What about you?" I ask. "Are you the one to stay in the same place, or do you find that dull and repetitive?"

"It'd be selfish of me to say that I'm the same as you."

I'm curious to know what's holding him back, but I'm careful not to pry. "Maybe we ought to be selfish once in a while," I say. Before he has the chance to muster a response, the waiter brings out our food.

We eat in silence, or I eat, and he watches me. When we're done, we saunter back to the house in no rush, his hand intertwined with mine. It scares me how much I relish Ace's presence. He causes me to feel nervous, but at the same time, excited. As though the enigma itself isn't enough to run from.

"Can I use your shower? The upstairs one is broken," I ask when we get inside, and he nods.

His bathroom is enormous, especially his shower. It can reasonably fit five people in here comfortably. I pick up the body wash that's on the shower floor, smelling it. Flavors of woody citrus swirl in front and all around, filling the shower with the scent of him.

Ace is standing in his wardrobe when I come out of the bathroom, removing his shirt. As if he senses my presence, he turns, and his eyes scan me. I don't move—the way he looks at me insinuates an unfamiliar covet. I intend to tear my gaze away, but I can't. I'm stuck, frozen in his existence.

The sound of his phone ringing startles us both, and he tears his eyes away from me. Taking it out, he briefly glances at the caller ID. I can't see who it is, but his face stills. He strides toward the back door and slides it open. He closes it behind him, but I hear the faint words. "Hey, baby, is everything okay?"

Baby? I stand there, frozen in time. Feeling stupid. So incredibly stupid.

Ace returns, and I wait for an explanation, but he doesn't give one. He doesn't owe me one. He doesn't owe me anything. "Sorry, I have to go." He collects his keys off the nightstand and swings a t-shirt over his shoulder.

11

Innocent Phenomenon

Gazing out my window, I observe the sun setting. It's a delicate hue of deep orange and pink. It's a shame it will dim into darkness within a few brief moments like all good things tend to do.

"Are you sure you don't want to come home for a few days?" my dad asks through the phone. "I can come to pick you up, Cals."

"No, Dad… I'm fine, really," I say.

Today's my mom's birthday. We both know it, but neither of us mentions it. It's been like that for the past two years. I truly detest it. We're both trying to think about the accident less often, but my dad does a far better job at it—or maybe a better job at concealing it.

"Look, Cals, I know we don't speak about her much…but it doesn't mean that there's even a second that goes by where I don't think about her. That I don't wish I could change it. That I don't wish it was me instead of her in that damn car that night."

I squeeze my eyes shut. The pain in my chest becomes unbearable. "Dad, don't say that."

"Why? It's all I think about." His voice breaks, and causes my chest to heave.

I open my eyes, focusing on the lake in the distance. The dusk colors bounce off it, and it's the most exquisite view I've ever seen. "Mom wouldn't want that for us."

He sighs. "I know. God, I know."

It doesn't make it any easier, though. I experience firsthand the guilt that comes with surviving the crash. I spend most of the time wondering if it would be more serene for my dad if it were me instead of her.

"I should go. I have a lot of reading to do for my class. Is Uncle Dave with you today?" I ask. As long as he has someone with him today, it's all that matters.

"Yeah, he went to put flowers on Mom's grave," my dad says. Neither of us has been able to go there since the burial. Something about that place compels my skin to crawl. I don't want to remember my mom like that—buried six feet under.

"Come visit soon. Don't forget about your old man. I miss you," he says, and the pain tightens, engulfing me.

"I miss you too, Dad."

I hang up and continue staring out the window. I'm not fine, not really, but I can't have my dad worrying about me, he's already troubled with other afflictions. He has close friends and his brother, my uncle, to keep him company if he needs it. I'll only be a burden.

Changing into a hoodie and sweatpants, I mindlessly walk downstairs. I sought to keep my mind occupied the whole day. I attended my classes and then caught up on university work. Now that I have nothing left to do, my mind keeps straying to a place where there's emptiness.

Liv and Zach aren't home. Friday is usually date night for them, or a party. I assume it's the former, since they didn't pester me to come like they usually would if it were a party. Ace has been in and out all week, but we haven't talked since the night he walked out without enlightening me of the reason.

My mind occasionally wanders to him… "Occasionally" is the wrong word for the circumstances. "He's deeply embedded into my thoughts" would be a better way of putting it.

I open the cupboard, and in front of me is exactly what I need to numb tonight—alcohol. I hate alcohol. I hate how it makes me feel—almost as if nothing is real. But that's the point right now, I require an escape from reality. Will I ever get over the fact that my mom, my lifelong best friend, is gone? Everyone says time heals all wounds, but how long? Or is my wound an empty hole incapable of mending?

Taking the bottle of vodka, I make a mental note to replace it, whoever's it is, even though I doubt they would mind. Alcohol isn't scarce around here.

It's the last moments of dusk, and I leisurely walk toward the edge of the deck in the middle of the lake. There's no cloud in the sky, and I twist the lid of the bottle, taking a mouthful. I cough from the taste and almost throw up. How anyone drinks this for *fun* is beyond me. Perhaps they drink for the same reason as I am right now—to anesthetize the pain.

It's not long before it's pitch black, but the darkness engenders the brightest stars. I lay on the wooden planks and look up. The breeze wafts, encompassing me with its chill. I wrap my arms around myself.

The stars burn with the glistening of electric light. I envision that I see my mom—in the stars, in the lake. She's all around me, yet I'm still so forlorn.

My head spins, but I only took one sip. Occasionally, there's a shooting star, I don't understand why people wish upon them. They're simply an innocent phenomenon.

It's at times like this when darkness overcomes and the silence engulfs the night. This is when my guilt and truly traumatized heart kick in, no distractions, no noise, just my wandering mind to keep me accountable for all the pain I could've avoided.

I see him before I hear him. Am I that delusional? The dark silhouette moves toward me. "I come here sometimes to clear my head." His voice is rough.

"Ace?" Shouldn't I be angry at him? I can't remember.

"Were you expecting someone else?"

I wasn't expecting you. "Um, no, but—"

"Good." He drops against the wooden pillar. I roll my eyes and push the bottle of alcohol toward him as a peace offering. "I don't drink," he says. I scrunch my face but then recall that I've never seen him with a drink before.

"I don't either," I say.

He inspects me, then the bottle, and raises an eyebrow.

"I don't," I defend.

We sit in silence for a few squandered moments before I speak. "I remember one time, my dad and I went out on a lake just like this one back at home. I was only about five or six. We were in a wooden boat, and I climbed on the front of it, as far as I could go, and extended my arms. With the breeze in my face, it felt so liberating. My dad told me to get down before I hurt myself. I didn't listen," I recall.

"I ended up falling in the lake, and with my luck, there was a submerged rock below. I sliced my arm open and had to get stitches. My mom was so mad at my dad that day," I say. I remember being angry at my mom that day too. I wasn't fond of the way she yelled at my dad, blaming him for what happened when it wasn't his fault.

"I can picture it," Ace says, chuckling. "It seems as though you haven't grown out of your clumsiness."

I don't find myself clumsy, simply unlucky. Wherever there's trouble, it has a way of stumbling upon me. "Have you ever felt guilt eating up at you, strangling you with no way to escape?" I ask, squeezing my eyes shut.

"All the time," he says. "All the damn time."

I'm unsure of the reasoning for the following words which attain their escape. It's not because I require Ace to feel sorry for me or even pity me—those are the last things I need. Maybe it's because I'm over not talking about her. I'm through with keeping everything bottled inside. Or maybe, I have the relentless feeling that Ace and I are alike in many aspects.

"My mom died two years ago on Christmas Eve in a car accident," I say. I don't look at him. I lie still on the wooden deck, directing my attention to the one star that shines brighter than all the rest.

When Ace doesn't utter a single word, I take a deep breath. "It was my fault. If I didn't make her turn around because I forgot my stupid journal, we would have already been home—" I begin. My heart quickens frantically.

"It's not your fault," Ace interrupts, leaning over me, so I'm forced to look at him.

"It is."

"No, Calla, it's not. You can't blame yourself for that."

"Ace, if I—"

"Fucking don't," Ace warns and locks his hand on mine. "Don't do that. No amount of guilt will change the past. Don't blame yourself. It's unfair, and it will destroy you."

He gazes at me like I'm the stars when all I've ever felt before was the darkness that encircles them. He makes me feel insanely sane for the first time in my life. "It already has, Ace."

The silence is becoming more frequent between us, more delirious. But he's here—sitting next to me on the pier, in the middle of the lake, and the moonlight pours over his skin.

I'm uncertain if it's the alcohol or the way he looks at me, and a smile surfaces on his mouth—*definitely the alcohol.* I don't know what I'm doing, but I'm suddenly on his lap. My knees are on either side of his hips, and I observe how drained he looks. *Where have you been, Ace?*

He's rarely at the house, disappearing all the time without any warning.

I trace the dark circles under his eyes and detect the way his body stills. My fingers trail down to his lips. My thumb brushes against them delicately, bordering the shadows, savoring every single moment—every single touch.

Ace arrests my fingers with his hand, and my eyes pounce to his. They're sinister and filled with darkness but, at the same time, entrancing. I'm incapable of looking away even though I'm crumbling underneath them. His eyes have the whole world in them—his damn eyes are destroying me.

"Make me forget," I say, my voice breaking. "Make me forget about everything. It's killing me inside."

Ace brings his hand to my cheek and gently wipes away the tears escaping my eyes. Every single stroke of his fingers against me is igniting a fire inside.

"Ace, please," I beg. I need the despair, the suffering to fade, even if it's for a brief second. It appears he's the only one able to give me what I need.

"Calla," he cautions. My demand has stunned him. His eyes meet mine again, and there's something different inside them. I may be reading too much into it, but it's as though his own demons are dancing directly in front of me.

"Tell me to stop," Ace says, leaning into me.

Don't stop. "Stop," I breathe, but my body is uttering the complete opposite as my hands tangle in his hair, drawing him even closer.

"Mean it, Calla," he drawls in a low voice, tightening his grip around my waist.

My body burns everywhere he touches me. His calloused fingers graze my bare skin where my shirt has lifted. I *need* him to continue because no one has ever made me feel like this. I don't wish for it to end.

His lips faintly brush against the corner of my mouth, waiting for my consent—waiting for me to change my mind.

I gasp at the subtle contact, craving more. "No, I can't."

"Fuck," Ace swears, and suddenly, all I can taste is him. His mouth moves along mine, meticulously unhurried.

I never understood how people could be addicted to drugs. I've never even sampled them. My dad would have lost it, you know, him being the sheriff and all that. But at this moment, I'm an addict who can't get enough. All the hurt in my mind, all the frustration and anger subside. Every thought in my head is exploding into a dark craving.

I'm addicted to the way Ace makes me feel. Of course, don't get me wrong, I've kissed a handful of guys before, but no one has ever made me feel like this. Not even close. I wonder if it's because we're surrounded by the stillness of everything around us, the stars, the moon, the lake—the tranquility of time.

His lips are demanding against my own, and there's nothing gentle about them. Ace is far from gentle. His hands are on my waist, luring me closer even though there is no space between us.

He runs his tongue along my bottom lip, asking for permission, and I let him. Pleasure darts through me as our tongues dance together in perfect sync. I don't know how I've ever assumed kissing Ace would be anything less than this.

I hate that I relish it so much.

The last bit of rationality left inside me advises me to get out of this situation, but my body is glued to Ace's. What is he doing to me? He's breaking down all the barriers that I've formed to guard myself.

He pulls away. His voice low and rough. "We shouldn't be doing this."

"Ace," I mumble against him, bringing his lips back to mine, not prepared for this feeling to end. Not willing to accept the reality, which is on the verge of crashing back.

I need more. More of him.

"Calla," he warns, and it's the finality of his voice that brings me back down to Earth. We're both trying to catch our breath. "We shouldn't. Not like this," he says, firmer this time.

"Why does your mouth have to do that thing again, where it ruins everything?" I heave away. Ace reluctantly lets me go, and I suddenly remember exactly why this isn't a good idea.

Baby.

We're just friends.

I've never met someone who's been able to keep my attention for long enough.

Three reasons that seep into my mind like poison. "Are you trying to flirt with me or start a fight?" he asks, irritated. He's irritated…at me? The audacity. *Don't start this, Ace.*

"Neither." I get to my feet. My head spins, but I'm soberer than I've ever been. I don't want to argue with him, and there's the need to detach myself from the situation. How can we go from making out to the verge of an argument in less than a second?

"Where are you going?" he asks.

I ignore him and continue walking. I'm unsure of what time it is or how long I've been sitting out on the deck. How long was I here before he came and ruined it all? And why? Why can't he leave me alone? Does he get a kick out of playing with my emotions?

"Calla, wait." He catches up to me. Why am I so angry at him? But that question is not worth answering, because I already know.

I hate how he makes me feel like nothing matters when I'm with him. I hate that even though he orders me to stay away, he's always the one who finds me. He's always there when the only thing I'm seeking to do is fit in and start over. But most of all, I hate that somehow, during all these weeks of Ace being an asshole, I find myself wanting to spend time with him. I find myself *liking* him. He understands me in a way no one else has. I grasp him for who he truly is—and we're not so different after all. Both of us push away everyone who aims to help. Both of us have a tremendous amount of healing in front of us.

But I don't need complicated. I don't need *this.*

"Fuck, Calla. Just wait." He touches my arm.

"What?" I twist around, facing him.

"That shouldn't have happened—" He runs his hand through his hair. I can't shake the feeling of it through my fingers moments ago… *No, no, no.* I want to rip it out.

This is the last thing a girl wants to hear after kissing someone. *It shouldn't have happened.* I'm convinced he doesn't say it to his other companions.

Was it that dreadful for him? Oh my God, what am I doing with Ace? My heart is thrashing out of my chest. I'm livid at myself for allowing this to happen.

"Why? Because you're bored with me already? Because you disappeared for a week after a girl called you? Because we're friends?" I'm not yelling, but it seems like it because everything around us is silent.

"No, Calla. Because you were drinking and you're not in the right emotional state. I'm not good for y—" he starts, but I've had enough. I can't allow him to finish that sentence. I've had enough of him determining what's good for me and what's not.

"Ace, I swear if you say what I think you're about to say, I will...I will..." Ugh! I place my hand on my forehead, massaging it, and the sharpness of a headache forms.

His lips twist into a grin, the one that causes both dimples to emerge, and I'm inclined to smack it off his face. He's so infuriating. No one has ever made me feel this much anger, irritation, and apparent yearning all at once.

"You'll what?" he challenges.

"I-I-Screw you, Ace," I stutter.

His smile grows, and he raises his eyebrows. "Is that what you want?"

I can't believe the words that are deriving from his mouth. Why does he think he can say things like that, and most of all, why do his words make my heart race more than it already is?

"Absolutely not." My voice betrays me and comes out with a hint of uncertainty. All I can imagine is his hands on me...his mouth on mine.

Ace takes a step closer. It's like he knows what he can do to girls with a single word, a look, a touch. It's like he's playing with my feelings—one minute he wants me, the next he doesn't.

"Ace," I whisper, stepping closer and setting my hands on his hard chest. I glimpse at him through my lashes and bite my lip, feigning an innocent act.

"Hmm? Did you change your mind?" He smirks arrogantly, his mood shifting once again. The asshole is smirking, and I do my best to keep it together. To not punch him—not because I don't want to, but because his face is made of steel. He's been hit too many times to feel anything.

I rise on my tiptoes and lean closer. The inviting scent of Ace lures me in. His eyes widen, and he thinks he's got me wrapped around his finger like everyone else. He's wrong. And I do like him. I like him a lot, but I'm not stupid, and I'm not a game.

My lips brush his cheek before whispering, "Stay the fuck away from me." It takes everything I have to leave him standing there dumbfounded, questioning what the hell just happened.

When I return to my room, I slam my door harder than necessary and instantly regret it. I hope I didn't wake Zach and Liv. I glance at the time, and it's three in the morning. I've been out for hours. I turn the light off and collapse on my bed.

It's evident when Ace comes into the house, because he slams his door even harder than I slammed mine. He's pissed off, but I am too. He's been temperamental with me from the start. And from the start, I knew that he was someone I didn't want to deal with.

But here I am.

I toss and turn, unable to fall asleep, because Ace is downstairs—only a floor away. Hours later, when the light seeps through my window, I finally drift off, but I wish I didn't, because my dreams are filled with everything I'm endeavoring to escape.

Everything that's him.

12

The Carnival

Mia prepares a coffee order, her head bobbing to the beat of the music that streams through the old stereo on the paint-peeled wall.

"Do you believe in fate?" I ask her. A question that's been running through my mind all day.

I'd like to believe fate is real, mainly because the thought of everything being a coincidence is a terrifying one. The belief that everything happens for a reason makes the terrible things in our lives a part of something greater. Maybe I'm overthinking, once again.

"Have you been spending time with Brody? I swear, if he's trying to get crazy ideas into your head about his theories, you have to be blunt with him." She shakes her head.

I like Mia. She has grown on me and is one of the minimal friends I have. She's different, and she doesn't worry about what people think of her, which I find vastly refreshing, especially when I'm the complete opposite.

I laugh. "It's just a thought."

As if on cue, Brody steps out from the green door at the back.

I still haven't seen inside it, and I'm not sure if I want to. It almost feels like an intrusion because he spends a great deal of time there.

"Well, then..." Mia pauses and turns to Brody. "Brody, thoughts on fate? But please make it quick. We do have customers."

Brody assesses Mia, he seems surprised by her question. A spark flickers in his eyes. It's like he's been waiting for her to ask him a question like this his whole life. He's passionate about this stuff.

Mia mentioned that she finds all this absurd, and she'd rather go on with her life without unrealistic theories. But I am intrigued, I always have been. I can sense that Mia is as interested as I am, even though she may say otherwise.

"Not everything is defined by fate, and fate is almost always cruel and unfair."

What did fate do to him?

With that, Brody throws his denim jacket over his shoulder and marches toward the door. That man constantly behaves like he's on a mission, and I guess he is—his whole life is a mission, by the looks of it.

I'm about to probe Mia further about Brody, like how he ended up in this small town when he visibly comes from a place far from here, but when I turn to face her, she's staring behind me. Her eyes widen, an indication that there's a certain someone there. I don't like the feeling. I slowly turn and pray it's not who I think it is.

Nate. *Thank God.*

His caramel locks compliment his blue eyes, and he's unpleasantly happy. Almost too happy. He removes his keys from his pocket and deposits them on the counter.

"Hey, Calla." He sits down on the stool in front of me. He doesn't seem to screen what we both know, he's not here for his daily milkshake. He's here to see me. I don't mind as long as he comprehends that our relationship is purely platonic, and I think I've made it crystal clear.

"Hey," I say, before taking the coffees that Mia prepared to a couple at the corner table. Nate's eyes are on me, and when I return, he doesn't waste an opportunity.

"I was thinking, you know…" Nate begins. I'm trying to concentrate on what he's saying, but the café door opens, and I can feel *him* before seeing him. The atmosphere shifts. I don't have to glimpse behind Nate to know that *he* is here.

Ace.

It was easy to keep my distance from him over the weekend, he wasn't at the house. It's like he's living two entirely separate lives, one during the week where he attends university and does ordinary things and then the other…well, he fights some weekends, but that doesn't justify his disappearance the rest of the time.

Ace trails behind Liv and Zach. From the corner of my eye, I notice he turns his head in my direction. I don't acknowledge him, but my heart doesn't hesitate to skip a beat. How long will this senseless crush last?

"Calla?" Nate calls.

"Hmm?" My attention snaps back to him. I have absolutely no knowledge of what he's been saying.

"So, what do you say?" He leans closer. I lean away from him.

"About?"

"The carnival…" he says. I stare at him blankly. The carnival?

"Uh, yeah, sure," I say, agreeing without giving it a thought. My heart is still thumping inside my chest from seeing Ace.

Nate smiles at me wholeheartedly, and I'm unable to return his smile because all I can see is Ace. I turn around, Mia is looking at me, wide-eyed. I told her all about Ace over my shifts on the weekend. It's hard not to when she can see right through me.

I sigh and walk over to collect some cups from the table behind Ace. "Hey, did you want to come to the carnival with us?" Liv asks.

"I would, but I think I just agreed to go with Nate." I peer over my shoulder at him. He's still sitting behind the counter. He grins when he notices me looking at him.

When I turn back to face Liv, I can feel Ace's gaze piercing through me. I try to withstand the urge to look at him. However, I fail, spotting the way his hand curls around the side of the table so brutally that his knuckles turn white.

"That's cool. We can meet up in there," Liv says, and I nod in agreement. It will be better to go as a group, so Nate doesn't get any funny ideas. "It will be just Zach and me," she adds.

"I'm going," Ace interrupts.

"But you just said you're—" Zach begins.

Ace glares at him. "I'm going to the carnival."

Of course he is.

✦ ✦ ✦

Nate arrives at the house earlier than I expected. "Hey, come in. Just give me a minute." I open the wooden door to let him inside.

"Take your time," he tells me as I rush back upstairs to grab my bag, the old stairs creaking beneath my feet.

I let my hair out of my braid and untangle it with my hand. There's no time to style it, so I leave it down, it hangs in waves halfway down my back. I glance in the mirror, taking in my appearance. Washed-out denim jeans with a white spaghetti-strap bodysuit. I grab a light gray knitted cardigan out of my wardrobe, throwing it over my shoulders before heading back downstairs.

Nate has made himself at home. He's lounging on the sofa with his legs stretched out on the coffee table. I'm glad everyone has already left for the carnival, and it's just me here. This would be extremely uncomfortable with Liv and Zach.

"You ready?" Nate stands abruptly when he hears me coming toward him.

"Yeah." I nod while I slide my feet into my black boots.

It's a little past five, but the sun is already setting. It's my favorite part of the day. There's something magical about sunsets—the way the entire sky changes color and transforms into this fairy-floss pink.

It's only a fifteen-minute walk toward the carnival across the parklands. When we get closer, music faintly sounds in the distance.

"How's your dad?" Nate attempts to make small talk.

Nate and my dad get along, but I feel it's only because our dads are fishing buddies. They go out almost every weekend on his beloved boat. "Yeah, he's doing good," I say, staring at my feet as we walk.

"And you? How are you?" He comes to a halt in front of me, forcing me to arrive face-to-face with him.

"I'm good," I say. Nate raises an eyebrow. I offer him an assuring smile. "Really, I'm fine."

It's not a lie, not really—I'm fine. I'm not crying anymore. I'm getting on with my life, like everyone expects me to. I can even say that a few times in the last month, I felt happy, but I only felt that when I was with *him*. I refuse to think about that.

The parking lot is already crammed with cars. The closer we get to the entry, the smell of popcorn and candy intensifies, filling the atmosphere. When I was younger, my parents took me to every single town fair. They let me go on every ride I desired. It was the only time I could eat as much sugar as I was able to fit into my small belly. Those memories seem like a lifetime ago.

I can see why sugar isn't a good idea—children run past us, giggling and screaming. I can almost feel the parent's headaches as they carry their children back inside the gates and scold them.

The gravel crunches underneath my boots. I wrap the cardigan tighter around my body when the cool breeze sweeps across my cheeks.

We step up to the booth. "Two people," Nate says to the man behind the counter. He pays for both of us, and the man hands him two wristbands, which obtain our entry into the carnival. We step out of the way to let the people behind us through. Nate takes my hand, placing the wristband on.

There are rollercoasters and stalls in every direction I look, but the tall Ferris wheel stands out the most, with the enchanting lights fluctuating in colors. Teenagers are walking around in small groups, and the game stalls are crowded with people tossing balls at targets or desperately trying to hook a duck to their rod to win prizes.

From a distance, I locate the whole group, even Theo and Josh are here. So is Ace. Theo sees me and grins, motioning for me to come over. Liv and Zach share cotton candy while Josh attempts to pick some of it off for himself, which results in Liv smacking him.

Once we get closer, Nate does something that makes me think he doesn't get the platonic thing. He grabs my hand in his, it's cold and uncanny.

Confusion spirals inside of me. He smiles at me like he doesn't believe there's anything wrong with his actions. I remove my hand from his, but not before Ace notices. His jaw tightens as his eyes flicker from me to Nate. Why is he even here if he's going to act like someone kicked his puppy the entire time?

"Hey." Theo wraps me in one of his big bear hugs, snugly embracing me.

"Can't—breathe," I manage to mumble into his chest. He releases his grip on me.

I introduce Nate to the group. Apparently, Nate already knows Josh and Zach, as they share some classes together. Everyone appears to like him, except for Ace, of course—that goes without saying. I ignore Ace's demanding glances and attempt to enjoy myself.

"What flavor do you want?" Nate points to the candy stall, which has various sour straps on display in clear tubs.

"Strawberry," I say. Nate nods, staggering toward the stall.

Ace seems to be gravitating toward me. I stand next to Theo, and Ace stands next to Theo. I talk to Liv, and Ace somehow gets involved. I glower at him, trying to remind him to stay away. He grins, showing off his adorable dimples—my stomach fills with these imprudent butterflies that I can't relieve myself of.

Nate gets back and hands me the sour strap. I take a small bite. "This is cherry," I say, disappointed.

"Yeah, you said cherry, didn't you?"

"No, I said strawberry. I don't like cherry-flavored anything, I thought I told you this before?"

Ace snickers under his breath. All eyes go to him. I didn't realize he was listening to my and Nate's conversation. I recall telling Ace that small fact somewhere throughout the weeks.

Nate glares at Ace and takes my strap, swapping with his forcefully. "Uh, thanks," I mumble under my breath, feeling the uneasy shift in the atmosphere.

We head toward some games that Josh and Theo want to play, they're like children. Nate walks on one side of me while Ace on the other. If this isn't awkward, then I'm unsure of what is.

Nate notices Ace's actions and throws his arm around my shoulders. I roll my eyes and keep in mind that I must have a serious conversation with him later, regarding where we stand. Before I have the chance to move his arm off me, Ace moves closer, grazing his arm against mine.

Shifting from one foot to another, I watch Theo and Josh shoot basketball hoops to win a plush toy. Josh pushes Theo lightly when he goes to take his turn, and he misses. This results in a wrestling match in the middle of the carnival.

An arm wraps around my waist, and I'm ready to ask Nate what he thinks he's achieving. The smell of Ace fills my lungs, and my breathing accelerates hastily.

He drags me into a narrow, restricted gap between two stalls. Ace braces his hands on either side of me, against the wall. I glance up, meeting his consuming stare. If this is his definition of staying the fuck away from me, this guy has some grave issues.

"What are you doing, Ace?" I hiss with my back against the coolness of the metal.

"Are you trying to piss me off? Make me jealous?" he asks.

"What?" I ask, perplexed. Make him jealous? "What are you talking about?"

"You and Nate?" he growls, hurling goosebumps up my arms.

"We're just friends." It's not any of Ace's business. His jaw clenches. "You know, like you and me," I say, adding fuel to the fire. His eyebrows furrow together, and his eyes darken before he closes them—slowing his breathing.

We stand like this for a moment, and I absorb all his features. The dark circles under his eyes seem to have worsened since the last time I saw him. I guess mine aren't any better, I simply do an excellent job of covering them up. His soft lips are carved into a thin line, and my chest heaves when the memories of the enticing kiss we shared stream through me.

Ace opens his eyes, ensnaring me. He's calmer, his eyes are softer. He cocks his head to the side and challenges me. "Are we just friends?"

My eyebrows crease in puzzlement. I want to voice that we're not even friends, but all I'm able to do is nod.

Ace scoffs at that, shaking his head. A cunning smirk arises on his face, and he skims his thumb down my cheekbone. "If we're just friends, then why do you act like this when I touch you?"

My body trembles, but regardless, I open my mouth to deny it.

Before I have the chance, he takes my hand, placing it on his chest. "Calla, if we are just fucking friends, then why do I feel like *this* every time I'm around you?"

Between breaths, his heartbeat thunders under my hand, like mine. I can't think straight. He's intruding on my mentality, and my thoughts are all over the place.

"Ace," I mutter, and he leans closer as if it's an invitation and not a warning. His breath tickles my lips, and I strain to recall why this is a bad idea. "We can't keep doing this. You're the one who said we shouldn't… You're messing with my head."

He laughs and shakes his head again. The sound fills my ears, and I don't ever want it to cease.

"I'm messing with your head? You have no idea what *you* are doing to me. You have no idea how fucking pissed I was when I saw you with that fucking idiot," he says.

"I don't understand…"

"Fuck," he curses. "I can't stay away from you. I've tried, but I fucking can't. Give me a chance to prove myself."

"What, like a friend?" I scoff.

He closes the small gap between us, and his lips skim mine. It's not innocent, because nothing about Ace is innocent—it's almost unholy. I should pull away before I lose myself again, but I can't seem to. My senses are seduced by his mouth. I'm lured to him.

"No, Calla. Like you and me. I'm done playing these games."

"I don't believe you," I utter, the words coming out in a whisper.

"Then let me change your mind."

My heart flutters, and for some unknown and distant reason, I believe he will.

I clasp my hands on either side of his face, bringing him closer. Ace presses his hot tongue to the seam of my lips, and I open my mouth, allowing the kiss to deepen. With every stroke of his tongue, a deep feeling elicits in my core. I close my eyes, and the surroundings disappear, leaving him and me, rapt with each other. The warmth swells through my entire body.

This feels good. This feels right. We pull away to catch our breath. His hand rests on my ear, his thumb caressing my cheek. I can see all the emotions swirling in his flawless eyes. Finally, I know I'm not the only one feeling *this*.

13

Every High Has a Low

It's dangerous how one person can suddenly walk into your life and turn everything upside down. It's frightening that every minute I spend with Ace, it's like nothing else matters. And I'm absolutely terrified that Ace may leave my life as quickly as he came. But something is telling me he's not going to. Something drives me to give *this*—whatever it is—a shot, because I don't want to be left with a *what-if.*

Maybe it's the way he makes me feel *something* more than anyone else has, or perhaps it's the way he portrays himself that hides who he truly is. He puts on a hard exterior, and it's not until some of his walls collapse that I recognize he's not really that asshole which he makes everyone believe he is.

"There's something I want to do," Ace says, still leaning over me.

"And what's that?" I bite my lip to conceal a small smile.

"Come with me."

"We can't just leave everyone. I can't leave Nate," I say, but he narrows his eyes at me as if that's the most ridiculous thing I've ever said.

"I'll be back. Stay here." Ace strides out of the snug space that we've been confined to for the last five minutes.

Not even a minute goes by when he comes back and beams at me. "Let's go."

"What did you tell them?"

He smirks, and my cheeks flush in embarrassment. Is he implying something?

"Ace!"

"I'm joking." He shoots me a wink and takes my hand in his, it's warm and fits effortlessly with mine.

Ace leads me through the stalls in the opposite direction of the group. It isn't until we stand in front of the Ferris wheel that I realize this is what he wants to do. He pays for the ticket, and the operator who looks bored to be on the job opens the cabin door for us, rushing us through.

Ace takes the seat opposite me, but the space feels so small and intimate. My knee is between his. He places his hands on either side of it, his fingers stroking my thigh.

Our silence is more powerful than words could ever be. I want to ask him who *baby* is, and where he disappeared to that time, but it feels wrong to spoil this moment.

I look out through the open bars and watch the town unfold in front of us. The darkness of the sky separates civilization. I've always been fascinated with the world above us, with the galaxies and stars. I can watch them for hours. The feeling that seduces me is marvel and contemplation—wonder in many phases, such as wondering what I cannot truly decipher with my eyes. Wondering what is really occurring in other galaxies and wondering about alternate realities, different possibilities.

We're at the highest point and come to a sudden halt. These

things occasionally stop to let people in and out, so I wait for it to start moving again. So when it doesn't, my eyes snap to Ace. He doesn't seem bothered.

"Why are we stopped?" I ask.

"It must have broken down. I'm sure they'll fix it soon," Ace says blankly. I close my eyes, trying to remember how to fill my lungs. "What are you doing?" he asks, amused.

"I'm scared of heights," I reply, almost to myself, in the form of a reminder. I don't know what I was thinking. *I wasn't thinking*—I'm irrational with Ace.

"Then why didn't you say so before we got on?" His lips curve at the edges.

"I-I forgot," I say.

"You forgot you were scared of heights when getting on the tallest ride here?" He laughs.

"Yes," I reply, annoyed that he's laughing at me. It sounds thoughtless, but Ace makes me overlook my fears, and I probably wouldn't have remembered if we didn't break down in the middle of the freaking air.

I place my head in my hands and count to ten to calm myself.

"Hey, look at me," Ace says.

I shake my head, but he peels my hands away from my face and takes them in his own. He kneels in front of me and glances up to meet my gaze, composure encloses me. I haven't known Ace for long, but the connection between us is remarkable. I'm drawn to him in a way I've never experienced before.

"We're all afraid of something."

"What are you afraid of?" I ask, drawing my attention away from the fact that we're still not moving.

He doesn't reply, and I think he's not going to answer. "Myself."

He drops his gaze from mine, and his mouth sets into a hard line. "I have these…episodes sometimes, where I can't control my anger," he explains.

It surprises me that he's this open with me. The first day I met him, I remember how enraged he was, to the point that Zach had to stop him from destroying things in his room. I also recall that Zach didn't have a scratch on him.

"What causes, um…these episodes?" I question.

He shrugs, not answering. He's told me this as a reminder that's he not good for me. But a reminder for who—himself or me?

"You haven't hurt anyone," I state.

"I might," he tells me, his grip tightens around my hand.

"You won't."

He looks at me and clenches his jaw. "You don't know that. Fuck! I don't even know that."

I lay my hand on his cheek, and he drops his gaze from mine. "You're not a bad person, Ace. I can see that, I can see you. You may have done bad things, but…" I shake my head, trying to find the appropriate words to make him understand. "It's in the past. You can only move on if you accept it and stop letting it have power over you."

Ace meets my eyes—guilt and pain are eddying in the deepest parts of him. He takes my hand, the one that's on his cheek, and brings it down to his mouth and brushes his lips against my fingers, coercing my heart to soar.

I forget we are stopped mid-air, so when we begin to move, it startles me. Ruining our moment.

On the way back to the house, we get ice cream, and I laugh more than I ever have before. My cheeks hurt from the unfamiliar movement. Even though the crisp wind picks up through the night, my body is high on endorphins.

"You're not going to be sleeping anytime soon, are you?" Ace asks when we step into the house.

I shake my head. My sleeping pattern is terrible, but I'd rather stay awake if that means escaping the nightmares that sleep entails.

"Movie?"

A small smile shapes my lips, and I nod. I like to be alone, but I find myself desiring to be alone with Ace even more. A part of me wants to spend as much time as I can with him before tomorrow, in case *this* only lasts till then.

"I'll be down in a few minutes," I reply as I head upstairs. I have a shower and brush my teeth.

Heading to Ace's room, I'm unable to stop my hands from shaking. His bedroom door is open, and I pause in the doorway. Ace is sitting on the bed with a movie ready to go on his plasma TV. He grins at me and pushes play on the remote. I instantly recognize it—*The Lion King*—according to Ace, the best movie ever made.

Comfort submerges me as I sit next to Ace, and he wraps one of his hands around me, pulling me closer to his side. I trace the tattoos on his hand. I hadn't really looked at them properly, but now I'm memorizing every single line. I'm not particularly into tattoos, but on him, they're appealing.

I glance up to Ace, and he's already watching me, his mouth tugs up at the corners into a smile. How long has he been viewing me instead of the movie? My eyes set on his mouth, and, as if reading my mind, he lowers his lips to mine.

I can never get used to kissing Ace. The way his mouth moves against my own forces the whole room to rotate around me. I climb on top of him without breaking the kiss. Ace places his hands on my hips and pulls me closer—as if there's a way to mold us together.

Heat radiates from his body through mine. We take time exploring each other, but it all feels so familiar like we've already become accustomed in another life. His rough fingers skim my bare skin where my shirt has ridden up, and they travel farther upward, grazing the bottom of my breast. Heat settles between my legs when I recall I didn't put a bra on.

Pulling away from him, I tug on his shirt. Why did he choose today to leave it on, of all the days? I want to feel the smoothness of his skin, the ridges of his hard muscle underneath my fingers.

He understands, removing with one swift movement. I waste no time running my hands against the hardness of his chest, down his defined abs and digging my nails into him.

"Calla," he murmurs under his breath and lowers his lips to my neck, sucking and licking. Claiming me. I can't control the moan that streams from my lips.

My heart slams against my chest, and I can't get enough. The feeling is cosmic. He easily flips me over onto my back, pinning me to the bed, keeping our kiss intact. Never faltering. His tongue teases me, and the rich taste of Ace overpowers my rationality as I buck my hips grinding on his huge erection.

He pulls away too soon, both of us trying to catch our breath. "Did I do something wrong?" My voice comes out in a pant.

"No, the opposite, actually. I don't want to rush into things, and you're making that *very* difficult."

"Oh, I'm sorry."

"You don't need to apologize, Calla. I'm going for a shower," he tells me, jumping off the bed and heading toward the bathroom, leaving me hot and bothered.

"A cold one?"

"Hmm?" His head snaps back at me.

"Nothing." I bite my lip, holding back a smile.

✦ ✦ ✦

It feels like the middle of the night when I hear pounding and someone calling my name. "Calla! Calla! Are you here?"

For a moment, I feel as though it's a dream. I don't open my eyes, waiting for whatever it is to pass. It doesn't. Finally, cracking my eyes open, I glance around the room. The light peeks through the curtains, and I realize I'm not in my own bed.

I don't remember falling asleep last night, even though typically I have to force myself to sleep. I also didn't have a nightmare, for once in a long time. In fact, I didn't dream at all.

My heart flutters when I see Ace's arm wrapped around me. His dark hair is messy, and his soft lips are parted—so peaceful. I don't want to wake him. He needs to sleep, he's always exhausted.

I move Ace off me as lightly as I can, but he grumbles and wraps his hand tighter around me, hauling me closer into his hot chest. "What the fuck is that noise?" he asks, irritated.

I quickly untangle myself and get up, heading toward the door because I know exactly who that voice belongs to. I step out of Ace's room, and Nate is about to storm upstairs when he notices me. I look at a wide-eyed Liv by the front door, regretting her decision to let him in. She gives me an apologetic smile and closes the door on her way out.

Thanks, Liv.

"Where did you go last night?" Nate asks. "I looked for you everywhere." His eyes dart behind me.

Ace wraps his hand around my waist, making Nate's eyes narrow in frustration, and a flicker of hurt crosses them.

"Sorry…I…" I begin, but I don't know what to say. What did Ace tell everyone?

"I see." His jaw tenses, but he continues. "My dad has been trying to reach you," Nate says. I try to recall where my phone is. I think I left it upstairs in my room after I had a shower last night.

"Your dad had a heart attack," he says. The world stops spinning, and the ground swallows me up. There's a lump in my throat that I can't swallow.

My dad.

Heart attack.

I must have heard him wrong, my dad is only in his mid-forties. My eyes widen, and my chest tightens like I'm about to have one too.

"He's in hospital, stable condition," Nate quickly adds.

Silence. I don't say anything. I'm trying to still my breathing as the fire claws up in my throat.

Everything's okay. He'll be okay.

"Calla? Calla, did you hear me?" Nate asks. I try to zone him out, I need my mind to relax before I can respond.

"Shut the fuck up and give her a minute." Ace glares at Nate and gives my hand a reassuring squeeze.

"Don't tell me what to do. I know her better than you do."

"Clearly fucking not," Ace snaps. Ignoring both of them, I rush upstairs to pack some of my clothes. I need to see my dad.

Footsteps round the corner into my room. I barely glance toward my door, but I know it's Ace. I throw some clothes into a duffel bag and race past him into the bathroom to grab my toothbrush.

"Is there something I can do?" he asks, but what he means is, *do you want me to come with you*? It's too soon, we both know it.

I shake my head. Even though Ace makes me feel calm, it's not the time for him to meet my dad, especially when I don't know what's going on between us and when my dad is in hospital.

"At least let me drive you?"

"It'll make sense for me to drive her, since I'm going with her," Nate says. I turn around. Nate is leaning on the door casually, he offers me a comforting smile.

I sigh. It does make sense for Nate to come with me. We're practically family, but something about this feels like he has ulterior motives. I don't have time to argue, so I only nod. It's a chance for Nate to see his family too. Plus, I don't trust myself driving, I feel like I'm going to be sick.

Ace's jaw ticks in annoyance, he's glaring at Nate. Nate crosses his arms and grins at Ace, looking pleased with himself. Too pleased for my own comfort. I need to diffuse the situation before Ace wipes the grin off his face.

"Can you wait for me downstairs?" I ask Nate, hoping he will take the hint. He looks at Ace and smiles again before turning on his heel and heading down.

Ace's hands are curled into fists, his knuckles white. Ace isn't a fan of Nate, but now is not the time to start a fight.

Ace watches me pack my bag, running his hand through his hair and rubbing his temple every now and then. I finally finish and turn to look at him. His chest has faint pink lines from my fingernails digging into him last night. I blush at the thought. That memory feels so distant now, so far away. For every high, there's a low—a high *always* must come down. That's what makes the world go around.

"How long will you be gone for?" Ace's voice is blank, emotionless.

"I don't know." I shake my head. "A few days, a week, maybe

more." I shrug, I don't know what state my dad is in. He needs me, I can't lose him too. He's the only close family I have left.

Ace's facial expression doesn't give anything away. I turn to my desk and take a pen and a sticky note, scribbling my number on it.

"Here," I say, handing him the sticky note. "Call me or text," I say, but add, "You know, only if you want to, you don't h—"

"I want to," he says. He takes my hand, gently pulling me to his bare chest. He smells like soap, and my hands run up his back. Ace buries his head in the crook of my neck and kisses my shoulder.

When I get outside, Nate is waiting by the driver's door of my car. I open the trunk, throwing my duffel bag inside. Nate extends his hand. I'm confused, but then I understand he wants the car keys. I give them to him.

I open the door to the passenger side of my car. Ace comes to my side and slips his hand around my waist, my stomach erupts with need at his touch.

"What are you doing?" I ask, my voice dry.

"Making sure that idiot—" he nods toward Nate, who's glaring at us through the window "—knows you're off-limits," Ace says, smiling. I hold onto his biceps as he clasps my cheek with one hand. He leans toward my lips, brushing them with his.

One hour. For one whole hour, Nate and I don't say a word to each other. For some people, that would be awkward. For Nate and me, it's ordinary. I kind of like that about him. He likes to think things over before talking about them. "It keeps me from being irrational in the heat of the moment," he once told me after our first argument.

I call my dad on the way there. He's too calm about the fact that he had a heart attack. He assures me he's fine, but his voice says otherwise. He always downplays these situations, and even if he's okay, I need to see it for myself.

"Cals, you shouldn't worry about me," he says, but I tell him I'll be at the hospital in about an hour.

"You and Ace?" Nate hums five minutes after I end the call. "I don't like it." He maintains his eyes on the road. I turn slowly to look at him, his face is vacant, and his hands are gripping the steering wheel a little too tightly.

"It's not your business, Nate," I say, and his head snaps toward me.

A small curl covers the left side of his face, and he shakes his head. "Something about him isn't right. I can feel it," Nate tells me, and I roll my eyes.

"You don't know him," I defend.

"And you do?"

My eyes travel back to the road, and I watch the scenery unravel—green meadows with trees as far as I can see. It's beautiful, really. The road is long but narrow and stretches for miles. If I put my window down all the way, it'll feel like I'm flying.

That's the feeling I get when I'm with Ace. Like I'm flying—floating in the reality of me and him. But I only know the Ace that's with me. It alarms me that I might not know him at all and how quickly he might change his mind about us. *Us.* What were we again? *Me and you*? What does that even mean, Ace?

He has secrets, a past, and even though I don't care what he did or what he *thinks* he did, which renders him to believe he's a bad person—I can't help but question the concealed.

"I'm getting to know him," I tell Nate.

He shakes his head again and scoffs. We don't speak the rest of the way, and Nate sneaks glimpses at me every few minutes as though he wants to tell me something but doesn't.

We pull up at an old hospital building, and I get out. The air here is visibly different, thick, and harder to breathe. Has it always been like this? I don't quite remember anymore.

"I'll find a parking spot and meet you inside," Nate says. I nod and walk toward the entrance, putting one foot in front of the other.

Would my dad look like he just had a heart attack? But what would that even look like?

I identify myself to the nurse at the front desk. "Floor seven, room twenty-five," she informs me. I take the lift and prepare myself for the worst, so much so that when I see my dad, I'm shocked.

He appears to be exactly the same. His chocolate-brown hair is cut short, and his hazel eyes light up when he sees me at the door. If it weren't for the blue hospital gown that envelops him, he wouldn't look any different.

"Cals, I told you, you didn't need to come."

Rob, Nate's dad, is sitting next to the bed in the hospital chair. He rises and gives me a small hug. "I'll give you two some privacy. I'll go find Nate."

I nod. "What happened?" I ask my dad.

"It's nothing, Cals. I didn't even know that I had a heart attack. I was at work, and I felt a tightness in my chest, but that's all. It was one of the guys that was adamant I go to the hospital to get it checked out. Turns out, it's a heart attack," he says. "Honestly, I'm fine," he assures me when he sees my concerned face.

"I'd like to stay home for a little bit," I finally reply.

"You don't need to do that. You should get back to university. You don't want to miss anything," my dad says, and once again, I roll my eyes.

"A few days won't kill me, and anyway, I'm ahead in my classes," I explain.

It takes a little more convincing, but my dad finally agrees. I don't know how long I sit here with him, simply talking. It feels like hours. "How's the university newspaper going?"

I press my lips together. "I haven't been able to write anything."

My dad shuffles, sitting upright on the stiff hospital bed. "Your mom was like that sometimes. She would go for years without writing anything, and then an idea would pop into her head, and she'd spend the next few months in her office."

The doctor arrives and advises that he wants my dad to stay overnight to keep an eye on him. If everything goes well, then he can come home tomorrow.

I move the chair that I've been sitting on for the last couple of hours near the window. Rising on my tiptoes, I reach for the pillow in the cupboard above.

"What do you think you're doing?" My dad's voice comes out gruff.

"Making my bed for the night," I reply, motioning to the chair.

He shakes his head. "Go home, Cals. Get some rest." I don't want to leave him, but he doesn't want to hear it. Sighing in defeat, I tell him I'll return first thing in the morning.

I drive my old Mazda back to my dad's house. *My house*. I recognize the roads like the back of my hand. I've lived here for eighteen years. I drive past the park where Mom and Dad used to take me for picnics when I was little. It looks the same, but the unfamiliarity that rushes over me is strange.

I pull up to the four-bedroom house. It's a lot smaller than the place I'm living in now. Only one story, with a white picket fence, but it was more than adequate for the three of us. This house holds countless memories, which is the main reason my dad hasn't sold it. I doubt he ever will.

When I get to the front door, my phone lights up. As if on cue, my heart races. I don't recognize the number, but I have a feeling it's Ace. No one else calls me.

"Hi," I breathe into the phone.

"Calla." His voice is low, and goosebumps coat my skin. I unlock the door and walk toward my room.

"How are you? Is everything okay with your dad?" he asks.

"Yeah, my dad is doing good," I say, relieved. I explain what happened, and Ace listens, conveying that everything will be okay. I believe him.

When there's nothing else to say, Ace asks, "Did that fucking idiot try anything with you?"

"No, I think you've made yourself clear." I laugh, placing my keys on the dresser.

"Good."

The phone goes silent, and I want to ask him something. "Ace..."

"Yeah?"

"Are you...you know, still seeing other girls?" I squeeze my eyes shut. I didn't want to have this conversation on the phone, but there's no telling how long I'll be here.

"Seeing other girls?" he asks. I can almost feel the stupid smile on his mouth. "What do you mean *seeing* other girls?"

"Like, you know...doing things that you did with them before?" I bite the inside of my cheek. I want to know where I stand with Ace, so I don't feel like an idiot.

"What things have I done with whom, Calla?" he persists. I presume he's smirking right now, asshole. He requires me to spell it out for him.

I don't say anything, letting the silence determine my next words.

"Calla?"

"Mm?" I ask.

"I don't want to *see* anyone else but you."

There's no way to halt the smile that etches its way onto my lips. Ace says all the fitting things sometimes, but how long will it last before everything changes again? Is it too good to be true?

Getting off the phone to Ace, I plan to shower, only to realize that I didn't pack any underwear. How did I forget underwear? I browse my old drawers, only to find everything lacy. There's a reason I didn't take them with me, they are so uncomfortable. I don't remember why I purchased them in the first place. However, it's all I have right now.

I scroll through Instagram on my phone, something I usually *never* do. All my photos are from two years ago. I haven't posted anything recently. My feed is filled with people from my high school—my ex-best friends, the school's popular girls. It should be no surprise that I was one of them. I was the cheer captain, after all—isn't that how it works?

Clicking into my phone camera, I turn it toward me, wondering how someone can take a sexy photo and post it online for the whole world to see. That might have been me two years ago, but not anymore.

I lie on my back and take a picture, the red lacy underwear, and bra the center of attention. My face is barely in it, only my bottom lip, which I'm mindlessly biting mid-photo.

Running my hands through my wet hair, I decide to delete it. Even though it makes me feel good about myself, I can't imagine someone seeing it by accident. I press the delete button, but my hands are wet, and it somehow calibrates to *send*.

Shit. No, not send. I tap my index finger on the back button.

It results in making things a hundred times worse by sending the photo to the most recent number.

My face turns scarlet. *No, no, no.* This cannot be happening.

My phone rings. I know it's Ace without checking the caller ID. I don't answer, I can't. I'm so embarrassed. I throw the phone to the other side of the room, hoping the ringing will subside, and it does, for a moment, enough for me to read the short text message that weakens my knees.

Pick up the phone, Calla. Now.

14

Beautiful-Eyed Monster

Five minutes have passed, the longest five minutes of my life. My phone hasn't stopped ringing, but I have somewhat relaxed. If by *somewhat* I mean my whole body is shaking, and I'm on the verge of losing my sanity, then yeah, I am somewhat okay.

I reach for my phone and swipe my thumb over the screen to answer it, placing it to my ear. "Calla." His voice is profound. Even though he can't see me, I cover my face with my hand.

"I didn't mean to send it to you," I say, stumbling over my words.

"No? Who did you have in mind, then?" he asks with bitterness to his voice.

I smile. "Ace, are you jealous?"

"I want to see you."

"I'm coming back in a few days."

"No, I want to see you *now*," he emphasizes.

Impatient as always. "It's a two-hour drive." I close my eyes and lie on my bed.

"I'll be there in less than one," he says, determination dripping from his tone.

"Ace, that's reckless." There's silence, and I press my lips together. "I'll wait. Please drive carefully."

Ace instructs me to text him my address, and I do. My hands are sweaty as I brush my teeth and pace around my bedroom. Luckily, I took all of my posters down before leaving for university.

I glance in the mirror for the fifth time. Should I put clothes on? I check my wardrobe and find a silky robe. I try it on in front of the mirror and then take it off again. I look like a foolish idiot. What am I doing? The nerves are forcing me to become feverish.

I leave the lace underwear since I don't have any others but shove the silky robe back in the wardrobe. Instead, I go to my bag and pull out a long white t-shirt, yanking it over my head.

The sound of Ace's motorcycle jolts me from my thoughts. It rumbles as he pulls into the driveway, cutting the engine. Is he here already? That was definitely less than two hours.

I unlock the front door. He's on my porch, dressed from head to toe in black—my favorite "color" on him. I open the door wider for him. Ace's gaze travels over my body, and a small, deliberate grin forms on his face. "You look…nice."

He's aware of what's underneath my shirt, and I clear my throat, swallowing. "Hmm?" I close the door behind me. I turn to find him observing me, his thoughtful eyes never leaving mine.

Wrapping his muscular arm around my waist, he brings me to his chest. "I said, you look nice."

I take a moment to regain my voice, so he doesn't realize what he's doing to me. "Nice?" I raise my eyebrows.

He braces his other hand on the door behind me and brings his lips centimeters from mine. "Calla, you look fucking perfect."

Heat sweeps my cheeks. So much for regaining my voice. Ace chuckles and pulls away when I'm unable to speak. He shoves his hands in his pockets and glances around the small living space, absorbing it. "Give me the grand tour."

I roll my eyes. "It's not much, but it's my family home. The home that I grew up in. The only place that holds most of my memories with my mom." I say the last bit quieter—almost to myself.

"Then, it is everything to you," he says, glancing at me.

I smile. "It used to be. I don't think that's the case anymore. It gets claustrophobic if I spend too long here."

Maybe that's why it took me the longest time to cope with my mother's death. I was trapped in this house, where everything reminded me of her. My mom was the life of it, and when she died, it was as though everything died with her—including me.

"Is that why you decided to move away to college?" Ace asks.

"I guess that's part of the reason. I needed to get away. To remind myself that there's something out there for me, and my dad convinced me." I don't know why I'm talking so much. I haven't opened up this immensely to anyone. It's effortless to converse with Ace, he understands. It's as though he's just as fragmented as me. We're both trying to pick up the pieces that shattered us.

He nods. "If you stayed here, the guilt would eat you up inside." He hit the nail on the head. I'm too stunned to reply. Is he speaking from experience, or am I that easy to read once again?

"This is the living room, and the kitchen is there." I motion toward the right, shifting the conversation. "I don't cook, though."

"If you had tried my pancakes, you'd know that I'm an amazing cook," he states, raising his eyebrows.

"Ah, yes. If I remember correctly, they looked better smeared on your face," I reply.

He shakes his head. "You're a menace. I still can't believe you did that."

I shrug and lead him down the hallway to my room. He halts, observing the pictures on the walls. "Who's that?" he asks, motioning to a baby picture of me. I'm about two or three years old, with chocolate cake smeared all over my face and my body. It even found a way into my hair.

"That's me."

"You were blond?" he asks, glancing at my dark hair, and as he does so, his eyebrows crease.

"Lots of babies are born with light hair, and then it changes over the years. It's the same with blue eyes." I take his hand and pull him away from the wall of shame. There are other embarrassing photos, such as middle school ones with braces and acne, which I do not want him to witness.

"And this is my room… Where my boyfriends got thrown out by their collars by my sheriff dad and never spoke to me again," I recall. My old bedroom walls are pastel peach, with a desk by the window.

"So, there were a lot?" Ace asks.

"Hmm?"

"You said 'boyfriends,' I want to know what I'm up against."

I roll my eyes again. "There weren't many, and none of them were serious." None of them made me *feel.* Ace turns his head to quell an emerging grin.

He skims his fingers over my mom's journals on the bedside table. I don't blame him—they are beautiful, really. The covers are different colors and embedded with elegant, flowing ornaments of interwoven arabesques. My dad always bought the journals for my mom. He said her words belonged in something as beautiful as their meanings.

My dad must have brought them into my room. He's never

inquired as to why I haven't read them. I'm unsure if he, himself, read them. I used to spend countless nights awake, marveling the covers, tracing them with my fingers, wondering what was hidden behind them. The day I decided to move to college, I threw them in the attic.

"My mom's journals," I say. "I haven't read them yet."

Ace glances at me. "Why?"

I shrug and walk over to him. "There's a part of me that thinks if I allow myself to read them, I will lose her completely." I shake my head. "I don't know…it's stupid."

Ace steps in front of me. "Why do you do that?" he asks, brushing a strand of hair behind my ear. He holds my face in his hands. "Why do you try to diminish something that clearly means a lot to you?"

I drop my gaze to the floor. "I don't know. Because it *is* stupid…"

"I don't think it's stupid," he replies sharply. I bring my eyes to meet his. "I understand what you mean. It's like there's a part of her that you still don't know, and when you uncover that part, there'll be nothing more."

I tilt my head, analyzing him. "Yeah."

"But even though I understand, I don't think it's true," Ace continues. "Especially not with words. If you read the same thing over and over, you'll still interpret it differently each time. There will be something that resonates with you that day, whether it's based on your mood or something that you're seeking to find." The pad of his thumb brushes my cheekbone.

"And even if you still think that you'll lose her after you complete the journals, you can read one word a day. It will take you your whole life to get through it," he finishes with a sincere smile.

"How do you always say the right things?" I sigh, my own lips twisting up at the corners.

Ace shrugs. "Maybe it's because I've done all the wrong things."

There's a brief moment before our lips meet where a glimpse of his real self flares through—darkness, repentance, and the dimness of chaos. I step on my tiptoes and brush my lips against his. He tastes like desperation and self-destruction. I taste myself in him.

Ace kisses me, softly at first and then with pure hunger like he's been deprived all his life—deprived of me. Like he's been concealing himself for the longest time. Like he's been withering away, and now he's fighting for exuberance.

His calloused hands travel down to my thighs, pressing me against the wall and gripping me tighter. Making me neglect everything that happened today. "Tell me to stop, and I will." He positions one of his hands on my inner thigh. A blaze erupts inside of me. Oh my…

"Don't," I mumble against his lips, unable to say anything else. Unable to tell him how much I like this side of him. Unable to tell him how much I like *him*. The tentative, gentle, caring side—the more time I spend with him, the more he proves to be nothing like I thought in the first place.

I squeeze my eyes shut. Being with Ace is like a breath of fresh air after I've been drowning for so long. And here with him, I'm finally living instead of existing.

Tears slide down my face. Noticing my mood shift, Ace wrenches away.

"Calla, we don't have to do anything if you don't want to. Fuck… I'm so sorry. I shouldn't have." He drops his hands to his sides and takes a step back. The blaze flickers out.

I meet his eyes. The way he looks at me makes my head dizzy. "Ace, I want to. I really *really* want to."

His eyebrows furrow together. He brings his hand up to my cheek and brushes the tears away. "Tell me what you're feeling."

I shake my head, not knowing how even to begin to explain it. "Being with you is so intense. I can't control my emotions."

"I know the feeling," he says. I take his hand and pull him closer.

Ace regards me with hesitation.

"Please don't stop," I beg. I bring his lips back onto mine. He kisses me delicately this time, savoring every moment as his lips glide along mine, and he gently bites my lip. He lifts me, and I wrap my legs around his waist.

Ace inhales deeply, and I can feel his thick erection against me, hard as steel. I trail soft kisses down his jaw with both of my hands around his neck. He positions me on my bed, and I remove my shirt, revealing the red set that got us here in the first place. His eyes peruse me, and his sharp jaw tenses. I'm entirely naked underneath his gaze.

He's already seen you naked.

Unconsciously, I place my hand over my chest to cover myself.

"No," Ace states and takes my hands, locking them on either side of me. He leans down and brushes his warm lips against the hollowness of my throat and then down my chest.

Every kiss is faint, gentle. My heartbeat turns erratic for his touch, and he knows it. Heat blossoms between my legs, and I'm dying for him to touch me there.

He traces the material of my bra with his index finger, and I shudder. Ace continues to kiss down my body, leaving me panting.

"Is this okay?" He tugs on my underwear with his fingers and looks up to meet my eyes. I nod, biting my lip. He lowers his mouth, taking them off with his teeth, and a husky sound escapes his throat.

He kisses and licks the bare skin of my inner thigh, and I gasp at the tingling sensation building in my core. Then, slowly, he inches closer to where I need him the most, and I shudder when he wraps his entire mouth around my sex, sucking and twirling his tongue, forcing my eyes to roll back into my head.

I tug on his hair, bringing him back up to my face. He takes his shirt off before I have the chance to direct him. I adore feeling his warm skin against mine, and I'm fond of kissing him. I love kissing Ace.

I straddle him with his fingers between my legs. Ace's lips never depart mine, but he still succeeds to murmur against them. "Calla, you're incredible."

Moving my hips back and forth on his hand, I set my own speed. His lips curve into a smile while he watches me with longing, and his fingers toy with my nipple—driving all my sensations wild. His tongue fills my mouth, and I'm lost in his presence.

Never have I done something like this. It's almost as though I'm a different person when I'm with Ace—more confident within myself. He soothes my soul and brings me back to life. I've never felt more in control with anyone, including myself.

Ace's erection digs into my leg, and a deep groan from the back of his throat collides with my moans. His middle finger pumps inside of me, curling, as his thumb circles me, and I buck my hips to meet his rhythm.

"That's it, ride my fingers," he urges against my neck, and that's all it takes for me to dig my nails into his shoulder and tilt my head back.

"Ace," I moan his name, and he lowers his mouth to my jaw, my neck, my chest while I experience pure exhilaration racing through my body. Finally, my head collapses against his shoulder, and I pant, catching my breath.

"That was…"

"Nice?" I ask breathlessly.

He laughs. His hot breath hits the crook of my neck below my ear. "No—enticing. You're fucking enticing, Calla." He sets a soft kiss on my shoulder.

Both of my hands locate the waistband of his jeans, but he catches my fingers. "Not tonight, not like this."

And I know what he means. Not when my dad is in hospital. Not when I revealed more to him than I've told anyone in the last two years. He kisses my mouth, disrupting me from my thoughts.

We talk for what seems like hours while he twirls my hair between his fingers. I almost fall asleep on his chest, but I coerce my eyes to remain open while I stifle my yawns. I'm unable to let this raw moment come to an end.

"Ace?" I say when we fall into our secure silence.

"Hmm?"

"Why did you hate me when we first met?" The question has been on my mind for weeks.

He stiffens and doesn't answer for a few minutes. "It's the other way around."

"I didn't hate you. I don't hate you," I say, confused by his response.

"I need you to." Ace's fingers trace my bare back.

"Why?" I ask, but I can't keep my eyes open any longer. I fall into the darkness, and I don't have a single dream.

I wake up with the sun piercing through my curtains. A recollection from last night floods my memory, but Ace is gone. I check my phone, and there's a text from him from five in the morning.

Sorry, I had to go. I'll call you.

I don't know whether I should reply to his text or the direction of my feelings. Am I upset that he just left without waking me? Getting dressed, I make a cup of coffee and rush out the door to pick my dad up from the hospital. The only thing on my mind is Ace and how he made me feel last night, like no one else previously had. Everything with him is considerably intimate and genuine.

For the next couple of days, I spend time with my dad. The doctor informs us it's unlikely for another heart attack to happen. My dad takes care of himself, he's in perfect health.

"Thank you for coming, Cals, but you can see for yourself, I'm fine." My dad sets a kiss on my head on his first day back at work.

I haven't called Ace or texted him—he said he'd call me. I'm hesitant to take matters into my own hands and seem like a needy girlfriend, because I'm neither of those things. Every night that I lie in my bed, the memories of what happened a few days ago play on repeat. An addiction that I never knew existed.

By Friday, Ace still hasn't called. Today is the day I'm driving back to the university. There's no point in staying. All I did was sit at home while my dad went to work. He seems fine, but it's still difficult to leave him. I pack my bags and, for merit, throw my mom's journals in too.

The drive back to the house passes quickly, maybe because I'm anxious to see Ace. We haven't spoken in days. Has he changed his mind about whatever this is? I wouldn't be surprised if he has.

My tires crunch on the gravel as I park my car in front of the house. Liv and Zach aren't here, but Ace's motorcycle is near the front. Taking a deep breath, I cut the engine and climb out of the car. I stick my key inside the front door lock and twist the handle. When the door opens, the disturbing noise from Ace's bedroom makes my stomach drop.

My duffel bag falls from my hands onto the ground with a loud thud, and I rush to his room. Twisting the doorknob, I sigh in relief to find it unlocked. I sure as hell didn't want to attempt to kick down a door. Is that even possible? They make it seem so easy in movies.

Everything in his room is a disaster. His books are scattered on the ground while his bookcase is in a different position, and his desk chair is broken into pieces. It seems like a wild animal has stampeded through his room. But Ace isn't here.

I follow the sound of glass shattering into the bathroom, twisting the handle and holding my breath. Not knowing what to expect, my hands shake. My eyes widen, and my lips part when the door swings open. The scene unravels right before me.

There's so much blood, but that's not what scares me. Ace is repeatedly punching the broken bathroom mirror. His knuckles are bleeding to the point where I don't think he can feel it anymore. There's no emotion in his eyes, solely complete nothingness. I assume he's having one of the episodes that he told me about, but I also remember Liv assuring me he doesn't have them often anymore.

Rushing toward him, I set my hand on his arm. "Ace." It's like he doesn't even hear me at all. He retracts his fist again and again, and it collides with the already-shattered glass.

Blood is smeared on the glass shards, and it's dripping down his knuckles. "Ace, stop, please!" I yell, but nothing. Tears build in my eyes. I'm helpless and under pressure, I don't know what to do. It's grueling to watch him hurt himself without even realizing it. My whole body shakes.

I do the only thing I can think of. I push Ace a little, so I can get between him and the mirror. I shut my eyes and wait. What am I waiting for? He won't hurt me. He only wants to hurt himself.

I slowly open my eyes, and his are glaring into me. Instead of blankness, there's anger in them, and I'm relieved there's at least some sort of emotion in the pure darkness of his gray eyes.

"Why the fuck would you do that?" he growls. His jaw clenches.

"You're bleeding." My voice is barely audible as I gently touch his hand.

He recoils. "Calla, I could have fucking hurt you, and you're worried about a scratch?"

It's not a scratch. Ace's knuckles are entirely busted on one hand, and I don't care if he can't feel it, he's making a mess on the bathroom floor. Liv isn't going to be too happy about the chaos he made.

"You probably need stitches," I mutter.

"Stop! Stop caring about me. I'm a fucking monster!" He slams his knuckles one more time into the glass next to me. He wants me to be scared of him. He wants me to abandon him, to leave him standing there with the consequences of his mistakes. I don't. I don't even flinch.

I bring both of my hands up and place them on either side of his face, compelling him to meet my gaze. His beautiful eyes are his prominent feature, and I love the way they engage with mine. No one has ever looked at me the way Ace does, and it's tantalizing, to say the least. All I want is to understand what's running through his head.

He instantly calms, his expression softens, and the connection between us—it's almost electrifying. "Not all monsters are bad, Ace."

He didn't expect me to say that. He takes a deep breath and leans down, placing his forehead against mine. And with every second that passes, his breathing returns to normal.

"What the fuck are you doing to me?" he murmurs. Then, wrapping his hands around me, he hauls me closer into him. My cheek is against his chest, and his heartbeat is astonishingly slow for someone who just beat up a mirror.

I glide my hands up his back, and his muscles contract at my touch. I don't know how long we stand like that, but eventually, I take his hand and run it under cold water, washing all the blood off.

"Ace, you should get stitch–"

"No," he interrupts.

I sigh and lead him back to the room where more chaos lies. "Sit. I'll go get the first aid kit."

"No," he says, gripping my hand tighter.

"Ace, don't move," I warn him, pushing him gently onto the bed.

"Or what?" He raises an eyebrow, testing me. His lips turn up at the sides. It's barely a smile, but it makes me unsteady. I'm glad he's still able to find a way to joke after what happened.

I brace my hands on his knees and lean over him. He lifts his head to meet my gaze. "You don't want to know," I whisper. Turning around, I hurry to the kitchen to retrieve the first aid kit.

When I get back, Ace is precisely where I left him. I stand in front of him and set the box on the bed, opening it. I examine the back of his hand, and when I'm satisfied that there's no glass stuck in the cuts, I clean it with alcohol wipes. He watches me the whole time. I'm surprised the shards aren't as deep as I thought, except for one. He really should get stitches, though.

"Against all odds," I reveal while cleaning Ace's wounds. I can feel his gaze on me. "The first three words from my mom's journal," I explain. I read one each day, not allowing myself to read any further.

"Against all odds," he murmurs, and half a smile graces his mouth.

When I finish bandaging him, he reaches out and takes my arm, pulling me toward him. He buries his head into my chest, and I barely hear the "thank you" that follows.

Threading my hands through his hair, I twist a small curl around my finger—it's soft. Ace lifts me onto him, and I place my legs on either side of his body. This position feels so familiar. Connected is the word I have been using, but it's so much more than that.

"Ace, have you talked to anyone about…this?" I ask, concerned, looking at his bandaged hand.

"No."

"Are you goin—"

"No."

I sigh. I can't force him to do anything. I'm scared that the more I persist, the further he'll push me away. I'd do the same if it came down to it.

"Ace…" I begin again. I run my fingers over his cheekbone and down his strong jawline to get his attention.

"Calla, no," he tells me, finality and sharpness peak in his voice.

He doesn't want to talk about it, and I want to wait until he's ready, but I'm worried about him. My eyes drift up to his, and his lips catch mine in a soft kiss. He curls his hand around my nape, his rough thumb gliding over my throat. I close my eyes and get lost in his existence.

After a minute, he pulls away and murmurs against my lips, "I'm sorry I didn't call you."

"You should be," I tell him, and he smiles, placing a kiss on the corner of my mouth.

Ace is the biggest paradox I've ever known. He hates himself for something he did, but he's also in love with himself to the point of outright narcissism. He's an arrogant asshole one second but then sweet and alluring the next. He confuses me in every way possible, but I can see myself, maybe, possibly, and rapidly falling in love with him. Despite all odds.

"Are you free next Saturday?" He skims his left hand up my shirt, and I shudder in response. "There's someone I would like you to meet."

15

The Storm

People come, people go, and that's just a way of life. They almost always leave something behind, either a treasured lesson or a particular memory that will cross your mind when you think of them.

I haven't seen Ace since the day he shattered the mirror all over the bathroom floor. That was on Friday. I promised myself that I'd bring it up the next day, I couldn't let this go. Ace wants to hurt himself. He's convinced that he deserves it, and it's breaking me apart. After I cleaned his hand that night, we fell asleep.

Sleep. Such a simple thing, really. You close your eyes, and you disappear into your most vulnerable state. Some people have dreams, others have nightmares, but the best sleep is filled with nothingness. Unfortunately, sleep is also something that I haven't been getting these last few days. My usual few hours a night have turned into two hours if I'm fortunate. It's, for the most part, my fault. I force myself to stay up until I'm confident that my mind is so exhausted that it can't deliberate any ways to torment me. But, sometimes, it still succeeds in finding a way.

My nightmares are always based around the same thing, the car accident. And even in my nightmares, I still can't save her. I can't do anything to change the sequence of events, all I can do is watch them unfold in front of me. One hour, that's how long it took for the rescue team to get me out of the car. One hour may not seem like a long time, but when you're crushed in a vehicle and counting the seconds, it feels like days.

For one hour, I had to sit and watch my mother deteriorate into a vegetative state. She wasn't responding, but her heart was still beating. They declared her brain dead at the hospital. A few days later, my dad was forced to make the horrible decision to take her off life support. Do I wish it was me instead of her?

Every damn day.

"You can't change the past." Brody's voice startles me. I'm too consumed in my own ominous thoughts while I cut the strawberries.

Brody's bloodshot blue eyes scan the café as if adjusting to the light. Did he just wake up? Is there even a bed behind the narrow green door? Perhaps it's a typical office, but the chances are slim considering Brody's character.

"Pardon?" I ask, because this must be a coincidence. He certainly can't know what I was thinking about.

"It's a waste of time and energy to analyze the past. To try put pieces back together, to justify what could have happened, when in reality, there's nothing you can do to turn back the clock," he says.

My mouth gapes open. I can't speak, I'm lost for words. *He can't read minds,* I remind myself. *It's impossible, right?!*

"Living in the past only fucks up the present," he adds, running a hand through his unkempt hair, and I swallow hard.

"Have you been reading your horoscope again?" Mia asks him and shakes her head as if this is normal, but I guess it's normal for him. Brody shrugs casually, as if that didn't happen, and asks Mia if they need anything from the grocery store.

I slouch in a booth across from Theo and Josh on my fifteen-minute break, replaying Brody's words. My fingers toy with the plastic straw on the table. Theo and Josh whisper to each other and continue to glance behind them.

"What?" I ask, following their gazes. Behind Josh is a guy that I recognize from some of my classes. His arm is draped over a petite girl with pigtails, and she's leaning into him.

"Nothing," Josh mutters under his breath and stares down at the table. His lips form a line, and he rubs his forehead. I've never seen Josh like this before, almost despaired.

"Josh has a secret boyfriend that's currently getting too cozy with a girl," Theo explains, nodding behind him and shoving a chip into his mouth, this results in Josh elbowing him in the ribs.

Josh glares at Theo. "He's not my boyfriend. We've just been seeing each other when no one else is around. He hasn't...come out yet."

"So...secret boyfriend," Theo says mindlessly. Josh must have kicked Theo under the table, Theo's head snaps up to Josh, and he coughs. "What's your problem? I almost choked on my food."

"Does this happen often?" I question Josh, tilting my head toward the guy. Josh fiddles with his drink, considering his answer.

He looks at me and shrugs. "A few months now."

"Have you talked to him about it?"

"He keeps saying he needs time. He's worried what people will think, what his family will think..." Josh says.

"You should really consider talking to him again if it makes you feel like this. Perhaps he's not ready for you. You can't wait for him and sacrifice your own happiness," I say.

"Yeah, Evans. Calla is right. I'm over seeing you down because of him," Theo chimes in and throws his arm over Josh's shoulder. Josh shrugs it off, uncomfortable that both our attention is on him.

I glance at the clock on the wall above the counter. "Sorry guys, I have to get back to work."

I make my way to the counter for the final hour of my shift, continuing to think of Josh's situation. Would I be able to be with someone who acts a particular way with me behind closed doors and completely different in front of everyone else?

The answer is a definite no, but then again, it's not that simple. From what I can gather, Josh has always been accepted in his family, in his friendship circle for who he is—this resulted in him embracing it and being confident within himself. Many others aren't as lucky as Josh.

I finish my last order and wipe the bench down. I turn to find Ace standing in front of me, his side against the counter. Five days it's been since I last saw him. No calls, no texts. Nothing. It's not a surprise, maybe only another disappointment. Although I had a premonition it would eventually go back to this, I didn't think it would be so soon and out of nowhere. I could've asked Zach or Liv where Ace was, but I didn't. If he wanted me to know, he would've told me.

"Calla," he drawls as a way of greeting.

I don't want to have this feeling that encompasses me every time we see each other. A weakness that floods through my veins every time I hear his voice. It's strange and unsettling that I have this reaction about a guy who came into my life so recently.

"You're back," I say, keeping my voice neutral.

"That's not the reaction I was hoping for." His mouth spreads into a guileless, boyish grin as he continues to perforate me with his conspicuous stare.

"So is your arrogance," I point out, not falling for his charms.

"What fun would it be without it?" he asks, preserving the same expression.

Ace does an excellent job at masking his genuine feelings. He'd rather make a joke than admit something is bothering him. For him to let me in as much as he already has must be a big deal to him. But it's the same for me. I've never spoken to anyone about my past, about my mother, about my feelings. Not as much as I have communicated to Ace in the last month.

"How long till you disappear this time?" I ask, my voice coming out icier than I intended it to. I can't lie and say it doesn't bother me, it does. We've come this far, and I wish he'd open up to me.

"Well, I have training soon," he answers, but he knows that's not what I mean. "You can come, but I can't guarantee it will be any fun."

"I'll come."

He raises an eyebrow, surprised. "You want to come?"

"If that's okay? I'm finishing up here in a few minutes."

Ace's training is at the same club as his fights. The building that is usually packed with a crowd is empty on a weeknight. Ace leads me through to the back with my hand in his. The bright lights are on, illuminating the paint-peeled walls and the floors that have been scrubbed clean, the smell of bleach fills my nostrils. My eyes dart to the fighting ring as we move past it, blood still stains the floor where many have fallen after defeat.

I don't realize I've stopped to stare at it until Ace gently tugs on my hand, leading me through a door. The lights in this room are dimmer and have a red luminosity to them. In front of me is a fighting ring, similar to the main one, but this one is cleaner, with no traces of blood. To the side are a boxing bag and other gym equipment such as weights, machines, and stretching mats.

"I told you this isn't going to be very fun," Ace reiterates as he lets go of my hand.

I take a seat at the chair by the wall. "Let me be the judge of that."

Ace pulls his shirt off and turns a playlist on, which starts blasting through the speakers in the room's four corners. He picks up a skipping rope and warms up. My eyes widen at how fast his feet move on the rope, and my mouth gapes open. Ace forms a crooked grin as he picks up the speed. Sweat beads on his forehead and chest, glistening vividly under the light.

After he's warmed up, he takes out the boxing gloves from his bag and saunters over, handing them to me. "You do need to work on your technique."

I scrunch my eyebrows. "I'm not going to hit you." Is he insane?

"Aren't you mad at me?" he asks.

Yes, I'm mad at him for disappearing again, but this isn't necessary. There are other ways to sort our issues out—by talking, perhaps? "I'm not going to hit you, Ace," I state.

"Afraid that you'll hurt yourself more than you'll hurt me again?" He grins, bouncing on the bottoms of his feet around me.

I narrow my eyes. Why is he doing this? I snatch the gloves from him and slide them onto my hands. They are too big for me, and I clench my fists, getting accustomed to the fit. I stand, and Ace's grin widens to show most of his top teeth.

"You know there are other ways to sort out our issues," I say once we're in the ring. Ace isn't wearing any protective gear, and that doesn't surprise me. I've concluded that he's crazy or underestimates my capabilities. I don't blame him, considering the last time I punched him.

"But this has proven to be our personal favorite," he remarks with a glimmer in his eyes. "Come on. I can take a hit. You should know that," he encourages me, motioning for me to land a punch on him.

Oh, so cocky. I allow myself to swing for him, but he steps to the right, dodging my hit. I narrow my eyes and try again, and again. He manages to duck out of the way. I clench my teeth together, getting discouraged by this ordeal. Ace tilts his head to the side in an awfully smug way. I take the opportunity, punching him in the arm, not using full force.

He grins. "Good."

We continue this for what seems like an hour but is probably minutes. I'm out of breath and panting. The whole time, Ace makes me work for it. He bounces on the pads of his feet, forcing me to chase him around the ring. I land three punches on him, but I think it's because he allows me to.

I eye him and go for the fourth, but Ace corners me between the ropes and cases one hand around my waist, hauling me closer to him. The sweat of his body clings to my shirt. I'm meant to think this gross and disgusting. However, I find myself not caring, even finding it a little appealing.

"And you said this was going to be boring?" I'm out of breath, but Ace doesn't seem the slightest bit winded. His stamina must be tremendous.

"Nothing can be boring with you," Ace reasons. He leans down and brushes his lips against mine. They're tender and inviting, making me delirious, especially after the exercise. He pulls away too soon, grinning at me.

I hand Ace the gloves. He walks over to the punching bag and begins his proper training routine. I stand to the side, watching him land punches with incredible force, one after another. His already massive biceps become more prominent under the pump.

"About the incident the other day..." I begin, not knowing whether this is the right time to bring it up—not knowing whether there'll ever be a suitable time.

Ace glances at me without losing his momentum. This time, no smirk, no invitation. "I don't want to talk about it."

I was expecting that, but I'm not going to give up that easily. "Maybe you need to. It's not something that you can just ignore," I say, keeping my eyes on him.

"I'm dealing with it," he almost growls, punching the boxing bag repeatedly, harder this time—using all his power. The sound of his gloves connecting with the bag echoes off the walls even though the music is still playing in the background. The bag is held to the ceiling by rusted chains, and I eye them deviously.

"That...did not look like you were dealing with it. How often do you have these episodes?" I press further.

His jaw tightens at my question, and he focuses on his technique—a way to avoid looking at me, to avoid this conversation. "Not often," he says, but the way he turns his head farther away from me and his voice becomes edgier is proof that he's untruthful.

"I see the lies right through you, Ace."

"You. See. Nothing." With every word he seethes, he hits the boxing bag harder and harder. I didn't know it was possible to have this amount of strength. On his last word, he powers through with a colossal amount of might. The chains that hold the bag give in, and everything comes crashing to the floor in front of Ace.

"I'm trying to help you. I want to help you!" I exclaim, wishing he'll understand—that's all I want to do.

He turns to glare at me. Conflagration dances in his eyes, and he shakes his head as though he's trying to eradicate my words. "I don't need your help or your compassion. I don't need that look that screams pity. I don't need you to come into my life and try to fix everything that's wrong with me," he snaps.

I take a step toward him, allowing him to know that he doesn't scare me. He can snap at me all he likes, but it doesn't alter what happened the other day. "Then what do you need?"

Ace looks straight into my eyes. "I don't need *anything* from you." His words force me to recoil, like a slap in the face. I know this is him shutting me out, and that's what hurts the most.

"Fine." I cross my arms in defense.

"Fine," he growls.

On the drive back, it's silent except for the roar of the engine. I try to avoid touching Ace in any way that I can, clinging to the sides of the motorcycle instead of him. It's colder today and reminds me that winter is closing in.

I understand where Ace is coming from. I get it more than anyone else, but I can't do nothing about it and overlook the problem. I can't tread on eggshells around him, hoping that what I decide to bring up won't make him launch me away at any given moment.

✦✦✦

There's a certain amount of tiredness that equates to insanity. I'm about to reach that frontier. Later tonight, I may have to take the sleeping pills that I've barely touched since my therapist prescribed them. Otherwise, I'll turn into a walking zombie.

I descend the stairs, hoping that Ace is still in his room so I can make a swift escape to class without running into him. I pause on the central stair, checking for any movement. His door is shut, and I breathe out a sigh of relief. I have no desire to talk to him after the events that occurred yesterday.

My eyes widen as I open the front door. I'm face-to-face with Nate's hand, which was raised to knock. "Hey! Um…" His eyes widen, and he begins rambling. "I just thought we could walk to campus together…and uhh…I got you coffee." He offers me the takeaway cup and flicks the small golden curl that obscured his vision toward the back.

I bring the cup to my nose and inhale. The smell of coffee hits me, and I'm on cloud nine. I enjoy smelling coffee more than drinking it.

"Caramel latte on almond," Nate says boastfully, and I'm surprised he even remembers my coffee order after the cherry incident.

"Thank you. I needed this." I stifle a yawn with the back of my hand.

"Are you still not sleeping?" He looks straight at the undereye bags that I tried to cover with a ridiculous amount of concealer, but clearly, it did little to help.

"Is it that noticeable?"

"No, no, you look beautiful," he reassures, and I sip my coffee, unsure how to respond to the unwanted compliment. I'd rather he tell me I look bad and make a joke out of it instead of lying.

We have only spoken briefly since he drove me to see my dad in the hospital. I figured it was because of Ace, but it seems like Nate is over it now, as he's grinning from ear to ear. What has got him in such a chirpy mood this morning?

I'm about to step out onto the porch, but the dark, angry clouds form in the distance, a promise of a storm later. I appreciate storms. Something about them is soothing, especially when you're in the comfort of your own home, relishing the appreciation of nature's power and how destructive it can be.

"Hold on, I think I might get a jacket." I turn around but stop in my tracks when Ace's door opens. The early morning sun hits his body in all the right places, accentuating his already tanned chest and the crests of his abdominal muscles. He courses a hand through his damp hair as he steps out of his room, and his gaze coasts to mine.

I hold my breath. My heart accelerates and…nope, not today. "Actually, don't worry, let's go." I turn back to Nate, bumping into him.

"Huh? What about your jacket?" he asks, not noticing Ace and blocking the doorway.

"Don't need it. Let's go. Now." I push him toward the porch with one hand while clutching my coffee with the other. I slam the door behind us, but not before I notice the way Ace's eyes dart from me to Nate and then back to me. His expression shifts rapidly to envy. The green-eyed monster.

Nate escorts me to my class and tells me about some camping trip that supposedly the whole university is going on for Halloween. He's exaggerating—I doubt the *whole* university is going, but I tell him I'll think about it.

We pause outside my lecture class. "You know I'm always here for you, whatever you need," Nate says, his eyes tight and full of concern.

"Yeah, of cour—"

"Move."

I don't even need to turn my head to know who that voice belongs to. I'd recognize it anywhere. "Dude, I'm not even in the way," Nate argues.

Nate is right, we're not in the way, but I stand farther to the side, pulling Nate with me. I don't have the energy to deal with Ace today.

"What's his problem?" Nate asks when Ace walks into the room with looks that could kill.

I shrug and tell Nate I have to go. He takes me off guard by wrapping his hands around my waist and pulling me into a hug. I return it, patting him on the shoulder after a few seconds, so he receives the message to let go.

Theo isn't in class today, so I don't have to sit anywhere near Ace. I choose the farthest spot away from him, at the back. But as I thought, it's no use, because Ace makes his way next to me.

"Calla." He falls into the seat next to me and turns his massive body to face me. I ignore him and keep my eyes on the professor, but I can't seem to concentrate on anything he's saying.

Ace pokes my arm lightly with the tip of his pen and trails it along my skin, leaving goosebumps as if he'd touched me himself. I snatch the pen with my other hand and place it too forcefully on his desk.

"For fuck's sake, Calla!"

"What, Ace?" I hiss, still not meeting his gaze.

"What was that?" he asks.

"What?"

"You and Nate? Don't you think he's a little too comfortable with you?"

I scowl at him, trying to figure out if he's joking, but his jaw tenses in annoyance. "You are such a hypocrite!" I scoff. I can't believe that out of all the things he could say, he decides to bring up how *comfortable* I looked with Nate.

The professor's head snaps to us. "Mr. Blackwell and Miss

Maven, I see you two have a lot to say. How about you share some things that you learned about each other while interrupting my class?"

I shoot Ace an annoyed look. "Well, my partner is an arrogant asshole with an ego bigger than his head, but I already knew that from the start," I mutter under my breath, loud enough for some students to hear but not the professor.

"Sorry, could you speak up, Miss Maven?"

Ace raises an eyebrow and smirks in a challenging manner. If it were any other day, I would have apologized to the professor and put my head down, but I'm already irritated, and Ace is not making this easy.

I smile at him sweetly before clearing my throat. "Ace has multiple personalities, and I still don't know if it's an actual issue or only him being a conceited hypocrite."

I look over to him, and he's grinning, so I take it as my cue to continue. "He almost always contradicts himself. If I didn't know better, I'd say that it's on purpose. And I still haven't discovered any of the secrets that he is adamant about keeping because he thinks he needs to suffer for his past."

Ace's grin is wiped off his face, and now he's gripping his pen so hard it's threatening to snap. I catch my breath before continuing, "Ace doesn't let people in, and the only time he is himself is when he's telling you how bad of a person he is, and when you finally think you're making some progress, he puts on a more prominent shield."

"But don't we all put on a front?" Ace asks me.

"To some degree, yes, but—"

"And wouldn't you say that you're not all that you make yourself out to be?" he interrupts.

"What's that supposed to mean?" I cross my arms over my chest, narrowing my eyes at him.

"Well, look at you. You're trying so hard to blame yourself for something that wasn't even your fault, and in the process of doing that, you've changed who you really are."

Ace has no idea what he's talking about, and I can't believe we're having this conversation in front of the whole class. "You don't even know who I am."

He cocks an eyebrow. "I know that you're not the person that you make everyone believe you are. You're not ignorant, antisocial, or even shy, for that matter, and you always have something to say. But no one here, in their right mind, would have guessed that you were the cheer captain in high school and also the…hmm…what do they call them? The Queen Bee?"

My eyes widen, not because it's not the truth, but because I don't remember telling Ace any of this. "In fact, now, you'd rather keep your mouth shut and have people assume things about you than have them know the truth and feel sorry for you."

There's silence, and everyone is gaping at us, whispering with their peers. I want the ground to swallow me. I'm grateful when the professor finally speaks, shaking his head. "Don't interrupt my class again, Miss Maven and Mr. Blackwell."

I sink lower in my seat and wait until everyone returns to taking notes. "How did you know all that about me? I never told you."

"I didn't, but it's not hard to guess. Nate wouldn't have even looked at you twice if you weren't all those things. All he cares about is his image."

"You may think you somehow figured me out, but you don't know anything about Nate," I say, not even comprehending why I'm defending him. Everything Ace has said is the truth, but I don't want to acknowledge it, neither to myself nor to him.

Ace shrugs and doesn't say anything for the next twenty minutes. I can't stop replaying what he said. I'm not trying to blame myself for anything, because everything *is* my fault.

"I'm sorry," Ace finally speaks, his voice on the edge of a whisper. "For last night." I ignore him. Now is not the time to talk about this.

"Calla," he says, and I roll my eyes.

I pick up my stuff and walk out of the lecture room without saying anything. Instead, I mouth a quick "sorry" to the professor, who is frowning at me on my way out. A pounding builds in my head, I can't deal with this today. I massage my temple, trying to relieve the throbbing. Footsteps are behind me, and I know that it's him. I hasten my pace.

"Calla! Wait."

I proceed walking, needing to get away from him, requiring fresh air and a clear head. I open the door leading outside, and it's raining. Of course it is. I'm stubborn, so the option to turn around and face Ace is not an option at all.

I place one foot in front of the other until the coldness of the raindrops run down my heated body. The calm that I usually feel when it rains is masked by my sudden urge to cry, and I blame all these emotions on my period, which came a few days ago.

Ace grabs my hand, twirling me around to face him. When I'm in front of him, he pulls us both to the side, under cover of a building to shield us from the rain.

"I'm sorry. I shouldn't have snapped at you like that last night. I'm-I'm just not used to talking about that with anyone," he explains.

"Maybe you should go see someone. I'm worried about you, and since that's not the first time…" My voice trails off. "How often has this happened?"

"I'm not going to see someone, Calla," he says, keeping his voice composed but not giving me an answer to the other question.

"Why? You're harming yourself, Ace."

"I told you. I'm dealing with it," he says. His cold eyes pierce into mine, and I recognize it's hard for him to talk about something he wants to keep buried within himself. It's unhealthy.

"What's that supposed to mean?" I persist.

"Just trust me."

I shake my head, unable to let this go. How do his friends continue to let him suffer without seeking help? I don't understand, but then I'm reminded that it's Ace. He won't let anyone help him, and he'll pull away as soon as they start.

"Please, Calla," he says, taking my hand in his. His touch immediately clouds my mind.

I sigh. I don't know what to do when placed in this situation. I could persevere, but then it would result in Ace distancing himself from me. "Promise to tell me if you have an episode again."

Ace hesitates.

"Promise me," I demand.

He exhales a deep breath, understanding that I'm not going to yield until he does. "Yes, I promise."

16

Unveiling Secrets

My eyes shoot open, and there's a trail of wetness on my cheeks. I wipe them with the back of my hand. Just another nightmare, if only that nightmare wasn't so close to reality.

In the shower, the scalding water pounds on my skin. I'm hoping to burn away every negative memory in my mind. I wish it worked that way, but it doesn't. I still remember everything, every detail, right down to the very last breath.

The mirror is foggy with condensation, and I wipe it with the end of my towel, quickly glancing over my appearance. My hair is darker now that it's wet, and my eyes have more green in them, like my mom's. My face is flushed a bright red from the heat of the shower.

Wrapping my body in the bath towel, I pad on the wooden floors to my room. Running my hand through my wet hair, I open my bedroom door with the other.

I don't know if I'm clumsy or if it's something to do with the way Ace is sitting on my bed—unexpectedly and too handsome to even be real—that causes my feet to slip on the floor.

Grabbing the door for support, I attempt to steady myself, but it slides out from my reach. I squeeze my eyes shut and brace myself for the fall, but it doesn't come. Instead, a pair of sturdy arms are around me. "Falling for me already?"

I open my eyes, unable to stop staring at him, or speak, for that matter. The smell of his body wash, and minty toothpaste crams my lungs. I'm intoxicated, and my head spins in agreement. "How long have you been waiting to use that line?" I ask.

He grins at me. "Since I missed my chance on the stairs."

I roll my eyes. "What are you doing in my room?" I brace my hands on his bare chest for support.

He looks down at my hands and smiles. "We have plans." He assesses my expression to see if I've forgotten.

I didn't. The opposite, actually. I've been looking forward to it all week, hoping that Ace didn't change his mind. I was beginning to wonder if he'd disappear this weekend like he always does, and I'm glad he didn't. I'm desperate to know more about him. I'm fascinated by every detail that he reveals.

"I know." I smile. "Are you going to tell me where you're taking me?"

He considers it for a moment. "No, you'll see."

I notice something in the way he says it, like he's nervous, but I quickly discard the idea. Ace, nervous? Not a chance.

We take my car, but Ace insists on driving. I don't mind. I'm too lost in my thoughts to acknowledge the silence between us, but it's not awkward. Not with Ace. His presence speaks to me more than words ever could. Our silence together feels more familiar than my own, even though I've spent a whole lifetime with mine.

Ace, too, is deep in thought. Occasionally, he runs his hand through his hair, which the wind ruffles anyway. His elbow hangs out the window, and his hand clutches the steering wheel. Is he having second thoughts about this, about letting me in? I hope not.

Twenty minutes into the drive, he fumbles with the stereo and eventually turns it on. The first thing that blasts out of the speakers is Hannah Montana, and I almost die from embarrassment. The last time I drove my car was when I came back from Dad's house, and I needed something catchy to keep me alert for the two-hour drive.

I immediately turn down the volume and change it to the CD Ace gave me. The song "Do I Wanna Know?" comes on. Ace turns to grin at me and sings along with the lyrics. He rests his hand on my thigh like it's a casual gesture. But there's nothing casual about it, especially not with the words coming out of his mouth.

The lyrics are incredibly fitting to our situation. *It's just a song. Control yourself.* But I can't. How long will it last? The feeling that erupts through me every time he touches me.

Ace rubs my thigh. I place my hand on his, hovering over the cuts that have almost healed from the mirror incident. I haven't been able to stop thinking about it.

I don't know where the confidence comes from, but I move his hand up a little. I swear the song is making me high or is it solely Ace?

He exhales deeply, but he keeps his eyes on the road. I don't push it any further. Instead, I take my hand off his. He travels it farther up my thigh. "Tell me if you want me to stop."

I don't. What I want is for him to stop the car, but I don't voice my ideas, and his hand treks up my skirt. You'd think someone who's been in a car crash would be against doing something like this—dangerous, reckless, and absolutely inappropriate. But Ace makes me disregard everything. It's just him and me.

He rubs me through my panties. The friction causes a need in me, and the arousal pools between my thighs. But he pulls away too soon. "Touch yourself."

My head snaps to his. "Excuse me?"

He takes my hand and places it where his was. "Show me how you touch yourself, Calla."

No way. I'm about to tell him no. For starters, I wouldn't touch myself in a moving car in pure daylight. This is insane. Ace turns his head toward me for a second, and his mouth turns up at the corners in a beguiling smile.

"For me," he drawls, his voice low and rich like some sort of decadence. That look he gives me and the two words that emanate from his mouth is all it takes for me to give in.

I take a deep breath and close my eyes, tilting my head against the seat. I've never done anything like this before. I've gotten myself off, yes, but no one has ever watched me. This feels dirty and inappropriate. But it makes me even more turned on when I can feel his eyes on me.

Ace holds my hand while I slip my other hand inside my panties. It's ridiculous how wet I am, almost embarrassing. I gather the wetness spread it, massaging it with two fingers. Heat fosters in the depth of my stomach, demanding release.

"Does that feel good?" Ace asks.

I manage to nod. If, a few months ago, someone had told me I'd be doing exactly this, I would have articulated they were insane. But now, everything has changed drastically.

Ace came into my life like a thunderstorm, all at once and without much warning. He has this unexpected energy about him, it engrosses and alleviates me. But there's a more profound feeling that lingers around us, something of attachment and affinity, like we've already crossed paths in another life. Perhaps

I'm merely idealizing.

While I continue to rub myself, quickening the pace, I pause to slide a finger inside and imagine it being Ace. My eyes roll back, and I bite the inside of my cheek. My breathing becomes erratic as small whimpers emit from my lips. I spread the gathered slickness over me and chase my release. It doesn't take long for me to dig my nails into his hand.

"Look at me when you come." He squeezes my hand, and I obey.

"Oh my God. Ace," I moan his name over and over when my climax washes over me.

His grip tightens on the steering wheel while his gaze flickers between me and the road, observing me fall apart next to him. Fall apart because of him. When my breathing returns to normal, I have time to reflect on what just happened. What is he doing to me?

Within ten minutes, Ace parks in the driveway of a small, pale blue house, and my breathing becomes uneasy. I rub my palms on my skirt, ridding the sweat that builds. It didn't cross my mind that the someone he wants me to meet may be his parents. He wouldn't do that to me without warning, would he?

We get out of the car, and Ace takes my hand in his—his thumb rubbing the back of mine soothingly. I have no idea what to expect. I look down at myself, criticizing my outfit choice.

"Relax, love. You look beautiful," he states. We walk up the steps of the porch, and my mind goes crazy with anticipation.

The door swings open, and a small girl, around five, jumps on Ace. He catches her in mid-air, pulling her up to his chest. She looks exactly like him. Her dark hair bounces on her shoulders in waves, and her eyes are the same as Ace's—like the sea on a stormy day. She's magnificent

"Acy!" she squeals, wrapping her small arms around his neck

and giggling.

"Hey!"

The small girl glimpses at me from Ace's arms and tilts her head to the side as if examining me. She gives me a short, unsure wave, and I smile at her. Her eyes sparkle in the glistening sun, and tiny, faint freckles that become more noticeable under the golden rays cover her nose.

"Hi..." I greet her, and Ace turns to me with a wholehearted smile. He doesn't say anything. Instead, he watches the interaction between this little girl and me. "What's your name?" I ask her.

She looks up at Ace. "Who's she?"

Ace laughs, a sound that I've adored from day one. "This is Calla," he says to her. They have an undeniable connection, I assume it's his little sister. There's no way she could be his daughter—the age difference doesn't add up.

"Calla," she repeats after him and looks at me. "My name is Ariella, but my friends call me Ellie," she says. It's easy to understand where Ace disappears every weekend. She's adorable.

"That's a pretty name," I observe, and she nods, looking up at Ace. "What can I call you?" I ask.

She thinks about this for a moment, looking at me with her almond-shaped eyes as if she can see right through my soul. "We can be friends."

I notice the way Ace's lips form a smirk, and his eyes flicker to mine. *Friends*. Is that what Ace and I still are?

An older woman in her sixties appears in the doorway. "Ace," she greets him. Her expression is gentle, and she smiles, allowing her wrinkles to become more prominent.

"Evelyn, this is Calla...a friend of mine," he explains to the woman, and her smile grows wider on her thin, frail lips.

"I see. It's nice to finally meet you, Calla." Her voice is filled with sincerity. Finally? Does that mean Ace talked about me previously, or is she simply saying this to be polite? I don't want to overthink it.

"Likewise." I'm not sure what else to say. Ace hasn't told me anything about his family, but he brought me to meet them. I'm a little bit out of place.

"I'll come back around four, dear?" Her eyes turn to Ace.

"Yes, I'll have to be at work at six," he states, placing Ellie down. She comes to my side.

Work? Does he mean he has a fight?

Evelyn nods. "I took out ingredients on the kitchen counter for cookies. Ellie and I were going to make some, but she wanted to wait for you."

"Cookies! We're making cookies!" Ellie exclaims, gazing up at me.

"I love cookies," I state, and she beams with excitement.

Ellie tugs on my arm and leads me inside while Ace and Evelyn finish up on the porch. "Acy likes you."

"Oh?"

"He only brings girls he likes here," she says nonchalantly, bobbing her head from side to side while skipping to the kitchen.

I love her already.

"Hmm, really?" I ask with my eyebrows raised. Does he now…

"Yeah, like Livvy! I love Livvy. She does my makeup and makes me look pretty," Ellie reveals, and I breathe a sigh of relief.

The inside of the house is much bigger than I expected. It's an open plan arrangement, the kitchen and living room are connected, and the large windows brighten the place. There are a few pictures on the walls, and I halt in my tracks to take a look.

There's one with Ellie on Ace's shoulders. It seems like it was taken not too long ago on the front porch. However, another photo catches my attention, and my eyes scan it. Ellie is holding a massive, purple helium balloon that's the shape of the number five. Ace is holding Ellie, and there's a woman to the right of Ace. She looks like she's in her mid-thirties with the same features—dark hair and vivid eyes. It must be their mom, and I wonder where she is.

"That's my mom," Ace says, startling me. I didn't realize he is paying attention to me.

"Will I meet her today?"

"No, she's working. She works most weekends," he tells me, and I nod. I'm starting to understand the situation.

"What does she do?" I ask.

"She's a nurse."

"And Evelyn?" I prompt. I hope he doesn't think I'm asking too many questions or overstepping any boundaries. Since I met him, he's been a closed book, and it's refreshing to see a different side to him.

"Evelyn lives next door. She's like family," he explains.

Ellie climbs onto the barstool behind the kitchen counter and examines the plastic cookie cutters. "I want to make the bunnies," she says, and Ace heads toward her.

I wash my hands in the kitchen sink and mix the ingredients for the cookie batter with Ellie's help. She's very clever for a five-year-old and knows the exact method. Ace isn't any help, I don't think he even knows how to make cookies. He's watching Ellie and me, occasionally placing his floury handprint on the sleeve of my shirt.

"Do you have a fight today?" I whisper while Ellie is busy mixing the frosting, stealing a few licks from the spoon now and then. Ace's eyes narrow, but he doesn't say anything, so I assume he does.

"Can I come?" I stack the dirty dishes inside the dishwasher.

"No."

"Why not?" I turn, facing him.

"It's not safe, Calla."

I roll my eyes. "It was fine last time."

"There are going to be more people this time," he says.

"Is everyone else going?" I ask. He doesn't answer me, placing the cookie tray into the heated oven. "You don't want me to come?"

"I don't want to be distracted. *You* distract me." Ace corners me between his body and the counter. My eyes glance at Ellie, but she's not paying any attention to us.

"Please?" I skate my hand down his chest. "It was hot watching you last time," I whisper so only he can hear and slightly graze my bottom lip with my teeth.

His eyes narrow. "Fuck, Calla. Why do you have to do that?" he asks, frustrated, taking my hand away from him and turning away abruptly.

Someone's in a mood. I smile to myself. "Does that mean I can come?"

"No."

I drop it for now, but he's an idiot if he thinks I'm not coming.

"Acy is taking me to Bella's birthday in a week. I have to make her a card," Ellie says when we finish cleaning up.

"We can watch *The Lion King* while you do that," Ace suggests, heading toward the living room.

"Nooo, we watch that every time," Ellie argues, grabbing an arts-and-crafts box from the cabinet.

"But it's the best movie," he tries to convince her.

"No," Ellie says, and I notice the resemblance in the bossiness trait. "Calla can choose." I laugh, and Ace pouts at Ellie, but she's not having any of it. She takes the TV remote off him and hands it to me.

Ace lies on the couch, and I sit next to him. Ellie positions herself on her beanbag beside us, focusing on her card. She glues glitter and feathers on the front. Ace wraps his arm around me, resting it on my leg, and I run my fingers over the dark ink that covers his skin.

"Do these mean anything?" I trace the outline of a small clock with no arrows.

"Some do. Some I got as a way to distract myself." He doesn't elaborate. For the rest of the time, we watch the movie with Ellie asking what colors she should use for her card.

The timer goes off for the cookies, and I turn to Ace, but his eyes are closed. His breath is moving gradually, in and out between his lips. I refrain from waking him. He needs sleep.

Ellie and I watch another movie while we wait for the cookies to cool. We decorate them quietly with pink-and-white frosting, drawing the faces of bunnies. I don't have younger siblings or even nieces or nephews, so I never realized how much fun it is to paint frosting on a stupid cookie, ensuring it looks perfect.

Ellie shows me her room—it's painted pastel purple, and silver stars scatter on the ceiling. "They glow in the dark," she says, and I'm suddenly envious of a five-year-old's room. "Acy has glow-in-the-dark planets in his room," she adds.

My eyebrows shoot up as I imagine what I'd encounter in Ace's room.

"Can you read to me, please?" Ellie hands me a book with dragons on the cover. Interesting choice, I bet Ace got her into this.

"Sure," I say.

We lie in the corner of her room under the canopy with fairy lights and blankets. I spend the next hour reading every book that she asks me to, while she listens without interrupting. "Can you come to Bella's birthday party with Acy and me?" she asks after I finish another book.

"I'd love to, but you will have to ask Ace if it's okay."

"It's okay. He likes you."

When it's almost four, we head into the living room to check on Ace, and he's still spread out on the couch. "Ellie, do you have whipped cream?" I ask her, and she bobs her head up and down in confirmation, pointing to the fridge.

I retrieve the whipped cream from the fridge and motion for Ellie to follow me. I place my finger to my lips to tell her to be quiet, and she nods with excitement. Filling Ace's hands with whipped cream, I find a feather in the arts-and-crafts box.

"Do you want to tickle *Acy's* face?" I offer Ellie the feather, and she takes it, giggling.

"Shh." I laugh. Ellie makes her way over to Ace and runs the feather down his face, but he doesn't budge. Her eyebrows furrow in confusion, like Ace's occasionally do, she's so cute.

"Here, let me try," I say, and Ellie passes me the feather. I trace Ace's face with it, remembering every single line like it's a roadmap to heaven. He looks so peaceful, his full lips parted a little, and his dark lashes cast a shadow underneath his eyes. I feel bad for trying to wake him, but damn, the guy sleeps like a log.

When he doesn't move, I stick the feather up his nose, and Ellie tries to cover her giggles with her hand. But that finally seems to do the trick.

Ace groans, and his hand shoots up to itch his face, getting the whipped cream all over his nose. His eyes fly open, and Ellie is already in fits of giggles, but it gets even louder when Ace tries to wipe his face with the other hand, not realizing there's cream on that one too.

"Ellie!" Ace complains, giving her a wolfish grin and rising.

"I didn't do it! Acyyy!! It wasn't me," she squeals, running away from him.

"No? Was it Calla?" he questions, his eyes settling on me in amusement. Shit.

"Uh." Ellie pauses, unsure of what to say, not wanting to get me in trouble. I bite my bottom lip and back away slowly.

Ace chases me toward the kitchen and grabs me by the waist, pulling me closer to his chest. I don't fight him, I adore playful Ace. I never would've thought he had this side to him, but the more I spend time with him, the more I unravel.

He kisses me softly—covering my face with cream—and then tickles me.

"Stop, Acy, it wasn't her." Ellie attempts to pull him away from me. He picks her up and tickles her too. Our laughter satiates the space around us.

And at this moment, standing in the middle of Ace's childhood home, laughing until I can't breathe anymore, I'm happy. I don't have to fake a smile or force a laugh, because it just happens with Ace. It's a linking I can't explain, and it's moments like these when I wish I could stop time.

17

Written in the Stars

The cold air nips at my face through the open windows on our drive back. "Are we going straight to the club?" I ask. We pass a forest, and I inhale the smell of pine—sharp, sweet, and elevating.

"I'm driving you back to the house. Then *I'm* going to the club," Ace states.

His hands tense around the steering wheel. I'm a little upset that he doesn't want me at his fight, even though everyone else is going. I twist the ends of my hair and stare out the window.

The rest of the car ride is silent, and my mind goes into overdrive. I'm anxious that Ace will return to his usual charming self and push me away. I hope I'm mistaken. He pulls into the driveway, cutting the engine, and hands me my keys. I take them, heading inside the house.

"Calla, wait," he orders, catching up to me and taking my hand between his fingers gently. I reluctantly turn around to face him. "You can come if you want," he says, his eyes tempering when they meet mine.

"I don't want to come if you don't want me there." I drop my gaze to the ground.

"I do. It's just I can't protect you when I'm in the ring and—"

"I don't need protection, Ace," I say, not even sure what he means by that. From what would I need protection?

Ace shakes his head. "I'm going to change. I'll be back," he says, advancing toward his room.

We take my car to the club, and everyone is already waiting for us there. Ace opens the door for me and takes my hand in his. Liv wiggles her eyebrows and looks down at my hand, which is intertwined with Ace's. She gives me a look that says we're definitely talking about this later.

There's a much bigger crowd inside than last time. Everyone is shouting over each other, and there's barely any space left to breathe. It smells like cigarettes, alcohol, and sweat mixed with blood.

Ace leads us to the back corner, where no one is allowed except for the fighters. I spot Dean, the school chancellor, talking to someone. His hands are in the air, and his face is red with anger. To be honest, it looks like Dean is about to throw punches himself.

"I have to go," Ace says, squeezing my hand in reassurance. He turns to Theo. "Make sure nothing happens to Calla." I roll my eyes. I don't need a babysitter.

"Of course, man." Theo throws his arm over my shoulder. Ace frowns before walking toward Dean.

I didn't expect Logan to be here again, and most importantly, I didn't envisage him to be a fighter, even though he's got the physical build for it. I guess there was a reason why he was lurking around last time. It's foreign to see the way Logan moves in the ring. He's not quick, but he lands each punch with everything he's got. My eyes dart to Ace, bearing in mind the last time he had a run-in with Logan. Ace is warming up and not paying any attention to him. My shoulders relax.

"What's the deal with Ace and Logan?" I ask Theo. He scratches the back of his head as if considering whether he should spill or not.

"You wouldn't believe this, but they're used to be close," Theo begins, unable to hold his tongue, but I guessed that part myself after their encounter at the football game.

"A couple of years ago, something happened between them. No one knows what, but it was odd…one minute, they were best buddies, and the next, they hated each other. Ace says they had a falling out, but that's all we could get out of him."

I open my mouth to ask another question, but the crowd erupts into cheers. I glance up to see Ace in the ring. His body glistens with sweat and tenses with every move, showing every single carved muscle. It's ungodly and puts dirty thoughts into my mind.

This time, Ace's opponent is speedy on his feet and strategic. He succeeds in getting a few hits on Ace, and I flinch every time he does. Ace doesn't seem troubled by them, and it causes me to consider whether he permitted them. He probably did. Otherwise, no one would bother gambling on any of Ace's opponents if he were going to overthrow them instantly.

It's not long before Ace's opponent gets fatigued and clumsier with his feet, stumbling from corner to corner. The perfect time to take him out, and that's precisely what Ace does, with one clean punch followed by another and another until his opponent tumbles to the ground and goes limp. The crowd cheers with excitement and collides their drinks together, spilling them. I'm glad we're not in the middle of all that chaos like last time.

Ace strides toward me, grinning, and in the moment, I wrap my hands around his neck, bringing my lips to his. His mouth curves against my own, and he sets his hands on my hips, pulling me closer to him.

"That was hot," I whisper between kissing. The blood from his busted lip runs down his chin.

"Blackwell," a voice interrupts. My head turns to the right, where Logan is still in his gray boxing shorts.

He examines Ace and then me with a dubious glare. "I haven't seen you so fascinated by a girl before. Usually, you get bored with them after a few days. Well, apart from..." He pauses for a moment and tilts his head to one side. His eyes flicker from Ace to me and then back to Ace again. "No..." he mutters in disbelief, his mouth forming a sardonic smirk.

"Logan," Ace warns, his hands clenching into fists by his side.

"It is, isn't it?" Logan asks.

"No," Ace snarls.

"You're fucked up," Logan says with amusement in his tone, crossing his arms over his chest.

Ace takes a step closer to Logan and clenches his jaw, anger radiating off him. "Shut the fuck up before you say something you'll regret."

I didn't realize two medium-sized guys were with Logan. One of them I recognize from the football game. They take a step closer as if waiting for a fight to break out, but they don't say anything.

"You want to take your anger out?" Logan shoves Ace, barely moving him. "How about we fight? It will be one hell of a match. Give the audience what they want."

Ace shakes his head and snickers in a way that implies Logan is an idiot—which I don't doubt that he is, but my stomach churns at the thought of them fighting, especially since they have history. Fighting with a stranger for money is one thing. Fighting for personal reasons is a whole other story.

Logan steps closer to Ace, provoking him. "You either agree to fight me or…" His smile gets broader and more malicious.

Ace's body trembles with rage. He knows precisely what Logan is implying. I scrutinize Theo, Josh, and Liv, they all wear blank stares. On the other hand, Zach steps closer to Ace as though he's aware this will set him off.

"Two weeks," Ace barks with wrath leaking from his tone and places his arm around my waist, turning away.

"Aren't we going to discuss the prize?" Logan asks with a glimmer in his eye, and Ace pauses, turning back to scowl at him. "Maybe I should see what it's like." Logan's eyes travel suggestively to me. "To fuck h—"

Before anyone has the time to react, Ace's fist collides with Logan's smug face. It's quick and vicious. After that, everything happens so quickly that it's hard to keep up. The two guys with Logan step forward, but so do Theo and Josh.

Logan holds up a hand, motioning them to back off. "Two weeks, Ace." He smirks, wiping the blood off his face and flicking it onto the floor. I grimace.

"What the hell was that about?" Josh questions Ace once we get outside. The cool breeze strikes us, and I wrap my hands around myself, shivering. Ace notices and tightens his hold on me.

"Nothing. Logan is just searching for trouble," Ace answers, looking toward Zach and holding his gaze as if silently conveying a message.

Ace and I tread to my car, and the rest of the group goes in the opposite direction as they couldn't get a parking spot next to us.

"What happens when you're in the passenger seat at night?" Ace asks me as we get closer to the car. I hesitate for a moment, unsure of how to answer his question. "You haven't even tried to get in the passenger seat?" Ace raises his eyebrows.

"You sound like you're trying to say it's all in my head."

"It is," he tells me, and I narrow my eyes at him. He's partially right, but I can't seem to get over it. Something about it terrifies me, and not even therapy seemed to work, maybe because I discarded the idea before stepping foot into the clinic.

Ace opens the passenger door and leans his elbow on the top of it, waiting for me to get in.

My heart pounds in my chest, and I shake my head. "No, I can't."

"Just sit inside. We won't drive." I hesitate and slowly move toward the car, trying to calm my breathing. *It's just sitting*, I tell myself.

Images of the accident fill my head. Ace takes my hand in his, and everything disappears. It's unexplainable how a wave of calm washes over me with his touch, and I slide into the seat.

"Okay?" Ace asks when he gets in the driver's side, and I nod.

"What was Logan talking about?" I try to get my mind off the car situation. Ace's whole body tenses.

"Nothing," he says sharply. He turns toward the window, not meeting my prying glance.

"It sounded like something," I persist. It seems like the more I get to know Ace, the more secrets there are between us.

"It was nothing."

"Ace…" I begin, wanting to tell him he can talk to me about anything.

"Can you just drop it? Fuck! It has nothing to do with you." He rubs his forehead and turns his head toward the window.

I guess that's the end of that conversation. I don't press him further. I'm afraid he'll shut me out entirely like he did after the mirror incident.

We sit in silence for a while before I can't take it anymore.

Usually, our silence is soothing, but this time it's filled with obscurity and uneasiness.

"Okay, I'm done sitting," I snap. Then, climbing out of the passenger seat, I stride to the driver's side. Ace sighs before getting out of the car as well.

"I'm sorry." He pulls me in for a hug. He brushes his lips against the top of my head.

When we get to the house, Ace says he has to go somewhere and walks off in the opposite direction. I'm left standing in front of the house, confused by the whole ordeal. I walk upstairs to find a pink sticky note in the middle of my door.

Meet me at our spot. There's a meteor shower tonight.

Our spot. There's only one place that it could be—the place we first kissed.

Did Ace have this planned all along? He must've placed the sticky note on my door before we left for the club. Why not ask me when we got back?

I put white sweatpants and a hoodie on, because it's freaking freezing, and I'm not about to turn into an icicle in the middle of the night. The colder months have always been my favorite. Something about being cozy and not drenched in sweat is comforting.

It's about a five-minute walk to the lake. It must be a new moon, because there's no light from it to illuminate my path, but I know the way. All the times I've been here, there hasn't been anyone else here—except during the bonfire. The place is secluded from the public, and there's no pathway, so passersby who take their midnight stroll won't coincidently stumble upon it.

My eyes travel to the end of the dock where Ace is, and my heart flaps inside my chest. He's lying on a blanket with his hands behind his head, looking up at the sky. Who knew Ace, the arrogant asshole that I once thought he was, could propose a lovely gesture such as this one.

"I didn't take you for a romantic." I stand in front of him, blocking his view of the cosmic sky.

He sits up, smiling, and grabs my hand, pulling me into his hard chest. I place my knees on either side of him.

"Only for you," he whispers against my mouth. He finds my lips with his like they were never meant to be apart. The taste of him is intoxicating. It's been less than an hour since I last saw him, but any time apart from him makes me crave him even more.

I lie next to him, placing my head on his chest. The soft sound of his heart beats in my ear, and I trail my fingers down his bicep.

"Is that where you go every weekend? To see Ellie?" I ask. Today's events seem so distant.

"Yeah, my mom works almost every weekend."

"Dad?" I ask in a small voice, pushing my luck. The air thickens around us, and Ace exhales.

"He disappeared a couple of years ago. He was a piece of shit anyway. A self-centered lawyer who thought the sun shined out of his fucking ass," he explains with bitterness.

I'm mesmerized by the sky. The clusters of glimmering stars scatter across it. It's better than anything in pictures or, in fact, better than any imitation at all. A bright light races across the sky every few seconds and leaves a glowing trail of smoke behind that eventually fades into nothingness.

For once, something about shooting stars feels magical, but why? I can't figure it out. Maybe it's the reality of them—the mystery. Or the way everything else becomes so insignificant. The universe is beyond anyone's conception. My eyes are glued to the infinite existence of stardust, swirling in a trillion different ways. The only thing on my mind is how perfect this moment is because of him.

Does Ace have the same nostalgic thoughts running through his mind as I do? I turn my head to get a glimpse of him, but his eyes are already on mine. A smile spreads across his tempting mouth, which sparks something inside of me—a need for him.

I need him in every single way possible.

Stretching my neck, I kiss him, flicking my tongue over his lips. He opens his mouth, allowing me to take control. Placing my hands on the back of his neck, I lure him closer to me, unable to get enough, like this is some kind of dream.

His mouth explores mine like we have all the time in the world. My whole body radiates with desire—a desire for him.

Ace sits up with me in his lap, and I push my hips against his. Feeling his hardness against me, I moan into his mouth, and his arms tighten around me. My hands travel underneath his shirt and up to his body—over every single muscle that's expanding underneath my touch. We both know what's coming, and I want him more than I've ever wanted anyone or anything before.

"There's something I need to tell you." He catches his breath and pulls away.

"Then tell me." I place my hands on either side of his face, his skin is hot underneath my fingers, and I brush his cheekbones with my thumb.

Ace closes his eyes as if reflecting upon my answer. "Calla…" I love the way he says my name. There's a moment of hesitation, where something crosses his face in the form of apprehension.

"I can't fucking lose you." His voice fills with an emotion that I haven't heard before from him. Vulnerability?

"I'm not going anywhere, Ace," I say, dragging out every word, so he understands. Is this why he's afraid to open up to me? Because he thinks I'll leave? I have reiterated time and again that I have no intention of doing that.

Ace's lips are back on mine, this time more demanding, like he's putting everything he has into it. It's passionate and consuming, it's more than I've ever envisioned it to be. Finally, Ace flips me over, laying me down on the blanket beneath him, and I pull my hoodie over my head.

His eyes scan my body, and he sucks in a breath, lowering his mouth onto my neck and sucking gently before whispering, "Fuck, Calla. Do you know how beautiful you are?"

He works his way down my body, kissing every part of me with his perfect mouth. Then, dragging his tongue across the areas he's kissed. If I didn't know any better, I'd say that my heart is about to explode from my chest into a million shattered pieces. Yet every piece would still find its way back to him.

Ace tugs at the waistband of my pants, looking up at me, asking for permission. I nod, and he pulls them off, placing them to the side.

I know the cool air travels across my body, but I can't feel anything except the way he touches me. His hot breath is between my legs, and once again, he tugs on my panties, asking for consent. I nod, closing my eyes, biting my bottom lip in anticipation.

He kisses each of my inner thighs, sucking gently, and I swallow hard.

"Look at me," Ace commands. My eyes fly open and land on his. My breath hitches in my throat, and Ace smirks before lowering his mouth directly in between my legs. One of his hands holds mine, and the other grips my thigh, this moment becoming much more intimate. He glides his tongue over me, and I shudder in response.

"Oh my God," I breathe when his tongue dips into me, and the tip of it curves. My back arches as pleasure streams through me, I've never felt anything like this before, and I'm high on endorphins, which swirl through my entire body.

My head tilts back, all I can see is the cosmos above me. Being worshipped by Ace's mouth while watching the stars is rather amazing, and some would say, a once-in-a-lifetime opportunity.

Ace groans against me, and the sensation sends vibrations through my entire body.

"Ace," I pant. His hand tightens around mine, locking me in place while his strokes quicken like he's writing our names in the damn constellation with his tongue.

He eases a finger inside of me while he devours me, whirling his tongue around the most sensitive area. I can't hold back the feeling that overtakes me when he wraps his entire mouth around my sex and sucks. I move my hips against his mouth as I throw my head back. Finally, my body shakes and I come, gasping his name over and over, and all I can see are stars behind my eyelids.

He moves back up toward me and cups my face. "I love hearing you."

My hands are on him, rubbing his erection through the material of his pants. He curses, pinning my hands on either side of me, trailing kisses from my jaw to my lips. "Do you have a cond—" I begin.

"In my pocket. Are you sure about this?"

"I want you," I tell him. He pauses like he's waiting for me to change my mind. "I want all of you, please."

I grab his face and lower it back to mine.

Between our kissing, I manage to slide his pants off, and he fumbles with his pocket, cursing when he can't unwrap the condom wrapper quickly enough.

"Oh my…" My eyes widen when my hand goes into his boxers

and wraps around *him*.

"What?" He freezes, pulling his mouth away from mine. He's on his knees in front of me.

I knew he was big from all the times his erection brushed against me through his clothes. But now that I'm experiencing it for the first time, I have doubts about how this will work.

The only person I had sex with was Nate, so I'm not sure if this is common or whether Ace is abnormally large. Flashes from the last time I participated in this unfortunate event with Nate fill my head. Oh God.

Thinking about my ex isn't helping. I shake my head to rid the thoughts.

"Um…I—you're…" I have no words.

Ace raises his eyebrow. "I'm what, Calla?"

I swallow hard. "You're huge. I'm not sure this is going to work." My hands stroke him, preparing myself.

He grins, the sheer male arrogance and ego at its peak. What did I expect after saying something like that?

"Don't let it get to your head, Ace."

"Too late, love." His grin is wider than the Cheshire cat.

I wrap my hands tighter around his shaft, and he groans. "Ahh, easy."

Ace watches the uncertainty on my face unfold. "Hey," he says, stilling my hand with his. "We don't have to if you're not comfortable."

"I want to," I say. And I do, I really do.

I run my hands down his body and flick my tongue over his neck, which earns a grunt from him. Gripping his hair with my hands, I pull him even closer and cover his mouth with my own. Ace's tongue fills my mouth, and he grasps my body tighter against his, leaving no room for anything else.

He slides one long finger inside of me again, and I gasp. Ace lowers us to the blankets as he deepens the kiss, igniting me everywhere like I'm a match.

His body settles between mine, and I can feel him right *there*. He doesn't move as he waits for me, and I give him a small nod. He slowly pushes into me, stretching me with his length. My hands are on his back, my nails digging into his skin from the stinging.

The pain doesn't last long, and the pleasant feeling of fullness encompasses me.

Ace watches my face for any sort of resistance or hesitation. I don't give him any. "Fuck," he groans into my ear as he holds completely still inside me. "Are you okay?"

I nod, giving him the go-ahead.

Holding his weight above me, he moves, savoring every thrust. I run my hands down his chest and his arms, his muscles contract with every movement. I never thought this could feel *this* good. Or is it just with him? Everything feels mind-blowing with Ace.

His eyes pierce mine, conveying every single undeclared emotion between us. I wrap my legs around his torso, and he takes my hand, bringing it above my head, lacing his fingers through it.

"You're incredible," he coaxes.

The bond between us is compelling. It's remarkable how one person can make me feel like this, like I have the whole world at my fingertips. Ace increases his pace, and his other hand wraps around my waist, bringing me even closer to him, making his thrusts deeper.

He runs wet kisses down my jaw, my neck, toward my chest. He takes my nipple in his mouth and sucks on it before connecting with my mouth again. His tongue is hot, and plays teasingly with mine. I close my eyes and let my head sink deeper into the blankets, allowing Ace to guide me in any way he needs. I'm getting close again, and so is he.

My eyes grow heavy, and he kisses me with unforgiving passion. "Ace," I moan between catching my breath. He interprets every single sign that my body offers him.

"Calla," he murmurs and lowers his forehead against mine, grunting. I come for the second time tonight. This time with him, trembling against his body and feeling the warmth of his chest as he collapses onto me. Our breathing is ragged, and my fingers trace his back.

When we are wrapped in the blankets, and I'm lying on his chest, I ask him, "Do you believe in fate?"

"To a certain extent, but not everything is defined by fate."

How ironic, Brody said the same thing. I scrunch my face at his answer, looking up at him, and his mouth turns at the corners.

"Would you like it if I told you that us being here was written in the stars?" he asks.

"Hmm, yes. I would like to believe in something."

"You and me, we're written in the stars, love." He takes my hand and kisses it. I hope he can't sense my breathing quicken, but I'm confident that after everything, he already knows what he does to me.

"Would you want to know when and how you would die?" I ask thoughtlessly. Perhaps the world above us is opening the door to philosophical questions tonight.

"I'd like to know when, but not how. So I know how long I have to make amends for my mistakes."

"You say that like there are many. Do you believe in the afterworld? Is that why you wish to make amends before your time is up?"

He scoffs. "No, I already know I'm going straight to hell if such a place exists." His voice drives a barrier up, and he doesn't elaborate.

We spend hours talking, and he opens up to me about his mom and Ellie. He tells me he wants me to meet his mom, and I'm apprehensive, not because I don't want to, but because I want her to like me. He teases me for my music choices, bringing up Hannah Montana, and I tell him that was a one-time thing.

I promised myself that there would be no boys in college—I didn't come here looking for that. But it's three a.m., and we are on the deck. We're laughing to the point of snorting and watching the whole universe above us. I'm happy for the first time in a long time because of him, and I know I'm wholly and utterly screwed.

18

Unexpected Turn

It's easy to get lost in an idealistic daze when it's just Ace and me. Time passes by almost at the speed of light, and I'm left wondering if any of it was real. The saying "don't judge a book by its cover" is undeniably true, especially with Ace. When we met, I had no idea there would be this segment to him.

Underneath the concealment of darkness and anger, there's a strobe of light. Ace is perceptive, thoughtful, and selfless, which wasn't evident through our first encounters. I'm glad I've decided to give him a chance, even when he irritated the shit out of me at the start.

I don't know what to call it, the thing that's happening between us. I like it, though. It feels fragile and powerful at the same time, but good. So good.

"Hey, did you think about that camping trip?" Nate's voice tugs me out of my thoughts.

"Shit." I jump, almost spilling the hot cup of tea that I'm carrying.

He constantly emerges out of nowhere, and most of the time, it's when I'm working. It's like he deems this the perfect opportunity to have a conversation. Doesn't he know what a phone is, instead of showing up to the place I work?

I've been jumpy since the weekend and Ace's confrontation with Logan. I can't get Theo's words out of my head—they *used to be best friends*. What did Logan know about Ace that he didn't want anyone else knowing?

"Sorry," Nate apologizes and cocks his head to one side as if waiting for an answer.

I walk to the table in the corner and place the tea in front of a middle-aged woman with glasses. She's one of the regulars—she comes in most afternoons and reads a book with her peppermint tea as if this is her way of diverting herself from the worries of the day she's had.

"Thank you, dear." She offers me a thin smile.

"Hmm..." I consider my options while I walk back to the counter, where Nate is still waiting for an answer.

I heard Liv, Zach, and Theo discussing the camping trip the other day, but I'm uncertain if they decided to go or not. It's for Halloween, and I'm hesitant about a camping trip that's filled with very intoxicated university students in the middle of nowhere.

"Come on, Cals, it'll be fun." Nate gives me puppy eyes. They don't work on me anymore.

Nate never used to act like this, even when we were together. He'd always cancel plans that we formed to hang out at parties and do drugs with his friends instead. Why the sudden change now? Is he really not making any friends here, not fitting in?

I reach for my water bottle and take a sip.

"Yeah, Cals, it'll be fun," Mia mimics Nate in a lesser voice behind me. I restrain a smile. I'm not sure if Nate heard that, and if he did, he's not reacting to it.

Mia and I have grown closer as we spend a lot of time together during work, so I told her about Nate. She's adamant that he still has feelings for me, but I refuse to ponder over that. I made it clear to him that nothing will happen between us. He'd be unwise to believe otherwise.

"Okay, sure, only if you come," I tell Mia, making sure she can see my pleading eyes. I don't need Nate to get any ideas if I agreed to come on this camping trip with him, so the only way to combat that is to bring someone else. Plus, didn't Mia say she thought he's cute or something?

"I-I…" Mia stutters when I put her on the spot, and I seize the opportunity.

"Perfect, that's sorted. You should get more people to come with us." I glance back at Nate, and he sighs, scanning my expression and rubbing his brow as if he were anticipating it'd be just us two.

"Uh, yeah, sure," he replies in a flat tone. He turns around and staggers out with a shake of his head.

"He's in love," Mia sings when Nate is out of hearing distance.

"He's not. I think he's lonely. It must be hard for him here," I counter. Nate has left all his friends back home, most of them decided not to attend college and chose a trade instead.

"You hungry? Come have dinner with us," Brody invites me when we're closing up. He doesn't look at me as he scribbles in his notepad, his broad shoulders tensing when he can't think of a word.

I glance at Mia, and she seems as confused as I am. I assume this doesn't happen regularly.

"Sure," I tell Brody, and he nods to himself before heading out.

Mia and I close up the store and walk to her house. "You know, camping isn't really my thing." Her boots click on the concrete beneath our feet.

My eyebrows crease. "Does it look like it's my thing? I don't even have a tent."

She laughs. "Don't worry. I'm sure Brody will have one."

We enter through the front door, and the smells of peppers, rich tomatoes, and onions engulf me. I didn't realize Brody would be making dinner when I agreed to come.

He serves the pasta in bowls in front of us and glances at me. His piercing blue eyes dive into my soul, and I drop my gaze to the food.

"The monsters that live in your mind really do exist. They just have the face of a human," he tells me when I have a mouthful of pasta, and I choke on it. I wipe my lips with a napkin, coughing, and reach for the cold glass of water.

"Brody! Did you just invite her so you can scare her? There's a reason why I can't bring any friends over here." Mia shakes her head. "You can't say things like that."

Brody shrugs and returns to taking notes while occasionally stabbing the pasta with his fork.

We head into Mia's room after dinner, and it's incredibly spacious. Her queen-sized bed is against the dark gray wall with a desk next to it. The rest of her room barely has anything, even though there's enough space to have a whole gathering. I guess she likes the minimalistic look.

"So…has Brody always been like this?" I ask Mia.

It can only go two ways with Brody, and neither of the possibilities is something anyone would consider normal. Some things he says, it's like he can see right through you, and the other things, I doubt anyone knows what he's talking about.

"No, he was in an accident a couple of years ago, and he suffers long-term memory loss," she says. "It changed him."

"An accident?"

"Yeah, I don't really know what happened, and Brody doesn't remember much, if anything. My family isn't close to him, so they never really bothered to find out what happened."

"What was he like before the accident?"

"Much different. The opposite, actually. He used to be involved with drugs and gangs, hence why my family cut all connections, but he's a completely different person now, as you can see."

I nod in agreement. I can't imagine Brody being involved with anything along those lines.

"Did you draw these?" I ask, studying the detailed sketches in amazement. There's one of a girl with thorns coming out of the back of her head and her hair braided tightly. The detail on it is extensive, from the moonlit background to the unique colors and shading. It's truly remarkable.

"Oh, yeah, they aren't the best..." She bites her lip, placing her hand over some.

"Not the best? They're incredible," I say. "You're majoring in arts?"

"Yeah. I've always wanted to be a tattoo artist, but I don't know...I don't feel like my work is good enough to be on someone's skin forever." She drops on her bed.

I sit next to her and lean my back against the wall. "You're not giving yourself enough credit. They really are amazing," I tell her, eyeing the drawings.

It all happens so quickly, and I freeze when she leans in, placing her glossy lips to mine. I can't move. Her lips are made of velvet and move gently against mine for no more than five seconds. The lip gloss she has on tastes like succulent strawberries, sweet and welcoming.

"Hmm," she sighs when she pulls away.

I stare at her, wide-eyed. "Mia?"

"Sorry, I needed to try something." She stares blankly ahead of her and brings her small fingers to skim her lips.

"Try something?" I question, not angry but extremely confused.

"I'm trying to figure out something," she says, reflecting. Is she confused about her sexuality?

"And, um…did *that* help you figure it out?"

"Not really, but it was…good," she admits and begins drawing on a new page as if nothing happened.

I've never had a girl kiss me before, and it didn't feel bad, just odd. But it's instantly forgotten, and I'm consumed by watching Mia draw.

"What was your life like before you came to live with Brody?"

"Strict. My parents are Mormon," she tells me like that explains everything. I notice the way she doesn't classify herself as one. "I probably sound like I hate my parents. I don't. I just don't believe in their way of life and them trying to force it onto me from the day I came out of the womb."

"I would never have guessed you've been raised as a Mormon."

"Good," she says with bitterness laced through her usual tender voice.

"So, what's the dream for when you finish college? What would be your ideal outcome?" I ask.

We all have a vision for ourselves at the end of this. My dream has been blurred for a while. But as more time passes, the clearer it's becoming. It's like I've finally gotten glasses after being blind for so long, I'm still adjusting to the fit. But New York City is becoming embedded into me.

"I'm going to travel for a few years. I'll start in France, Paris to be precise, since it's the city of love. Maybe I'll get lucky and find a companion that's willing to follow me to whatever end." She laughs.

"Then I'll go to Portugal, Spain, Italy, Croatia, definitely Greece and all its islands, that's what I'm most excited about. Ancient history, beautiful sunsets, and food. I'm already in love," Mia dreams, closing her eyes.

I watch her lost in her vision, a million miles from here. There's hope in the stillness of her face, in the depth of her soul, behind the tiny freckles that scatter like glitter around her nose. And in her presence, the ambiance embraces me and tugs me toward my own ambitions, making them clearer and more defined.

I picture an old studio apartment overlooking the New York streets, which hum with life. The anticipation flows through my bloodstream and floods my veins.

Ace is in the kitchen when I arrive home around eleven, and his eyes shoot up to me when I step foot through the front door. I'm uncertain of how to act around him. He isn't my boyfriend, so I shouldn't act like he is either. But it wasn't just sex—it was too intimate for that. Or am I analyzing too much?

He drops his dark gaze to the book in his hand without saying anything. I walk toward the stairs. I shouldn't be nervous around him after everything that happened.

"Sleep with me tonight." Ace shuts his book and looks at me. "Just sleep, nothing else," he adds when I don't say anything. We both know the only way we can both sleep is around each other, both of us don't want to admit it. Isn't it insalubrious to rely on a person for such a basic need?

"Okay, I'll just have a shower," I find myself saying.

"You can have a shower in my room," he tells me but quickly adds, "if you want. It's bigger, and you can use it…instead of sharing the upstairs one with Liv and Zach."

I nod. "Okay, I'll just get some clothes."

"Okay." A smile escapes his mouth, and everything is instantly back to the way it is when it's just him and me.

"Is the shower broken again?" Liv asks me as I descend the stairs with my towel and clothes under my arm. She knows that it isn't, since her hair is wet from the one she had ten minutes ago. Liv twirls around in the cheer squad uniform that she's designed while Zach makes her waffles.

"Uh, not exactly," I say, not meeting her eyes because I know she's giving me that look that says we still haven't talked about what's going on between Ace and me. I haven't told her as much as I told Mia, because either she's always with Zach or Ace is within hearing distance.

"Oh, got it," she says, smirking, and Zach looks up at me.

He's the least talkative out of the whole group, the most closed off one, and I don't know him at all, even though I live with him.

"What do you think?" Liv asks, standing in front of me with her hands on her hips. She's changed the one-piece cheer squad uniform to a two-piece with a skirt and a long-sleeved crop top that rests just above her navel.

"Much better than the previous ones," I admit.

"Much better? Girl, it's in a different class." She spins one more time, gloating at her skills.

I pad to Ace's room, and his eyes locate me when I open the door. He's typing away on his laptop, I assume it's an assignment.

I still have no idea how Ace has managed to score himself a bedroom that's double the size of Liv and Zach's *and* has a personal bathroom. But he can be very persuasive or demanding, whichever one you want to believe. They mean the same thing to him.

I emerge from the bathroom, studying Ace's books and running my fingers over the edges, not really reading the titles but aware that Ace is watching me. And being observed by Ace is intensely riveting.

He's sprawled out on his bed, and even though it's king-sized, he occupies most of it. His hands rest behind his head, and I keep my eyes away from him because I know too well how he makes me feel, how my thoughts jumble around him. How I lose connection to the existence, and I exist entirely in him.

"What are you majoring in?" I ask, tilting my head to the side but still not daring to look his way.

"I'm actually thinking of changing degrees," he confesses. I focus on gliding my fingers through the titles. *Benjamin Franklin, Ernest Hemingway, Nelson Mandela.*

"Hmm, really?"

He nods in my peripheral vision and continues, "I didn't know what I wanted to study, but since all my life I have read, I assumed literature would be somewhat okay."

Somewhat okay? That doesn't sound convincing. "It doesn't sound like you're very interested in it at all," I observe, gently drumming my fingers on his wooden bookshelf.

"My dad wanted me to be a lawyer, just like him." He almost scoffs at the last part. This is the first time he has mentioned his father without me bringing it up.

"And I'm guessing that's not something you want to do either?"

"If you knew my father, you wouldn't want to do anything that would make you relatively similar to him."

How can someone disappear and leave their five-year-old daughter?

"Lawyers want to become lawyers so they can uphold the law. But my dad is a lawyer so that he can abuse it. He'd fuck over his own family if someone made him the right offer," Ace speaks, his teeth clenching. He shuts his eyes.

"So, what's something that you're interested in studying?" I bid to change the conversation to something a little lighter. I stroll closer to him, and he sits up, so my legs end up in the middle of his.

"Maybe something to do with sports science," he considers and brings his arms around the back of my thighs, tugging me a little closer. "I got offered a contract with a club. Dean surprisingly has some connections, and this one isn't illegal."

"I didn't think you liked fighting?" I tangle my hands in his hair, something I do unconsciously now.

"It's not just that. Part of the offer is that it would guarantee me an all-paid scholarship at Palm Valley University."

My mouth drops open. Palm Valley is one of the most prestigious universities in the country, and grades alone don't guarantee you a spot there. You need a hell of a lot of money too. It's mostly filled with students from wealthy families, such as politician's offspring and even movie star's kids. Everyone who attends is guaranteed to have a job in their chosen career before they finish the degree.

"That's one hell of an offer. You must have impressed someone."

He tilts his head and glances up at me, a smirk forming on his charming mouth. "Have you not seen me fight?" He grips my thighs tighter, and I enfold one hand around his neck. "Oh, but you did, because I remember you mentioning that you found it… hmm, what was the word you used?" He cocks a dark eyebrow at me, commanding me to answer, and I roll my eyes.

There he is, the pretentious Ace that I'm captivated by.

"Hot, Ace. It's surprisingly hot watching you beat someone up," I answer sarcastically, with possibly some honesty behind my words.

I don't know what it is about seeing him fight that presses my buttons in all the right spots. But then again, Ace could simply look at me a certain way, the way he's looking at me right now, with his gorgeous eyes and a lazy smile, which incites my insides to catch fire.

"So, you perve on me during my most critical moments. I'll keep that in mind." He pulls me closer and rests his chin on my chest, still looking up at me.

"When do you start there?" I ask, curious. I continue to thread my fingers through his hair that I already made a mess of, and he groans in satisfaction.

"Why do you assume that I accepted the offer?"

Ace's phone lights up next to him on the bed, and my eyes unconsciously travel to it. I don't recognize the number. Ace doesn't pay any attention to it, he's focused solely on me.

"You'd be stupid not to. It's an amazing opportunity," I tell him, even though my mind races with questions. It's about a four-hour drive to Palm Valley University from here and a two-hour drive from my dad's house.

"I told them I'd think about it. It would be sometime next year."

"What's there to think about?"

He shrugs, but I can decipher by his expression there's a great deal to consider.

"You know, Ellie called me today and told me that you have to wear something pink for Bella's party on Friday that I didn't even know you were coming to," he says as his grin widens further, causing butterflies to erupt in my stomach.

What's he doing to me?

"Uh, yeah, she asked me to, and I said I'd come if it were okay with you," I admit, feeling a little guilty that I may have forgotten about it.

"You better not get jealous. All the five-year-olds love me." He winks, and I smack him playfully on the shoulder.

"I guess I have some competition," I joke, and he shakes his head.

Ace's phone goes off again with a few text messages, but he still doesn't bother looking at them. Instead, he lifts me by my legs, catching me off guard.

"Ace!" I yelp, and he chuckles. Before I know it, I'm lying on the bed with him hovering above me.

"No competition, love." He brushes his lips against mine, and I can't help but smile throughout the feverish kiss.

I move my lips with his slowly, tasting the distinctive taste of Ace that I'm becoming accustomed to. However, it's interrupted by the sound of Ace's phone ringing.

His chest heaves in a sigh, and he pulls away, reaching for his phone. He rejects the call, but his eyes scan the text messages as his eyebrows furrow in confusion. There are at least five messages.

He abruptly gets up and puts on a hoodie that was on his desk chair.

"I have to go." He grabs his keys off the desk.

What? I attempt to keep my expression intact even though I have no idea what just happened.

"Hmm? Are you coming back?" I ask, immediately detesting how my voice sounds, almost needy, and I wish I didn't ask. I rack my brain for some sort of explanation, hoping Ace would at least offer me one, but he doesn't. He never does.

"I don't know. You can sleep here if you want, but don't wait up," he says, fixing his hair, which I messed up a second ago. And with that, he leaves the room.

His motorcycle starts up and drives off into the distance. I can't seem to comprehend the unexpected turn of events. It's not hard to give me a few words to explain the situation unless it's something that he doesn't want me to know. Have we taken one step forward and two steps back?

19

Solemn Decisions

My mind continues to wander endlessly as I lie in my bed with the window open. I try to convince myself that I'm not bothered with the current situation, but I soon realize that my thoughts are betraying me. My emotions are the only honest factor. Once again, I remind myself that Ace doesn't owe me an explanation, and if anything, it's my own fault for having these feelings when I've been warned not to.

Occasionally, the chilly breeze drifts through my window, and I inhale the fresh air, striving to clear my mind, but I fail. After what feels like hours of lying on my bed, staring into the distance, I reach for my laptop.

I finally type up an article for the newspaper. Letting my fingers hit the keyboard, not fretting about the outcome. It's short and straightforward, but it takes my mind off Ace. I read over it once, making a few changes. Before I have the time to change my mind, I send it to the email address the professor has provided me with.

In the early hours of the morning, I assume it's around three, I'm encased with darkness again. Ace's motorcycle pulls up, and

I'm pitifully anticipating him to come into my room and explain everything. Wishful thinking on my behalf.

There are footsteps on the stairs, but after a few minutes, the silence creeps in, and I swear I'm hallucinating.

I don't sleep for the rest of the morning, I lie awake for hours. When the sun rises, Liv gets up and gets ready for her classes. Then, Zach begins singing in the shower—a common occurrence.

I get out of bed when I'm sure everyone has left, especially Ace. I devote my day to completing chores and catching up on class readings. The last thing I need is to attend my classes when I'm incapable of thinking.

In the afternoon, there's a knock at the door. "Hey! I looked for you on campus, but you weren't there," Nate chirps when I greet him.

"Yeah, I wasn't feeling too well this morning," I answer, and he nods, glancing at me, absorbing my appearance.

"I'm fine, just a headache," I quickly add, so he doesn't worry about me.

"I've been getting things ready for the camping trip," he finally says, excitement peeking through his voice. "Come, I want to show you something." He motions me outside, and I follow him.

When I step onto the porch, I realize he drove here. His pickup truck is parked on the grass, and on the roof of the truck is a large red tent. My eyes widen. I don't think he drove here with the tent on the top, so how long has he been out the front setting this up to show me?

There's a flimsy ladder from the ground that leads to the top, and Nate eagerly climbs up. He shoves his head through the small window flap of the tent on the side. "What do you think?" He grins.

What do I think? *Well, Nate, I thought you were going to have a separate tent, but here you are*. I bite my tongue, he's proud of himself, and I don't have the heart to ruin that.

"It looks big enough for the three of us." I give him a reassuring smile. I do appreciate his effort.

"The three of us?" His eyebrows furrow in confusion.

"Mia?"

"Oh…yeah." His face sinks.

"Did you ask any of your friends if they wanted to come? Maybe your housemates?"

"Yeah, they're coming."

He steps on the ladder and descends. Everything happens too quickly. He misses a step and tumbles onto the ground, smashing his head on a rock that's protruding from the grass.

"Nate!" I cry, rushing to his side. "Oh my God! Are you alright?!" I kneel beside him, and my eyes travel to the gash on his head.

"Fuck," he grumbles. His hand shoots up to his head, and he rubs it. The blood transfers onto his hand.

"Let's get you inside." I help him up by his elbow. I guide him inside to the couch. "Sit, don't move. I'll get you something to clean it up so we can see how bad it is."

He groans, and I retrieve a washcloth from the kitchen, dampening it under lukewarm water. The sound of Ace's motorcycle pulling up to the house sends my heart into overdrive. I ignore it, Liv and Zach will be home soon too.

I stand in front of Nate, delicately setting the washcloth to his forehead where the blood is pouring from. I've never been affected by the sight of blood, but this is too much. I can't get it to stop to see how severe the cut is, and that's a reliable indicator that he ought to get stitches.

He's going a little pale too. I open my mouth to let Nate know that I'm driving him to the hospital, but I freeze when his hands fly to my waist.

"What the fuck is this?" Ace scowls.

"Ace." I sigh. His eyes drill onto Nate's hands, which are still on my waist. I relocate them off me and take a step back.

"Calla," Ace growls my name and marches closer. His deadly stare solidifies on Nate.

"I was showing Calla our tent," Nate speaks proudly. I want to slap him for saying that. I don't want to deal with this right now. I haven't disclosed my intentions to go on the camping trip to Ace.

Ace's jaw stiffens, and if that's not enough, Nate adds, "For the camping trip that we're going on this weekend."

I hurriedly take Nate's hand and place it on his forehead, so he keeps the pressure on his wound before turning to handle Ace.

"The fuck you are," Ace says. He's directly in front of Nate now, looming over him like a caveman.

Nate stands and wavers to the side. I really ought to take him to the hospital before he passes out from blood loss. "Na—" I begin, but he interrupts.

"What's your problem?" Nate steps closer to Ace. This can't be happening right now. A wounded Nate and a raging Ace, this isn't what I had scheduled for my quiet afternoon.

"Nate, we need to go to the hospital." I set a hand on his chest in an attempt to move him back, away from Ace.

"No, Calla. I'm getting real sick of this dickhead thinking he owns you or something," Nate barks.

"You want to know my problem? You're my problem." Ace towers over Nate, his hands balling into tight fists at his side.

Shit. This isn't good. Where are Zach and Liv when you need them?

"Ace, stop this," I say, and his eyes flash to me for a second before glaring at Nate. "You have no right to tell me who I can and can't spend my time with."

This catches his attention.

"Calla." His eyes soften, remembering last night.

"No, don't 'Calla' me. I don't tell you who you can spend ungodly hours of the night with," I snap.

"I can explain." He closes his eyes for a brief second.

"I'm sure you can, but I don't have time for it. I need to take Nate to the hospital."

"I'm fine," Nate objects, eager to hear what's going on between Ace and me. He's always loved the drama.

"He's fine. It's just a scratch. If he wants something to go to the hospital about, I'll give him a broken fucking nose," Ace says, smirking. His mood lightens.

"You want to sort this out right now?" Nate asks him, tossing the bloody washcloth onto the ground.

"Nate, let's go," I reiterate, eyeing his head, which still hasn't stopped bleeding. I'm desperately seeking to diffuse the situation, but neither of them is making this easy for me. They're both behaving like children.

"No, Calla. I'm a little rusty, but I'm sure I can handle this fuckwit." Nate's eyes are on Ace, and I realize he doesn't know Ace could reconstruct his whole face with one strike. It wouldn't even be a fight. Ace knows this too, and he snickers.

"Nate! That's enough. Let's go!" I raise my voice, and he looks at me wide-eyed, blood running down his cheek.

I've never raised my voice at him before, but he's frustrating me. This whole scene that both of them have caused has given me a piercing headache. I massage my temple, aiming to alleviate the pain.

"Can you help me? I think I'm feeling a little light-headed," Nate finally says. I sigh, placing my arm around his waist, and he throws a hand over my shoulders.

"You can't be fucking serious?" Ace asks in disbelief.

"Ace, don't," I say, conclusiveness ringing through my voice, and Nate turns to grin at him.

I drag him outside, toward my car, before something terrible happens. I'm astounded Ace managed to keep his temper intact for the last five minutes.

"What was that? Are you trying to cause a fight?" I question Nate when I get into the driver's seat and turn the keys. The old engine coughs and then rumbles to life.

"Calla, I really don't like him. There's something off about him." Nate stares straight ahead.

"I'm sure he thinks the same about you."

He's quiet for a while, and I welcome the silence. It's not until I pull up at the old hospital building that he speaks again.

"So what? Are you two fucking or something?"

I shoot him a look, narrowing my eyes, knowing that I'm not going to be having this conversation with Nate, my ex. "It's none of your business."

Nate does end up having to get stitches, and I sit with him after convincing the doctor that we're family. Nate takes my hand in his when the doctor begins the stitches. I let him. He runs his smooth thumb over the back of my hand and cringes when the needle goes into his skin.

The doctor informs us that Nate might be a little delirious from the injury and the medication, but he should be back to his regular self tomorrow.

Luckily, he lives with roommates, so he has someone to keep an eye on him tonight. He provides me with directions to the house, and I end up taking a few wrong turns because Nate is high on medication.

At last, I park in front of the small building. Nate turns to me. "I love you, Calla."

I assume he's stating it as a way to thank me. The words have been thrown between us previously. "I love you too," I say and open my door to get out, to lead Nate inside.

"No. I'm *in love* with you."

Oh.

Oh, please, no. I can't deal with anything else tonight, and my head is spinning, knowing that Ace is waiting for me to return.

"I think you hit your head pretty hard. We'll talk about this tomorrow when you're feeling better." I hope he fails to recall this conversation by tomorrow.

"I'm serious. I'm in love with you. I'm a fucking idiot for ending us."

I stare at him dumbfoundedly. His eyes are lined with sincerity, but I hope it's the drugs. I'm uncertain of what to say. If he had expressed this two months ago, then things may have turned out differently. But the truth is, I don't feel anything for Nate anymore. I care about him, but that's not equivalent, far from it. He's like family.

"Nate, please. Can we talk about this tomorrow?" I drop my head in my hands.

"Calla..."

"Please, Nate. Tomorrow."

He nods, unwillingly getting out of the car, and I lead him to the front door before driving back to the house. I remain in the car out front, the silence devouring me. My mind dashes a million miles an hour, and I'm incapable of decelerating. The familiar starry night sky is covered with clouds tonight, like my thoughts.

I can't decipher if Nate's words had any truth to them. It's an onerous topic to cast on someone, and I wish it's a misunderstanding. He couldn't be in love with me. Absolutely not.

Ace is reading one of his books on the couch, or so it seems. His body is positioned upright and stiff, as if he abruptly placed himself there when he heard the turn of my key in the lock. It's been a couple of hours since I left for the hospital, and what I've come to discover about Ace, is he's the most impatient person I've ever met.

His abysmal eyes meet mine, and he peers behind me as if checking for someone. "Where's the idiot?"

I roll my eyes at his impoliteness, placing my keys on the kitchen counter. I get a drink before answering, "I took him home after the hospital."

"Fucking pussy," he mutters under his breath. He shuts the book and flings it on the couch.

I narrow my eyes at him. I don't know why it surprises me anymore, his insolence. I should have become accustomed to it by now, but I haven't, on the contrary.

"Nate is my friend." I take a sip of the water and set the glass on the counter, the droplets trickling down it.

And he is, for now. I'll have to determine how to deal with the situation in the next few days, once Nate comes to his senses. It doesn't make sense for him to love me. Our relationship wasn't exactly all that, and he was the one who broke up with me.

"Friend my fucking ass. His hands were all over you," Ace grumbles, and he stands from the couch, striding toward me. His posture is rigid, and he crosses his arms.

His sweatpants hang low on his hips, exposing his v-line, and I promptly bring my eyes back up to his, but he's already detected me checking him out. A wry smile etches onto his face.

"Does that bother you?" I ask, referring to Nate. It visibly does, but I want to hear him say it.

"Does that bother me?" He scoffs. "Are you trying to provoke me?" he asks rhetorically, stepping even closer to me.

As if on cue, my heart beats rapidly in my chest. My body craves his touch, but I set my hand on his bare chest, stopping him in his tracks. I'm not going to forget about last night.

"Where did you go yesterday? You just disappeared."

He closes his eyes and pauses before opening them again. I wait for an explanation, giving him a chance, the benefit of the doubt. Ace doesn't appear to get the message that I'm giving him an opportunity for redemption, so I twist on my heel and head toward the stairs. I refuse to wait for him to develop excuses. If he believes I'll put up with this, he's dead wrong. I may like him a great deal. Maybe even beyond that, but I won't allow someone to walk over me.

I don't have the chance to place a foot on the first step when my entire body is lifted off the ground. He picks me up and throws me over his shoulder like I'm merely a rag doll.

"Ace!"

What the hell is his problem? He can't do this when he doesn't get his way. I'm staring at his muscular lower back and his ass, in fact, a very toned ass.

No, not the time. I'm irritated with him.

"Put me down!" I smack my fists on his ass, but it doesn't accomplish anything except summon a low laugh from him. The vibrations from it pulse through my body, heating me in ways that should be impossible.

Ace doesn't set me down until we're in his room with the door closed. My feet touch the cold hardwood. I stagger, losing my balance from being upside-down, and my back meets the door.

"Don't walk away from me, Calla."

The way he's watching me is demanding and hot. So freaking hot. The low light in his room causes his muscles to appear more defined and his jawline more prominent than it already is.

But I refuse to fall for his games. I strive to push him away with one hand, but I swear he's built of steel, because he doesn't shift. Not even a little. I try again and glare at him. He appears to get the message that I'm pissed off. He takes a step back but braces his hands on either side of the door.

He glances down at me, smirking. "Has anyone told you that you look like a beaver when you're angry? With those flaring cheeks and scrunched-up nose."

He's comparing me to a freaking rodent. Insulting me…right now? I can't take any more of this from him. Games, he's playing games.

I raise my hand to slap him, but he catches my wrist without even blinking. He leans closer to me, and as if on cue, the back of my neck tingles. His lips brush my cheek. "Wanna try that again, love?"

And even when I'm undeniably mad at him, the fireworks in my stomach explode from the endearment. "Ace, I told you I'm not a second option, and last night, you made me feel like I was exactly that."

His eyebrows furrow. If I didn't know any better, I'd say he seems apologetic, but it's Ace we're talking about.

"I had to go sort some shit out with Logan," he begins.

"Logan?" I echo.

"A friend needed my help. Logan wouldn't let her leave until she called me. He used her to get my attention."

His jaw stiffens, and he glides his hand through his hair before placing it back on the door behind me. I feel foolish for getting upset over this, but he should have communicated last night before leaving me to question everything.

I'm still in the dark about what's occurring between Logan and Ace, but I'm allowing Ace to reveal it on his own when he's ready to do so.

"I told you, you don't have any competition. You don't have anything to worry about. I only want you," Ace reiterates.

I only want you. I acknowledge the words. They flow over me like a river, and my body temperature rises. "You didn't even explain. You just left," I argue.

"I know. Fuck, I'm sorry. I'm not used to explaining my actions to anyone."

Clearly.

"But I will, for you. For us. I want this to work. When I'm with you, it's as though I'm able to think clearly, see clearly. I can't explain it…" Ace shuts his eyes as if he's struggling to find a way. But I understand what he means. The feelings are mutual.

"Calla… I-" he begins. I forget how to breathe. Ace shakes his head, clearing his thoughts. It's one of the minimal times that I've seen him lost for words.

"I know what you mean. I think of it as finally being able to breathe after drowning for so long," I convey the concept to him without realizing I'm revealing the depth of my feelings.

Ace takes a step back and stares at me as if to perceive me more clearly. "Exactly."

He sits on his bed, and I join him. The air in the room thickens.

"I wanted to ask you…" I stare at my hands as they become the safest things in the room. "Are we…" I'm uncertain of how to go about phrasing the question.

"When I introduce you to someone, what do I say you are to me?" I squeeze my eyes shut. It's unclear why I'm embarrassed. All I want to know is where I stand with Ace.

He takes my hand in his, stilling my fingers. A wave of peace sweeps over me, and I open my eyes. "Well, you could introduce me as your boyfriend. That is, of course, if that's what you want."

"Boyfriend?" I mull over the idea. My tone is steady. However, my insides are anything but. Perhaps this means a great deal to me because Ace has never had a relationship.

I lift my head to glance at him. His eyes twinkle in delight, a sensual smile is plastered on his well-proportioned mouth.

"I'm not usually the one to care for labels, Calla. This is a first for me, so please tell me if I'm going too fast for you. But I'd really like to call you my girlfriend."

"Hmm, is that so?" I ponder, stroking my fingers against the inside of his palm. His whole body stills, and I attain consolation in knowing I have the same effect on him that he has on me.

"You're really making me work for it, aren't you, love?"

My hand brushes up his arm and to his strained biceps. "I'm keeping you on your toes. Wouldn't want you to get bored with me."

He shakes his head and gently places both of his hands on either side of my face. "Not in a million years."

He inclines, and his mouth joins with mine, setting every inch of my skin into an inferno.

20

Stars Colliding

The soft sun trickles in from the curtains. My eyes are still shut as I scoot my back closer to the warmth behind me. The unusual feeling of being energized overcomes me. I don't recall the last time I felt this way when waking up. I don't open my eyes, wanting to savor this moment.

Someone clears their throat next to me. A familiar sound that I'd recognize anywhere. "Calla, can you not rub your ass on me?" Ace sighs, digging his fingers into my hip to halt my movements.

My eyes fly open, and I turn around, meeting Ace's intense stare. His dark hair is scruffy, and my hand reaches for it. I thread my fingers through it, tugging at the little curls gently. I've been sleeping in his room, in his bed, the last couple of nights, primarily because he insists.

I don't mind. I haven't had any nightmares when I usually get them at least every second night. Ace's company succors me, and I recognize my presence does the same thing for him. The dark shadows that frequently linger under his vibrant eyes have faded, and he's even more handsome.

It takes me a while to comprehend what he said, but my hand travels down to his boxer briefs once I do. My mouth curves into a cheeky smile, and he groans.

"Give me a second," I say. I rise and head for the bathroom. I wash my face and use my finger to swish toothpaste around my mouth since I left my toothbrush upstairs.

I lie on his bed and continue from where we left off two minutes ago.

"Fuck, Calla," Ace warns, gritting his teeth. He grabs my hand to stop me, but I'm not having any of it.

"Ace, good morning," I say his name in the most compelling way I can. I keep my hand *there* and move it against his substantial erection. He closes his eyes and groans in pleasure, delivering vibrations against every part of my body.

He drapes his hands around my waist and flips me, so I'm on top of him. Our lips fit effortlessly, as if they were meant for each other. I run my tongue over his lips, appreciating the fullness of them. His hands travel up my shirt, and heat thrives deep within my stomach.

I shake my head. "Ah, no touching," I whisper against his mouth.

He narrows his eyes. "That's not fair," he mutters, sulking.

"Shh." I bring my finger to his lips, ignoring his protests. His mouth opens, gripping it softly in-between his teeth. I wrap my hand firmer around *him*. He releases my finger, bringing his lips to mine in urgency.

"Calla," he whispers.

The desperation powers through his voice to use his hands, to touch me everywhere. It's taking him everything he has not to. I continue to run my hands over him, kissing his jaw, his neck—driving him insane. His hands fly up to me, and I swat them away.

"Fuck," he swears, getting irritated.

I sit up, drawing him up with me, straddling him. I finally place his strong hands on my waist, and his mouth twists into a sinful grin.

In that small timeframe, before his touch has the power to rupture me, every nerve in my body is electrified. It's as though I'm waiting for the inevitable, but each time it ends up being more than I envision. The anticipation of us being together in a way that is more than words, connecting on a different level, in an entirely intimate way, is exhilarating, to say the least.

Ace's hand voyages up my shirt, leaving my skin flushed wherever he touches me. The way my body responds to him, immediately and with immoral passion, compels me to believe he's the only one who deserves it. The only one who is worthy of it.

He removes my shirt and pauses. His eyes rake over my body, consuming me darkly. I hold my breath, allowing him to do so.

Ace skims his tongue over his teeth, and my heart pounds in my chest. My mind is in complete denial. It's not difficult to figure out that what I feel for Ace is more than I've ever planned to, more than I've ever felt for anybody before.

I tug at the waistband of his pants, letting him know that I want him right now. "Off."

He raises an eyebrow and chuckles. "Bossy, are we?"

"Learnt from the best," I retort, and he laughs, the sound low and seamless.

Everything about him is so damn faultless, and I'm falling too deep. Or have I already fallen? I can't tell. Too many lines have become blurred, and the only thing left is the veil of admittance.

Ace ignores my demand and kisses my neck, gently sucking. It feels too satisfying for me to even worry that it may leave marks.

And being marked by Ace won't be so bad, will it?

His hands caress my body, tugging me closer to him like he wants to eliminate anything and everything standing between us.

"Do you know what you do to me?"

Ace takes my hand and brushes his lips against the inside of my palm before setting my hand around his neck. I shake my head slowly, my arms are around his neck, my fingers in his tousled hair.

"You drive me fucking insane," he utters, his eyes on mine. "I want you." He grabs my hips, and his fingers dig into my skin. "Nothing else. Just you."

"Mmm," I moan, trying to pull his mouth back to mine.

He doesn't let me. Instead, he places his hands on either side of my face. "There's nothing I wouldn't do for you. I want you to know that. Do you understand?"

This forces me to pause. Ace has a way with words, they pierce straight into my heart, but I don't want to be let down. I'm cautious about depending on anyone.

"Calla, answer me," he orders, his eyes not leaving mine. Ace hasn't let me down. I trust him with everything I have, and perhaps, it's foolish for me to do so.

"Yes." *I understand, and I trust you. Please don't make me regret it.*

"Good," he says. Then his mouth is back on mine, more persistent than ever before. My lips are already swollen, and the ache between my thighs grows.

Amid all the kissing, we manage to get each other's clothes off. I run my hand down his bare chest. His beautiful light brown skin is my undoing. His body feels exceedingly familiar, like it's been mine all along. Ace gets a condom from his bedside table and rips the wrapper with his teeth.

I sense everything, this colossal magnetic field between us. Electricity. Power. Fervency. He's the only one who's ever made me feel like this, the only one who makes me feel like he's breathing fire into me. Lighting me alive. Can he feel this too, or is it one-sided?

Ace's arm wraps around my back and his hand tangles in my hair. His other hand moves down my cheekbone, skimming my lips, and that's when the senseless kissing begins again. He rubs his erection against me, lubricating himself with my arousal, and his mouth wraps around my nipple.

He enters me slowly, and we fall into one another at precipitous speed, like stars colliding, but two things can happen when a collision occurs. The stars either form as one, or they collapse into a black hole.

We lock eyes together, and I'm safe. He makes me feel calm, high on endorphins. And that's when I realize we're collapsing into a black hole. Because nothing that feels this good can last. And nothing can escape a black hole, not even us.

✦ ✦ ✦

"My mom is going to be home," Ace tells me nonchalantly when we're almost at his house.

"Your mom? I'm going to meet your mom? And you couldn't tell me this earlier?"

He shrugs. I chew on the inside of my lip until the taste of blood seeps into my mouth. I glance down at my outfit, fixing my baby-pink dress, I tug on the ends of my hair.

"Hey," Ace says, placing his hand on my thigh and rubbing it gently, sending a reassuring sensation throughout my body. "It'll be fine. She's going to love you."

"Callaaaa." The front door swings open, and Ellie's voice pulls me out of my anxious thoughts. She's wearing a peach-colored dress with feathers at the front, and small silver wings protrude from her back. She twirls in front of me before wrapping her arms around my legs.

"Hi, Ellie." I squat down to hug her, careful not to bend her wings.

"Hey! What about me?" Ace pouts and crosses his arms, feigning to be upset.

"Acy!" She laughs and jumps on him. He catches her, picking her up in his arms.

A woman, which I recognize as Ace's mom from the pictures, arrives in the doorway. Her dark hair is pulled back, and her eyes are bright, like the clouds on a summer day. She's wearing a dark blue uniform, and I'm assuming she's about to go to work.

"Hey, Mom." Ace hugs her with one arm and balances Ellie on the other.

"Ace," she greets him, squeezing him back.

"You must be Calla." She turns to me with a wholehearted smile. "Ace hasn't stopped talking about you."

It surprises me that Ace has been talking about me. What has he said?

"Mom! What the hell?" Ace glares at her, but she waves him off with one hand.

"Language, darling." She throws him a disapproving look before glancing back at me. "Come in. I have to head to work now, but Ellie is so excited for this party." She leads us inside.

The house is filled with a sweet scent, and I inhale deeper. A hint of vanilla with chocolate. I notice the cupcakes on the counter, some of which have pink icing and some purple. All of them have white wings on top, sprinkled with gold dust.

"Come on. We have to go! We can't be late," Ellie gushes. She grabs the purple-wrapped box off the counter and orders Ace to get the cupcakes. He shakes his head at her bossiness but does what he's told. At least someone can tame him. It's ridiculous that it's a five-year-old girl.

Bella's party is every girl's dream. Children race through the house, almost knocking us over as bubbles float in the air and balloons drift from corner to corner. A stack of unopened presents stand in the corner of the living room, and an enormous cake, four-tier cake, covered with pink and white icing, sits in the middle of the kitchen.

We follow Ellie as she eagerly runs outside to meet her friends, forgetting all about us. Outside is even more extravagant than inside. There's a massive unicorn jumping castle and a coat of pink glitter covering what used to be the lush green lawn.

Ace greets a few people, but since most of the adults here are middle-aged women, we spend most of the time in our own little bubble, watching Ellie play with her friends.

When the time comes to sing "Happy Birthday," all the children eagerly pile inside around the cake.

"Come with me," Ace says, taking my hand and leading me outside without anyone noticing.

"What are you doing?" I arch my eyebrows.

"You'll see."

He leads me to the jumping castle, and my eyes widen. "Ace!"

"Shhh." He places his finger to his lips and tugs me with him, inside the enormous jumping castle.

He begins to jump, and I laugh. He looks so out of place, but he grabs my hand again, forcing me to jump with him. I can't stop laughing. This is the most ludicrous thing I've ever done, but also the most fun I've had in a long time.

I'm struggling to breathe. I really must do more exercise. I lie on my back on the floor of the blow-up castle, not wanting to get up. Ace lies next to me.

"I think you're the best thing that I could've found," I say. I gnaw on my bottom lip, dropping my gaze.

Ace leans over me and takes my face in both of his hands. He leans down, placing his lips to mine. Pulling away, he brushes a loose strand of hair behind my ear. "You are your best thing."

I'm unable to pinpoint where I've heard that line before. I'm unable to think. I'm drowning in the deep sea of his eyes, and there's nothing else I'd rather be doing.

Ace is different. He's the only person that makes my heart happy. And he's the reason I'm smiling again.

He grazes his thumb against my lips. "I really *like* you," he emphasizes.

"I really like you too, Ace." My cheeks hurt from smiling.

"I think I may be entering the *like-like* zone."

"The like like zone? What, are we ten?" I raise an eyebrow, prompting him for clarification.

Ace chuckles, and his thumb travels from my lips to my jawline. His fingers are rough and tender against my skin.

"I think I'm—" But before he has the chance to finish, we are abruptly interrupted by the shouting and giggling of small children around us.

21

The Camping Trip

My eyes fly open, and I almost shoot out of bed. I adjust to my surroundings. Ace's room, Ace's bed, Ace's arms around me. Everything seems familiar, more than familiar. Perfect. I can't comprehend why I'm suddenly awake. I didn't have a nightmare. Nothing appears to be out of the ordinary. That is, until I hear the noise again.

It sounds like a car horn going off outside. What idiot would be doing that at this time of the morning?

Ace groans next to me, and I move his arm off me. I have a pretty good idea who this might be. I pull the first hoodie that I can find in Ace's room over my head and sprint outside. If everyone in the house is still sleeping, they won't be for long with the commotion in the front yard.

I swing the front door open to find Nate standing by his car, rubbing his hands together to warm up. He grins when he sees me, reaching inside his pickup truck to pull out a takeaway cup of coffee.

"What do you think you're doing?" I ask through gritted teeth.

My eyes are wide, and I wrap my hands around myself, shivering. The temperature must be below zero.

"Camping time, BABY!" Nate yells. His excitement at its peak. He's wearing long pants and a windbreaker jacket.

"Nate, it's not even six in the morning!"

"Early worm catches the bird." He wiggles his eyebrows. He comes over, handing me the coffee and throwing his other arm around my shoulders.

The cup is warm in my hands. I place my other hand around it, holding it close to my chest, hoping the warmth will emit through me. "It's the early bird catches the worm," I groan.

"Isn't that what I just said?" He raises an eyebrow. "Never mind. Are you ready? Where is your stuff?" He assesses my outfit and looks confused. "Did you not get my text last night?"

"Uh." I pause. I hadn't even checked my phone last night. Ace and I were sort of…busy.

"Calla!" Ace's voice rings through the house, his footsteps head toward us. I have an uneasy feeling about this. Nate isn't bothered, not even a little. On the contrary, he's thrilled. A big grin is plastered all over his face.

As soon as Ace spots Nate and me on the porch, his relaxed demeanor turns into irritation. I can't blame him.

"I swear this better be my imagination, because I'm about to beat the fuck out of you." Ace runs a hand through his morning hair in frustration. Still, his eyes focus on Nate before looking over to me and examining my outfit—his hoodie and my light pink sweatpants. A smile appears on his face, but it vanishes when his eyes land on Nate's hand around my shoulder.

"Hey, man." Nate lifts his hands in defense. "I was just picking up Calla."

Ace glares at him. I step between them just in case Ace becomes irrational. I don't intend to take Nate to the hospital again. At the thought of that, the memories from that night come flooding back to me. Nate and I still haven't discussed the little... incident, and I'm sure as hell not going to bring it up. I'm hopeful it was the drugs talking.

"The only thing you're going to be picking up is your fucking teeth off the ground," Ace grumbles.

"Ace," I warn. There's no need for him to be disrespectful to the poor guy. Ace shoots me a look that says, "stay out of this," but he can't possibly think I'm going to let them resolve this on their own.

"Nate, seriously. It's six in the morning."

"It takes about an hour to get there. I've allowed for an hour and a half just in case we run into traffic," Nate begins. I roll my eyes. There won't be any traffic at six a.m. on a Saturday morning, certainly not around here. It's not as though we live in the city.

Nate takes a breath and continues. "We'll stop on the way to get food, alcohol, and anything else you need. That will take another thirty minutes to an hour. So, we won't even get to the camping site till eight-thirty, and then we'll have to set up..."

I yawn, zoning out.

"We have to pick Mia up," I add, because he hasn't mentioned that minor detail in his specifically outlined plans.

"What?" he asks when I interrupt him.

"Mia... We have to pick her up, because she's coming with us." He can't have forgotten again?

"Oh, yeah, that's right." He sighs.

"You're seriously not considering going with *him*?" Ace snaps, and I glare at him.

I understand this is not an ideal situation, but I've already agreed, and I told Mia to bring a spare tent, because I refuse to sleep with Nate. Not after he confessed his love for me, on top of that, everyone else will be there—Liv, Zach, Theo, Josh. I asked Ace to come, but he hasn't given me a definite answer.

"Let's go, Calla. You did pack your bags already, didn't you?" Nate interjects, raising his eyebrows. Ace's body stiffens next to mine.

"Not exactly. It won't take long. Wait here." I turn to head inside, grabbing Ace's hand and dragging him with me. I don't stop until we get to my room.

I check my phone, which is on my bed and has been there since yesterday afternoon. Low and behold, there are almost twenty texts from Nate informing me that he's picking me up 'nice and early' and an extended list of things to bring. I'll give him points for being organized.

I ignore them and instead text Mia to get out of bed. I sincerely doubt she'll cope with the horn being blasted near her bedroom window at six in the morning as well as I did.

"You can't expect me to be okay with this?" Ace asks, noticeably frustrated at the entire ordeal.

"Come with us," I urge him, and he scoffs.

I throw sweatpants and hoodies into my duffel bag. It's not a time to look presentable, more like try not to freeze to death in your sleep. It's one of the many reasons I don't do camping trips, especially in this season.

"I don't know what you want me to do, Ace. I already agreed to go with him, and Mia is coming with us. I'm sure there'll be a lot of other people there. Liv and Zach said they're going."

"I still don't like it." He crosses his hands over his broad chest and leans against my door frame. His substantial figure consumes most of the doorway.

"I'm not asking you to like it," I reply, and he presses his lips into a stern line. I throw the last of my stuff in my bag and stride to the bathroom to brush my teeth and change.

Once I return to the bedroom, I collide with Ace's chest. His facial expression is blank while he strives to bury his anger. He's following my every move.

I want to make sure he understands that he has no reason to worry. Setting my hands on either side of his cheeks, I bring his face eye-level to mine. "Ace, it's two nights, and I'll be thinking about you the whole time."

His eyes widen, and he clears his throat. His reaction is exactly what I was hoping for. "You're not sleeping with him." His voice is low, and it comes out as a growl.

"I know." I smirk. "Mia is bringing an extra tent for us."

A smile swells on his earnest face. With his hands on my waist, he leans in. "Music to my ears."

I place a small peck on his lips and pull away, heading downstairs before Nate decides to search for me. Just as I thought, as I descend the stairs, I spot Nate's foot on the first step. "I'm coming."

"About time."

"Fucking idiot," Ace mumbles under his breath.

Nate draws my bag from me and walks toward his car. I take the coffee cup off the counter, following him. Ace shadows me to the porch, and he tugs on my arm, causing me to stumble back into his chest.

"What are y—" I face him, but I'm cut off by his mouth on mine. I know exactly what he's doing, and I sense the death glare that Nate is giving us right now. It doesn't bother me. If this makes Ace feels better, more secure, then I'm all for it.

The car door slams loudly, and Ace chuckles against my mouth.

The drive to Mia's house is crammed with awkward silence. I turn the radio on. Nate's car is only a three-seater, so I force Mia to sit in the middle. She doesn't mind, although she clarifies that she's not impressed that we woke her up at this time of the morning. Understandable.

Nate pulls up at the shops on the way. Mia buys more alcohol than food, and I have to remind her that we're only going for two nights. One if we're lucky.

"Do you think I should get more?" She tilts her head to one side. I'm hoping she doesn't get alcohol poisoning.

The drive there takes an hour. Nate is not his regular talkative self. Mia, clueless to what happened before she got in the car, rambles about how she doesn't want our tent to be close to the water. The university guys always pull pranks by dragging the mattresses into the lake while everyone is asleep.

When we finally arrive at the camping site, I'm surprised to see that many people from university are already there. They are setting up their tents, already holding bottles of alcohol, typical college behavior.

I spot Theo and Zach and motion for Nate to park next to their cars. When we drive toward them, my eyes widen. A smile appears on my face. Nate's hands tighten around the steering wheel. He rolls down his window, spitting outside, like that's going to keep his anger in check.

It doesn't take an Einstein to figure out what has induced Nate to become so riled up, or more like *who*. Ace's motorcycle is parked next to Zach's car, and he's leaning against it. He smirks when he spots us, I'm baffled. How did he manage to drag Liv and Zach out of bed *and* arrive here before us?

"Didn't you say Ace wasn't coming?" Mia questions when Nate

parks next to Zach's car. Nate grumbles something under his breath that I can't quite catch, so I choose to ignore it.

"I guess he changed his mind." I shrug. I'm not precisely sure what Ace is doing here. He told me this morning he wasn't coming.

"Changed his mind, my fucking ass," Nate mutters. This time clear enough for us to hear. I narrow my eyes at him. I'm trying my hardest to be friends with Nate, but he's irritating me. He doesn't have the right to act like this about Ace and me. I can see whomever I please.

"Or he was planning on coming all along." Mia ignores Nate and sends me a wink.

I open the door to climb out of Nate's car, with Mia following. Before I can even set foot onto the ground, Theo's strong arms are around me, pulling me out of the vehicle.

"Hey," I say, laughing. Over the short period I've known Theo, he's become like a brother to me.

"I'm glad you're here. I thought this wasn't your type of thing!" Theo squeezes me.

"It's not, but I guess I can make an exception."

Theo laughs and puts me down. "It'll be fun. You'll see!"

Maybe it won't be so bad, but the only reason I'm having a change of heart is because Ace is here.

Theo and Mia dive into a deep conversation with each other about what drinking games they'll be playing tonight. I walk toward Ace. The cold morning mist still lingers in the air, it seems colder here. That's logical since it's in the middle of nowhere.

"I thought you weren't coming," I say to Ace.

"Did you really think I was going to let Nate have his chance? Not in a million fucking years." He intertwines my hand in his warm one, lifting it to his mouth, and his lips skim against my skin.

"How did you get here so quick? You better not have been speeding," I jokingly chastise him.

"Me? Speeding? Never, love." He pulls me closer, and I go on my tiptoes to meet his lips. They are home and taste like the sweetest candy, rendering me delirious.

"Hey! Stop fucking and come help with the tent," Josh jokes. He attempts to playfully punch Ace in the shoulder, but it's as if Ace knows what's coming, and he pulls away, dodging it.

"I don't think you should be trying to sneak in hits on an experienced fighter, Evans. It's not going to end up well for you," Ace notes.

Josh raises his eyebrow as if offering him a challenge. Josh smirks and brings his fists in front of him, jumping up and down in front of Ace. Ace shakes his head but plays along, and I decide to leave the two children for their playtime.

Mia drags the tent and the blow-up mattress that she found in the basement of Brody's house off Nate's pickup truck and onto the grass. "Have you done this before?"

I shake my head. "Have you?" She looks at me like I'm insane and crosses her arms, sighing. This is going to be a long morning.

After what seems like an hour, we've only put the pegs into the ground. We've concluded that parts are missing. I look around. Mostly everyone has already finished their tents. Josh, Ace, and Theo's set-up looks incredible. Their tent is massive, and it has a small undercover area where they set a plastic table and chairs.

Nate has finished his set-up too. He strolls toward us with a grin.

"Do you mind helping us? You seem like you know what you're doing." I nod toward his car, where he already ensembled his tent on top of it.

He grins wider as if he was waiting for me to ask and immediately gets to work. It takes him less than fifteen minutes to set up the tent and blow up the mattress. Apparently, no parts are missing.

We spend the rest of the day watching the nuisance the lightweight university guys are causing, stripping their clothes and swimming in the half-frozen lake. I wouldn't be surprised if we'll have to call an ambulance for hypothermia cases.

By mid-afternoon, at least a quarter of them are already passed out in their own vomit. I don't understand how they call this fun. Some of the groups are coming together to start a bonfire. I watch from a distance. Nate disappears somewhere with his roommates, and I'm glad he's making friends.

When the sun sets, Mia hands me a plastic cup, and I'm surprised it wasn't sooner. I bring it up to my nose, take a sniff, and almost gag. She didn't give me straight-up vodka but close to it. Gross.

"What's this?" I grimace at the cup, sniffing it again.

"Vodka, raspberry," she answers, taking a sip of hers and not even batting an eyelid.

Theo and Josh set up red cups on the plastic table to play beer pong, and other people gather around our camping area. I guess beer pong is the crowd collector.

"Is there even any raspberry in here?" I ask, and Ace takes the cup from me, replacing it with his. Mia watches us intently but doesn't say anything, only giving me an eyebrow raise when Ace isn't looking.

I bring Ace's cup to my mouth and take a sip, tasting nothing but raspberry soda. I'm reminded of the fact that Ace doesn't drink.

The sunset here is beautiful. The way the scorching orange colors bounce off the lake is mesmerizing. I wrap my hands around my body to accommodate for the sudden decrease in temperature.

Ace notices this, he takes my hand in his and pulls me off my chair toward his own. He drops into the seat and gently takes me down with him, my back firm against his warm chest. He wraps his hands around my waist and rests his chin on my shoulder. We observe Theo and Josh bicker over who gets to throw the ping-pong ball first.

A few people look over at us, and I feel safe in Ace's existence. It's like nothing else matters, just him and me. I run my fingers over his arms. He tightens his grip around me, sending the warm-fuzzy feeling throughout my body. Camping isn't so bad after all.

Throughout the evening, between roasting marshmallows and half-watching drunk Theo skinny dip, I search for Ace.

Josh sits down next to me around the bright, vivid bonfire as it crackles. The flames dance below the moonlight, but the fire's heat struggles to reach me. I rub my cold hands together. Only a few people are sitting around it. Most of them are passed out on the plastic chairs, but the very few who remain conscious are too drunk to form coherent sentences.

I follow Josh's gaze toward the shoreline of the lake. I make out two figures laughing. The guy chases the girl and wraps his arms around her waist, pulling her into him. It must be the guy that Josh is secretly seeing.

"Did you talk to him?" I ask.

Josh meets my gaze and exhales deeply. "Yes. He says he's not ready to publicize our relationship, and if I can't accept his decision, then..."

"Josh...I don't think this is just about that. It might be part of the reason, yes. But if he didn't want to publicize your relationship, he wouldn't be doing that with other people." I nod in the direction of the shoreline.

He sighs, tugging on his hair. He doesn't meet my eyes, and it's apparent that he doesn't want to talk about this. I relieve him from the topic.

"Does everyone know that you and Theo are related?" I bring my knees up to my chest.

"No, not many people do," he explains, but he doesn't sound surprised that I know. "Everyone assumes something is going on between us, but no one really asks any questions."

"Does that bother you? That people might have the wrong idea about you two?" I don't tell him that I use to think that too until Theo told me they were half-brothers.

"It doesn't bother me what people think." He shrugs, and I wish I could have the same mentality.

I go to grab my bag of clothes from Nate's car but halt when Ace hops onto his motorcycle next to me, it roars to life. A few people glance toward us but quickly lose interest.

Ace looks at me as if waiting for me to hop on, and when I don't, he says, "Come with me."

"Where are you going?" I shift from one foot to the other, biting my lip in anticipation.

"We," he corrects me. "And you'll see."

22

Ace of Hearts

I've never understood what it feels like to be so consumed by someone that even the air around them feels like the purest air I've ever breathed. And I've never expected the collision of stars that slammed into me, defining the moment when I first met Ace.

My hands wrap around his waist, and my head buries in the crook of his neck as I hide from the frosty air nipping at my nose. It's hard to believe that I've only known Ace for a few months. It seems like we've been best friends our whole lives. The comfort, the pull toward him from the beginning, is nothing short of incredible.

We don't drive for very long, maybe fifteen minutes. Ace slows down the bike, and I finally lift my head, opening my eyes. The lampposts light up the unfamiliar town, and even though it's late, people are walking, relishing the fresh air.

We pull up in front of a small ice-cream shop. The building's exterior is light blue, and the bright pink neon sign that says *OPEN* hangs on the glass door.

Ace cuts the engine and climbs off the bike. He holds out his hand for me to take as if it's something we've become accustomed to, but the feeling that comes when I take it is anything but average. No matter how comfortable I find myself around Ace, and no matter how much time I spend with him, my insides always dance with flames when he touches me. A fire inkling to spread.

"Best ice cream you'll ever taste," he vows, a smile appearing on his face.

"You've been here before?" I ask when he leads me inside.

"I used to come here all the time with my father when I was younger." His tone changes at the memory to something sharp and desolate. I'm inclined to find out more about his childhood, about the things that made him happy. I want to be the person he can talk to about anything.

My eyes scan the ice-cream shop, it has a vintage retro vibe. The checkered floor tiles bring out the baby-pink tables and light blue seats. The young woman behind the counter, with glasses too large for her face, greets us. The variety of colors and flavors draw my gaze. There aren't just all the flavors but all the possible combinations too.

It takes me ten minutes to decide what I want. Ace doesn't complain. He waits with his hands wrapped around my waist, his lips occasionally brushing my temple.

Ace opts for a chocolate milkshake with cookie dough ice cream mixed through it. I assume we're going to sit in one of the booths, but he takes my hand, leading me outside. We cross the road, and I realize we're walking toward the park.

There are lights on the ground, illuminating the path, and he doesn't let go of my hand. Instead, he grips it tighter. I bring the ice-cream cone to my mouth, and before I have time to taste it, Ace pushes my elbow, forcing the ice-cream to smear around my mouth and on my nose.

"Ace!" I shoot him a look of irritation, and he flashes me a boyish grin.

His eyes sparkle under the streetlight as he turns to face me and walks backward, far enough so I can't reach him. "Payback." He winks.

I realize he's talking about the whipped cream incident. That doesn't stop me from frowning, and his expression changes, from amused to concerned. Ace stops in his tracks, allowing me to catch up to him with a few steps.

He reaches for me gently. My mouth twists upwards, and I bring the ice cream up, spreading it all over his handsome face. The look he gives me is priceless.

"Now you've done it." He grabs me by the waist, pulling me closer.

He leans down and kisses me slowly, his tongue sweeping the ice-cream from my lips. The combination of strawberry and chocolate is mouth-watering. But the way Ace kisses me is incomparable, compelling my body to ache for more.

He pulls away for a moment, gazing down at me, skimming his fingers down my cheek. "Hmm, strawberry. My favorite." He returns his lips back to mine.

"How did you get into fighting?" I ask when we're walking along the pathway.

"Back in high school, Logan was into it, and we used to always practice in his garage. I went to a few of his fights, and he convinced me to participate. It only became serious after my dad left. It pays a lot, and I needed the money to help out my mom."

I nod in understanding. "Do you just do it for the money?"

He shrugs. "It's a sport. It gives me exhilaration. It's a sort of high that intensifies every time, especially after a win."

I nod in understanding. I've never been a huge sports fan, but I appreciate the skill that goes into it. It's intense to watch.

We stroll around the rest of the park in silence, but it's enough just to be in his presence. Ace's shoulders are stiff, like there's something on his mind, but I don't want to pry if it's something he's not ready to share with me.

Once we make our loop around to his motorcycle, Ace smiles. He lifts me, surprising me, and sits me on the bike like I'm going to drive it. I've never done this before.

"What are you doing?" I ask him, but he doesn't answer. Instead, he brushes his lips against my hair and turns the key, making the bike roar to life.

"Ace, I've never—" I try to speak over the engine. He places the helmet on my head, and my heart races with excitement instead of fear.

"Do you trust me?" He takes my hands, placing them on the handlebars, covering them with his own.

"Yes," I reply. I completely trust Ace, and maybe that should terrify me, but all I can feel is anticipation.

"I got you," he reassures me, and with that, he rolls the throttle toward us.

The bike slowly takes off, and the cold breeze smacks me in the face.

I keep my eyes open, unlike the other times, and watch the road hover beneath us. Everything feels too good, too comfortable, like something terrible is coming. But I shake the thought out of my head, not prepared to ruin the moment.

It's not until we've been driving for five minutes, I realize we're not going back to the campsite. A straight road stretches beneath us, and Ace tightens his grip around my right hand, which is on the throttle, pulling it toward us.

The speedometer climbs—my heart climbs, too, with the rise of the arrow. We pass sixty miles per hour. I take a deep breath.

Seventy.

All I can think about is the closeness of Ace's chest against my back and the adrenaline racing through my veins.

Eighty.

The bright, full moon lights up our path, making everything clear as if we are driving in clear daylight. My hands tighten around the handlebars, and Ace's warm breath brushes against my neck.

Ninety.

Ace loosens his right hand, giving me all the control of the speed. He still maintains control of everything else.

I'm not sure what comes over me, but I crave to go faster. Maybe it's the adrenaline, or perhaps it's the way Ace makes me feel like I'm invincible. Like nothing bad could happen when I'm with him. Like we're the center of the universe, and it's just him and me.

And I twist the throttle, gradually increasing the speed up to one hundred. We're flying with nothing in our way except for the endless possibilities and dire decisions.

I go to accelerate even more. "Ahh, easy, love." His voice is low in my ear, propelling goosebumps across my arms, returning me down to Earth. He brings his hand back over mine.

The speedometer drops, and Ace rounds a corner, taking the motorcycle onto a gravel path. It's not long before we pull up to a large wooden cabin, and Ace cuts the engine. It's then I understand he was never planning on camping, and I don't mind it at all.

Ace jumps off and offers me his hand. We climb the stairs toward the entrance. He retrieves his phone, activating the flashlight feature, and heads toward the mat near the front door, checking underneath—searching for a… key?

Running a hand through his tousled hair, he checks under a pot plant.

"Fucking prick," Ace mumbles under his breath. He forms a fist, and before I can stop him, it collides with the small glass window near the door. The glass shatters, causing the security alarm to go off. "Fuck!"

"Whose cabin is this?" I panic.

Don't some security alarms call out cops? I sincerely hope we don't get arrested. If my dad hears about this, he'll flip. The sheriff's daughter breaking and entering. I assume this place is only about an hour from my hometown, so no doubt my dad would hear about it.

"My father's," Ace replies. I breathe out at least half a sigh of relief. Hopefully, that means he has every right to be here, but I doubt that's the case, since he didn't even have a key.

Ace opens the front door lock through the window and swiftly walks inside, reaching for the lights. "I have about a minute to enter the code for the alarms. Otherwise, it'll send a signal to my dad's phone."

"I hope you know the code."

He winks and flips the plastic guard screen over, typing a bunch of numbers. The alarm is disabled within seconds, and I exhale, letting my shoulders relax.

I glance around the cabin, noting the expensive furniture. The entire cabin is massive and looks even more spacious, with the floor-to-ceiling windows covering most of the walls. Luckily, Ace didn't try to punch those, although I doubt they would be susceptible to shattering. I also wouldn't be worried about anyone invading our privacy here. There's no one around for miles.

"Wow." This is no dinged-up place, and it's worth a lot of money. "I'm guessing we're not allowed to be here," I state instead of asking.

"No one will find out. I doubt my dad has come here recently," he tells me with bitterness in his voice. I peer to see his expression, but his face remains blank.

My gaze travels to his hand, which is bleeding all over the floor.

"Is there a first-aid kit?" I keep my eyes on his hand.

"I don't know. It's fine." He wipes the blood on the front of his dark hoodie and creases his eyebrows, examining his hand.

"There are probably glass shards stuck in there. Let me at least take a look," I say with concern.

He doesn't reply and, by the looks of it, doesn't care that he's making a mess on the timber floors. He strolls over to the couch and sits down. I open a few cupboards, searching for the first-aid kit until I locate it.

Ace shakes his head at me, but his mouth curves up when I make my way over to him. I stand above him, taking his injured hand in mine, examining it. Ace sets his other hand on my waist and pulls me toward him.

"Ace," I warn.

"Calla," he drawls my name in a low voice, my toes curl.

I ignore him and grab some tweezers out of the first-aid kit, extracting small bits of glass from his knuckles. Ace rolls his eyes, but he reclines, tugging me toward him. I sit on his lap while I examine his hand.

"He used to bring me here all the time," Ace begins, and I glance at him for a second. His eyes are distant as he recalls the memory. He's talking about his dad. I don't say anything, afraid that if I do, he'll stop talking.

"He told me this was our secret, and Mom can't know about it." His face shifts into something dark. I have a feeling I know where this is going.

Placing the tweezers back in the first-aid kit, I wipe his hand with the alcohol wipe again after I'm confident there's no more glass. Ace doesn't notice.

"Ends up, this is where he fucked all his girlfriends the whole time he and Mom were together," he sneers.

I stop what I'm doing to meet his eyes, they're full of pain and rage. I wish I could take all that away.

I run my hand over his cheek, and he catches it with his. He holds onto it tightly, like he needs to clasp something. Otherwise, he's going to lose it. Lose all the control that he's desperately been struggling to hold in.

"I was so fucking oblivious to it. Maybe I knew all along. I just didn't want to believe it."

"You can't blame yourself for that," I say, but he shakes his head as if not hearing me.

"He packed his shit when Mom was at work. Didn't even have the decency to tell her he was leaving," he continues, swallowing hard. The words are stuck in his throat—is this the first time he has spoken about it? I wait for him to continue. I can see that there's more. More to the story.

"He didn't fail to make it clear how much of a disappointment I was to him. All he ever wanted was a son to follow in his footsteps, but all he got was me. An ungrateful, imprudent party boy that won't get anywhere. I didn't care what he said about me." Ace shook his head. "The thing that got to me was that he didn't even acknowledge Ellie, like she meant nothing to him."

I don't know what to say. Ace was only a teenager when this

happened, and Ellie…how could a father leave his three-year-old daughter?

"I beat the fuck out of him before he left. Luckily, Logan got there in time. We got drunk that night. And that was the last time I touched alcohol."

"Ace," I say his name, but it emerges barely audible. My mouth is dry, and I squeeze his hand tighter. "Your dad sounds like a shitty father. He doesn't even deserve the title."

Ace forces a laugh, the sound satiates the space around us, and my heart clenches. "You got that right."

"Ellie is lucky to have you," I say. "She looks up to you."

Ace brings his mouth to mine and kisses me. His lips are soft and gentle. The kiss is different from all the others, slower, deeper, passionate, like he's afraid that I'll disappear.

I'm here, Ace. I'll always be here.

"Calla, there's something I've wanted to tell you about that night."

"Hmm?"

"When I got drunk—"

The phone ringing startles me, and I almost fall off Ace's lap. He steadies me with his hand, and I wait for him to answer it until I realize it's my phone.

I quickly fish it out of my pocket and glance at the screen, half thinking it's Nate or Mia wondering where I am. But I'm surprised to see that it's my dad. I look apologetically at Ace, silently conveying that I have to take this.

He gives me a reassuring nod.

I stand, walking toward the back door. "Hey, Dad, is everything okay?"

"Yeah, everything is fine. I was just calling to check up. I haven't heard from you in a while, and your old man is getting worried," he says.

"About to get your SWAT team here?" I joke.

"Do you need one, Cals?" he asks, seriousness in his tone.

I laugh. "No, Dad, definitely not."

He asks me what I'm doing, and I lie to him. I tell him I'm camping with friends. There's no way he'd be okay with me being alone with a guy, even though I'm eighteen, especially when I haven't even mentioned Ace to him.

After assuring my dad that I'm okay and letting him know I'll come to visit in a week or so, I finally get off the phone.

"You wanted to tell me something?" I ask Ace when I get back.

"It doesn't matter," he states, standing up. "Wait here."

Ace gets a few blankets from the closet and heads over to the back porch. There's a large bed that hangs from the roof.

"I always slept outside when we came here. My dad hated it." He sets the blanket down and lies on his back with his hands behind his head, waiting for me to join him.

His eyes catch the moonlight, sparkling. How have I ever known a world without him? How have I ever kissed other people, touched them?

Ace and I are so alike, yet so different in many ways. We've both lost a parent, but mine was taken away from me, and his walked out. We both blame ourselves for the mistakes that were, perhaps, out of our control.

He starts a fire inside of me, and I'm like the ice for his underlying ire. I'd like to believe we were made precisely for each other, to balance one another.

Tonight, the moon is more beautiful than the stars around it, like it's taking all the energy from them. I sit on the swinging bed, kicking my shoes off and sliding my feet under the blanket.

"Do you think a parallel universe exists?" Ace asks me.

I lay my head on his chest, and his arms around me are like everything I thought I could never have. I'm addicted to the way they make me feel—the way he makes me feel. He takes my hand and brings it above us, intertwining our fingers together.

"I believe there has to be something…life outside of Earth itself. Look at the sky and all the stars and tell me we're the only ones here. It's impossible," I answer, looking up, watching everything above us.

Ace squeezes my hand in agreement.

"Why stars?" I ask Ace, looking up at him. He looks at them like he wishes there's another life out there for him, another chance, or something else to believe in.

There's silence for a moment, as if he's trying to think of the correct answer.

"Look up and tell me you don't feel a greater sense of power, like nothing else matters. Like everything that we've been taught to believe in doesn't exist when you're looking at the never-ending constellations. Your pain and everything you feel turns into numbness, and you begin to question everything," he explains.

"I've done things that I'm not proud of. I've made mistakes that might catch up to me in the future. But lying here with you and looking up at the sky that holds so many unanswered questions and offers no answers in return, it feels like this is where I'm meant to be at this point. Everything I've done has brought me to this moment," he says.

And just like that, we lie there for hours, talking about absolutely nothing, but to me, it means absolutely everything.

I wake to the chirping of birds, but the spot next to me where Ace was last night is vacant. The smell of coffee urges me inside.

"Sorry, there's no food. We'll stop on the way home to get some breakfast," Ace says, handing me a cup of coffee and kissing my cheek. The shirt that he slept in last night drapes over the kitchen table, and if waking up to a shirtless Ace isn't heaven, then I don't know what is.

"It's okay. Coffee is okay." I smile.

We drink coffee together and leave shortly after. This time he drives the bike, and I'm grateful for that.

"What are you doing?" I ask when he pulls up next to an old building.

"Getting a tattoo." He winks before taking my hand and walking toward the narrow pathway.

We enter through a painted blue door. A heavily tattooed female in her twenties meets us. "Ace." Her face brightens in recognition.

"Becky." He returns it and faces me. "This is Calla."

"Hey," I say awkwardly.

Her eyes travel to my hand, which is still in Ace's, and her smile grows wider. "Glad to see you finally found someone worth bringing here," she says. "What can I do for you today?"

Ace tells her he wants another tattoo, and she leads us through to the back, seating him in a chair. Ace shows her something on his phone, and they whisper back and forth for a few seconds.

"Don't look at it until it's done," Ace says to me. Becky takes the tattoo gun in her hand after wiping his arm with an antibacterial wipe.

"Does it hurt?" I ask when it touches his skin.

"No, I'm used to it by now."

Of course he is, black ink covers his arms and chest. I keep my eyes on his face the whole time, and he doesn't flinch.

He shows me his arm when he's done. There are four stars, and in the middle of them is a moon. The crescent of the moon is in the shape of a *C,* and from the smile on Ace's face, it was intentional. He got a tattoo for me, and it's the most romantic thing anyone has ever done. The moon. The stars. The whole freaking universe. It somehow became our thing.

"I want one," I state.

"You want a tattoo?"

I nod, and he tilts his head to one side, considering my answer. "Okay."

"Can you wait at the front? I want it to be a surprise." I know what I want, but I can't explain it to Becky without Ace hearing it.

He raises his eyebrows, and I give him a pleading look.

"Fine," he says, raising his hands in defense and walking away.

The tattoo hurts more than I expect, and Becky tells me I picked the worst spot for pain. She's done within a few minutes, and I glance in the mirror before thanking her.

"Are you done yet?" Ace calls impatiently before walking back into the room.

I lift my shirt high enough to show him, on the side of my rib, near my left breast, is a small 'A' with a heart underneath it—ace of hearts.

Some people say it's stupid to get a tattoo of someone's name on your body, and I didn't go that far. Maybe the initial of someone that you've only know for a few months is stupid enough. But I never want to forget Ace, no matter what happens between us.

He has utterly consumed every part of me and made me believe in everything I never thought existed.

23

Black Hole

I've slept more this past week than I have in the last few months. No nightmares. I'm smiling more, laughing more. I don't have to pretend that I'm okay, because I *am* okay. I finally might be more than okay.

"I still can't believe you ditched me last weekend and slept in an actual bed while my blow-up mattress kept going down," Mia sulks, eating a sandwich. There are only a few people left in the café, and I subtly stretch my body.

"Didn't seem like you minded sharing a tent with someone else." I wink.

It didn't take long for Mia to tell me that Theo slept in her tent. She texted me on Sunday morning, demanding to know where I was, and didn't fail to pop that minor detail in. She was adamant that nothing happened. "What do you mean nothing happened?" I asked her on Monday at work.

"You know, just kissing." She waved her hand like it's a small detail that seemed pointless to mention.

I guess kissing for Mia means nothing. My mind wanders to

the day in her room. I doubt Theo thinks that it's nothing. He's been acting strange all week, asking more questions about Mia. And she's not 'that weird girl' anymore, as he used to say when referring to her.

"You know, someone has a crush," I tell Mia.

"I don't think so." As if on cue, Theo wanders into the café, heading straight for us. I smile at him, and he echoes it, but his focus is set on something else. *Someone* else. I wonder who it could possibly be.

"Hey, guys." Theo leans against the front counter. His prominent muscly figure takes up most of the space. I look over at Mia and raise my eyebrows, conveying that Theo does indeed have a crush. She ignores my glance.

"Hey, Theo," Mia replies.

Theo shifts from one foot to the other. "Uh, did you want to go to the movies or something next week?" he asks Mia. His usual confident, playful self is nowhere to be seen. I haven't seen Theo like this…nervous.

Mia considers this for a few seconds. My and Theo's eyes don't leave her. She looks at me, scrunching her eyebrows together, before looking back at Theo. "Sure! We can go to the movies. Calla would love to come too," she adds.

"I would?" I ask, confused. I glare at Mia, trying to silently convey that this isn't what Theo had in mind. She ignores my subtle glances once again.

"Yeah, of course. Invite Josh. Maybe Liv and Zach could come too, and Ace?" Mia says to Theo.

"Uh." Theo scratches the back of his head. He opens his mouth like he wants to say something but dismisses it. Instead, he replies with, "Um, yeah, sure."

"Cool, it's a plan," Mia chirps and stuffs the remainder of her sandwich into her mouth.

Theo stands at the counter, glancing around, and turns to head out. "I'll see you later, then. I'll go tell the others."

"Yeah, see you," I say, giving him an apologetic smile on Mia's behalf.

"What was that?" I ask Mia when Theo leaves. He's obviously confused by what happened, as am I.

"What was what?" she asks.

"Is he not your type?" I persist.

"Mm, he's everyone's type, Calla," Mia replies nonchalantly like it's a no-brainer, and it isn't. Not with Theo's looks.

"Then what's the problem? He was clearly trying to ask you out," I tell her, but I'm positive she already knows. She's not stupid.

"And I agreed." She locks the front door after the last customer leaves.

"You invited the whole damn squad, Mia. I don't think that classifies as a date."

She shrugs. "Baby steps."

Whatever the hell that's supposed to mean.

It's Friday, and Ace has gone to see Ellie for the night. His mom is working a night shift. I would've loved to go with him, but I've already skipped two weekends of work. Even though Brody hasn't said anything about it, I don't want to seem unappreciative of this job.

Tomorrow is the big fight between Ace and Logan. Even thinking about it makes me nervous, and I'm not the one participating in it. Everything could go wrong.

I lie on Ace's bed, since I've practically moved into his room. It's more realistic, as I'm always in here. His room is much bigger than mine, and don't get me started on the size of his bed. It also means I don't have to share a bathroom with Liv and Zach, who knows what kind of stuff they like to do in there. I've witnessed them coming out together with red faces. It was either a steamy shower or, well…a *very* steamy shower.

My phone lights up with Ace's name. "Hey," I answer the Facetime call.

"Callaaaaa," Ellie sings into the phone, her bright green eyes looking into the camera, and she moves it so I can see her pajamas.

"Ellie, I love your onesie!" It's bright purple with a unicorn hoodie.

"It's my favorite. Acy bought it for me," she states. Ace takes the phone off her.

"Go get ready for bed. It's late. I'll be there in a second," he tells Ellie, his tone softening for her. She pouts but obliges, waving bye to me. I wave back.

"Are you in my bed? Wearing my shirt?" Ace asks when Ellie is not in the room anymore.

"Mm, yeah." I gently bite my lip.

"Are you doing that on purpose? Do you have any fucking idea what that does to me?" Ace asks. His hair is dripping wet, and his body glistens with the droplets. I assume he had a shower.

"How about you tell me?" I smile and lean back onto the headboard. I slowly pull up the shirt, watching Ace's face tense in anticipation.

"Acyyy, I'm ready for my bedtime story," Ellie calls, and a smile forms on my face. She's so cute.

"Fuck," Ace swears.

"Goodnight, Ace." I end the call before he has time to respond. I'm certain that he'll be calling me back later, once Ellie is asleep.

I'm bored, and I find myself not ready to go to bed yet. I pick up a book that's on Ace's desk and read the back of it.

Looking out into the darkness through the sliding doors, I'm unable to see anything. It's peculiar how my life used to be precisely this way. I wasn't able to grasp anything beyond the dimness of the past. Even though everyone kept signifying things would improve, I couldn't comprehend how it could possibly get better.

I was trapped in the inscrutable shadows, looking back on it instead of seeing the future. And now, I accept the past. I find myself welcoming what the future holds for me. Perhaps, I can even say that I'm excited about it.

I turn and spot a scrunched-up piece of paper next to the trash, like Ace threw it here from his bed but missed. I pick it up off the floor with the full intention of putting it inside the trash. Curiosity gets the better of me, and I unfold it, careful not to tear the page.

When I realize it's a page from Ace's journal, I want to throw it in the trash—I don't want to invade his privacy. But that changes when my eyes unintentionally skim over his writing.

I read the page once. Twice.

Three times.

I don't register it at first, not wanting to believe it. There must be an explanation, this can't be real. I'm being sucked into one of my nightmares. Sucked into a black hole.

My body shakes, and my lungs contract, not letting any air through. I physically cannot breathe. My mind runs at a million miles per second, thinking of every single scenario, of every single damn clue. This must be a mistake.

The last few months race through my head at full speed, and my vision blurs.

Stay out of my way.

Breathe in.

I need you to hate me.

Breathe out.

I'm not good for you.

The floor spins beneath me. I struggle to keep my balance.

I don't drink.

I squat down and place my head in my hands. I close my eyes in hopes that I'll wake up. But I don't, because this isn't a dream. It's much worse.

I'm a monster.

Ace's words hurtle through my head as I piece bits of the puzzle together. Everything makes sense, but I try to find another explanation. Anything that may vindicate this.

My heart hammers inside my chest. I keep reading the page that's filled with Ace's handwriting over and over until my hands are shaking so much that I can't focus on it anymore. My stomach flips with each word.

I reach for my phone and fumble with the screen. I can't control my shaking hands, so it takes me a minute to find Ace's contact.

"Did you miss my voice already?" he picks up. His voice, which usually provides me with solace, now delivers anguish.

I try to breathe so I can form words. Anything. The only way for me to believe this, is to hear it directly from him, and I can't wait until his return. I need to know now.

"Is everything okay?" he asks when I don't reply.

Everything is far from okay. "Is it true?" I finally manage to ask.

"What? Calla, are you okay?"

I open my mouth, but I can't say it. The words are stuck deep in my throat. Instead, I say, "I found a page from your journal."

Silence. A clear indication that he knows what I'm talking about. I want, no, I *need* him to tell me that this is not what it seems. I need him to prove me wrong.

"Fuck, Calla…"

"Is it true?!" I'm frantically begging for an answer.

"Let me explain…" Ace begins. But there's nothing to explain, it's a simple question.

"Answer me." My voice breaks. I hope with everything I have that this is a misunderstanding. The silence is killing me, and Ace's breathing deepens. A whole minute feels like an hour.

"Yes."

My heart shatters. I collapse onto my hands and knees, my breathing shallow and quick. I hear Ace's voice through the phone, but I can't focus on anything he's saying. I need to get out of here, out of his room. Anywhere but here, away from everything that's him.

Without complete control of myself, I manage to get to the front door without collapsing. I step outside, and the chilly breeze wraps around my skin—dragging me into its despair. The air out here is easier to breathe. Nevertheless, my lungs burn with every inhale and exhale. I don't realize I'm crying until my vision goes blurry again.

I look up at the sky to clear the tears that are now flowing, but instead, numerous vermilion shooting stars invade it. They're bright and illuminate the whole atmosphere in unimaginable ways.

The stars will burn in flames.

24

The Admission

A day ago, everything was different. But it all can change in the blink of an eye—life keeps reiterating that for me in more ways than one. It keeps exhibiting that nothing stays the same, and the more I attempt to hold on, the more it damages me in the process.

For the last two years, I've obsessed over this moment countless times. I've thought about all the things I'd say to my mother's killer if I came face-to-face with them. I laid awake countless nights staring into the hollowness and visualizing what could have been instead of what was.

My mother's case was a simple one, or so they say. The other car never hit us. My mom swerved off the road before we collided head-on. The experts said if we had crashed with the other vehicle, I wouldn't have survived the impact. I would've ended up like my mom.

They never found the other car, but it was evident from the whiskey bottle near the scene it was a case of an uncontrolled drunk driver. The fingerprints didn't match anyone on file, and there was no other evidence. They had little to no suspects and no witnesses except for me. I wasn't any help. I couldn't remember anything.

The case was a dead end, and even though my dad pulled every resource out of the book, worked every hour of the day, we never obtained answers. We had to live with the unknown.

"He's in the shower. He's been there for over an hour," Josh says. He paces in front of Ace's bedroom door.

Theo called me twenty minutes ago, frantically explaining that I need to come to the house immediately.

"We don't know what's wrong with him. He let Logan beat the shit out of him in the ring today. He didn't even try," Theo says with disbelief.

"Okay," I say and place my hand on the door to push it open.

"Hey," Josh says, stopping me. "I know he might have screwed up. Fuck, it's Ace, he definitely screwed up. And I don't know what's going on between you guys, but I've known him all my life, and I've never seen him act like this with anyone before."

I nod, not having the energy to say anything in response, and enter Ace's bedroom. If only Josh knew.

Ace doesn't acknowledge me when I open the shower screen, he doesn't even blink. I get in, fully dressed, and hold back a yelp. The water is scorching hot. It's like getting the shit beat out of him wasn't enough punishment. I turn down the hot water, making it bearable to an average person.

He's sitting with his head down, bowed between his knees, his boxer shorts still on. He makes no indication that he knows I'm here. Maybe he doesn't. He's too deep in his head, punishing himself over and over.

How many times has he done this? I've had little time to think about it, to really consider the situation. Everything has fallen into place—the non-drinking, the PTSD episodes, Ace warning me to stay away from him. He truly believes he's a bad person, and under different circumstances, I would too.

For years, I've convinced myself that the person who did this had no sympathy and no heart. How could they live with themselves after what they did, without owning up to it? But everything is not what it seems, especially when you only know one side.

The water pounds on his back and drips down his hair softly. The glass shower screen is thick with steam—suffocating us, pulling us into unfathomable veracity. It's compelling us to face reality.

I kneel in front of him, the water soaking my shirt and pants. Finally, he lifts his head. His eyes meet mine as he leans his head further into the stream of water. They are swollen but, nevertheless, still hold the vibrant blue and green. His face is covered with dried blood, and I almost reach out to touch him but stop myself.

It doesn't feel real. All this time, I believed I'd have closure if only I found out who caused my life to be thrown upside-down. Now, staring into the depths of the person who caused the tragedy, it's not what I'd imagined. There's no closure, or anything close to what I thought this moment would entail.

There's only heartache and grief.

Grief for my mother. Grief for this relationship, whatever it was. Grief for everything I was ever made to believe. But most of all, grief for the loss of the person I am when I'm with Ace, because I'll never be that again.

No one can ever make me feel the way he does, but no one can ever break me the way he has, either. The worst thing is, I blindly trusted Ace with everything that I had. And he showed me why I shouldn't have.

"Ace," I find myself saying.

He opens his mouth to speak, and the blood trickles from his lip. No sound surfaces, and he drops his head.

I don't say anything else. I don't know what to say. There are no words in the world that could do this situation justice. Instead, I grab the bottle of shampoo and pour it into my hands. I lace my fingers through his hair, scrubbing it gently, feeling it one last time against my skin.

My clothes weigh me down, but I wash the dried blood off his face. Pouring the body wash into my hands, I lather his neck, shoulders, and the arms that I've come to appreciate over these last few months.

He watches me. His blank eyes, devoid of hope, search mine for something I can't provide at this moment, or maybe ever. Forgiveness.

It breaks my heart to see him like this. Broken and empty. But what did he expect would happen? It would've been easier for both of us if he'd stayed away from me.

After I finish washing him, we sit under the shower stream. The silence is laced with every unspoken word, every emotion. How did it come to this?

I finally started to be happy again, and then the light was crushed quicker than it came. I've been thrown into the ocean, and I'm drowning once more with no one left to rescue me.

Standing, I offer him my hand. He glances at it but doesn't take it. Instead, he pushes himself off the shower floor and stands. I lead him out of the shower. I hand him a towel, getting one for myself from the cupboard to my left.

"Why are you here?" His voice comes out gruff, and for a few seconds, I'm taken aback.

"Did you want me to leave?"

He shakes his head in frustration. "Calla, you should hate me.

You should be yelling at me, you should be on your way to the police station or calling your dad to tell him. But instead, you're here, fucking washing me."

He's right. I should be doing all those things. But none of them will alter anything. They may, perhaps, even make the situation worse, if that's even possible.

I shrug and head out of the bathroom. I have some of my clothes in Ace's room from the last week, so I change into a dry t-shirt and jeans.

"I need to know the truth," I say firmly when he emerges from the bathroom.

He nods but doesn't look at me. The silence before he begins talking is deafening. My hands tremble in anticipation. Even though I have an idea of the events that he's about to recite, nothing can prepare me for the words which tumble out of his mouth.

"It was the night my dad left us. I wasn't in the right state of mind. Logan and I went to his house, and we drank. A lot. Logan could see my pain, and he offered me his dad's Chevrolet..."

"I didn't think anyone would be on that road. I've never seen anyone on it when it's that late," Ace says. He squeezes his eyes shut, as if the memories are too much, the pain too insufferable.

I can't stop thinking that none of this would've happened if I didn't make my mom turn around. We would've been home before sundown. Neither Ace nor I would have gone through such a traumatizing experience. Where would we be now? How different would my life be? Guilt pierces through me, a feeling that I've grown accustomed to over the last two years.

"I was driving too fast. The road was icy. I lost control..." Ace's voice shakes, but he continues. "From this point, I only remember bits and pieces. I remember getting out of the car. I remember dialing 911. I wanted to stay until the ambulance came, but Logan pulled me toward the car. He kept saying, 'think about Ellie, think about your mom.'"

He places his head in his hands. Affliction throbs throughout the room, brushing up against me and spiraling both of us into undeniable gloom.

"I wanted to turn myself in, but I couldn't…because of Ellie. My father left, and I couldn't leave her too. My mom only started her job at the hospital then, she wasn't getting paid much, and I knew my father wouldn't leave a cent to us," he explains.

My chest is constrained with his admission. My heart and mind are twisted against each other and ripped apart, forced to separate in times of conflict. I understand the battle Ace had to face, the decisions he was forced to make after his transgression. But it doesn't pacify the hollowness in my chest.

It's challenging to inculpate him for this. I anticipated that coming here tonight and hearing what he did to my mom would make this easier. I hoped it would make me hate him. I don't, and that hurts the most.

"There was a time when none of that mattered. A year after the accident, I was going to turn myself in. I called Logan to give him a heads up, but he talked me out of it." Ace swallows the lump in his throat.

"Does anyone else know? Apart from Logan?"

"Zach knows."

Of course. It all makes sense now. Zach has been distant with me, and he's the only one who knows how to deal with Ace's episodes. Pieces of the puzzle come together. Everything is more blatant than ever before.

"How could you spend time with me? Share intimate moments

with me? This 'you and me' bullshit, Ace. Were you ever going to tell me, or were you going to write it in your stupid journal? Maybe even write one of your autobiographies based around it?"

My voice is raised, and tears prickle in my eyes. I'm over crying. I'm over feeling helpless. I'm over feeling like this, for two damn years. I'm so tired of everything. Each screwed-up thing that keeps happening to me.

"I didn't know how to tell you."

"How about, 'hey, I caused the car crash that killed your mom'…this… finding out like this, after everything we've done together…it's like this was all a twisted game to you." My voice breaks, and I inhale deep breath. I have nothing else to say. I'm numb, but at the same time, everything hurts.

I can't think straight. I'm all over the place—stuck in a nightmare, unable to claw myself out. My tears are aching to get out, and my ears are bursting with the sound of my throbbing heart. There's warfare inside of me. I bite the inside of my cheek and push the tears back.

Ace drops to his knees in front of the door. "Calla, I'm so sorry. I'll do anything. I'll turn myself in…anything."

My heart tightens at the sight of him. I attempt to swallow the lump at the back of my throat, but it doesn't fade. I've never imagined that I'd see Ace in this position. Certainly not when I first met him. I tell myself to keep breathing. That's all I can do.

My feet move toward him. I place my hand on his cheek, savoring this moment—it's the last time I'll let myself do this. The warmth of him underneath my touch electrifies me. His regretful eyes find mine, and he places his hand on top of my own.

"You're not a bad person. You simply did a bad thing. You committed a crime. I don't think turning yourself in is going to achieve anything. You already suffer enough." I mean every single word that comes out. I had all night to think about this, yet it doesn't make it any easier, on the contrary.

"And I don't hate you...but I can't be with you. I can't see you. I can't be your friend. Every time I'll look at you, I'll see the person who took away my mom. I don't want to despise you, because what we had was good, even if it was all built on lies."

I trusted him more than anyone else. Ace knew all along. Knew me, knew what he did. And still, he let me fall into the cavernous despair of him.

Breathe. In. Out.

"Calla...everything was real. You and me, *we are real...*" he begins, but I shake my head.

There's nothing he can say that will change this. There are no actions that can be taken to mend this. And there's nothing more that I want at this moment than to rewind the clock.

I drop my hand from his cheek and force myself to put one foot in front of the other. I head out the door, leaving Ace on his knees—pleading for forgiveness. I don't think I'll ever face anything more difficult in my life.

That is until I hear the three words that make my heart clench in my chest. They make my breath hitch in my throat. They almost make me stop and go back.

Almost.

"I love you," Ace says.

The tears that I've been holding run down my cheek. And when they come, they don't stop. How many times can a heart break? Has mine ever been whole to begin with?

I can't do anything to yield this pain. My heart has been ripped out of my chest and crushed. I attempt to compose myself until

I'm out of that damn house, wishing that I never came here in the first place. Wishing that I stayed at home with my dad, believing that the person who took away my mom is a monster. Because this, knowing that Ace was the driver, hurts me more than anything ever did.

My vision is blurry, and I don't know where I'm going. All I know is that I need to get as far away as possible from him. But it's hopeless to run from the feelings that are breaking me apart piece by piece.

The streets are empty, with the occasional headlights shining my way. I keep walking, putting one foot in front of the other, letting my mind run wild. Thinking of every clue I missed this past fall, everything that has led up to this. How did I let my guard down this much? How did I fall in love with the person I hated for the last two years?

Without realizing that I was heading in this direction, I find myself in front of Mia's house. I don't have anywhere else to go. I can't go home to my dad, because he'll know something is wrong, and telling him about Ace—about everything—will do more damage than good. Maybe my judgment is clouded by the unnerving thoughts of Ace and the way I feel about him, even after finding out the truth.

"Baby girl." Mia opens the door. Her eyes fixate on me. "Oh, no." She wraps her arms around me, and that's what makes me break down completely. Sobs erupt from deep inside my chest, and I can't seem to get enough air into my lungs.

"Breathe, breathe." Mia rubs my back and squeezes me even tighter.

I haven't cried like this before. I'm drowning in my own tears, and no one can pull me up to the surface.

"I don't have…anywhere to go." I manage to get the words out in between the crying.

"You can stay here for as long as you need. Come on, let's get off the porch." Mia leads me inside and toward her room. "I'll get you a glass of water." She turns around to head to the kitchen.

"I love him," I admit out loud, not sure if I'm talking to myself or Mia.

She turns to me and holds my hand. "I know."

"But I can't be with him." I'm trying to convince myself, because all I want to do right now is pretend like this isn't real. I want to believe that Ace isn't the one who took my mom away from me.

"No. You can't rely on him to heal you when he's the one who broke you."

And I guess that's what I've been doing. I lost a piece of myself when my mother died. Ace mended that piece when he came into my life, or at least I thought he did. It turns out he was the very one who took it away in the first place. In the end, nobody can heal me except for myself, no matter how firm the bandage of love is.

I curl up on Mia's bed and cry. I cry for the girl who thought she was finally getting better. I cry for the guy who is as broken as me and made a poor choice. I cry for my dad, who'll never find out who took his wife's life. And finally, I cry for the sake of everything I've ever believed in.

Epilogue

2 MONTHS LATER

They say time heals all wounds, but how much time is enough to heal the countless ones of mine? Or am I a lost cause, with time being an irrelevant factor? Perhaps I have to face the fact that not everyone will get a Band-Aid or a cure for their lesions. And even if they do, a scar will always remain. A reminder in the form of a twisted memory of what you once faced embedded into your soul.

I've barely stepped foot outside in the last two months, and the only people I've had a decent conversation with are Mia and, occasionally, Brody. But he doesn't talk much, and when he does, it's intense and vague. I don't want intense and vague. Why can't anything be frank and straightforward for once?

Ace left for Palm Valley University, which is more than a four-hour drive from here. Good for him. It reiterated that I made the right decision for both of us. Would he have taken the opportunity if I made the decision to stay with him? Would I have allowed him to sacrifice his future for me?

It's pointless to think about alternate realities and what could have happened instead of what did. I made my choice, and I'll stick by it.

Ace isn't a bad person—I've always known that. From the first time I met him, his energy radiated a warm light clouded by the darkness surrounding it. He made a grave decision at the age of seventeen, and he's suffered for it every day since. But it's one thing to forgive and another to forget. With time I can forgive Ace, but I'll never be able to forget. How could I?

Mia offered to let me stay with her and Brody for the remainder of my university years. At first, I was hesitant. I didn't want to intrude, and two-and-a-half years is a long time to live with someone. But they had a spare room, and I convinced them to let me pay rent. Somehow that made me feel better instead of living there for free.

I focused on my college work. I handed in all my assignments on time and put in the extra hours of studying. I also got offered the position of the university newspaper editor. Apparently, the previous editor had other duties to fulfill, and Dean, Mr. Howley, was impressed by my consistent effort. He said I was the most dedicated student he's ever encountered, especially in my first year.

It's not hard to understand why. I busied myself tremendously, busied my mind in every way I could so my thoughts wouldn't wander to him. If that means spending hours doing extra work, writing papers, and editing articles, I'm happy to do it. Mainly when the stakes are high. My dream to live in New York City is only an arm's reach away. I've fixated a tunnel vision, and I'll do everything it takes to get there.

I spent Christmas with my dad and Nate's family. It was fine until Nate decided to put his two cents in. I assumed he was still bitter about everything that happened between us.

"What's wrong, Cals?" my dad asked me when I helped him

with the chocolate pudding.

I was about to make up some lie about not doing well on my exams, but Nate beat me to it. "She broke up with her boyfriend," he said, and I shot him a look of frustration. He's been a little cold since he found out I was acting like this over Ace. But he doesn't know the whole story. No one does except for Zach—he can't look me in the eye and avoids me like the black plague. I don't blame him. Ace had no right to throw such a burden on Zach—forcing him to keep a traumatizing secret that he had no choice in.

"A boyfriend? I wasn't aware of any boyfriends..." My dad rubbed his beard. I had to spend the rest of Christmas night convincing him that there was no boyfriend and managing to give Nate a cold glance now and then.

Brody eyes me up and down when I walk into the kitchen. "You headin' out today?" he asks in a raspy voice.

"Uh, yeah, I think I might go to a few classes. Get the rest of my stuff from the house, too," I say, unsure of how it's going to go. I have to start getting back into the routine of normal, whatever that is. I haven't known what normal is for a long time.

"Y'know, maybe you should have some green stuff before you go. It will get rid of the nerves," Brody says casually, barely giving me another glance. He's making his famous vegemite on toast, which is the grossest thing I've ever tasted. But he claims that me and Mia "don't know what's good for you, even if it hit you in the face."

It's not news that Brody smokes weed, but it's the first time he's offered any to me. He usually keeps to himself. If I didn't move in, I would've never known that he suffers from PTSD from his accident, and the "green stuff," as he calls it, helps him.

"I'm jokin', Calla," he says when I keep staring at him with wide eyes.

"He's not," Mia chimes in, and I manage to give her a small smile. She's the only person who's been there for me, day-in, day-out. It's nice to have someone who knows what you're going through even when they cannot help.

"I can get your stuff if you want," Mia offers. She must have overheard me.

"It's okay. I think I need to do this myself." I chew on the inside of my cheek.

I haven't stepped inside that house since I left Ace that night. Mia brought me some of my textbooks and clothes. The thought of going back there sends excruciating pain through my chest. It's all in my head. It's the fear of everything that I left behind—all the memories floating in that house waiting to invade my mind. I couldn't bring myself to do it until today.

I read one of my mom's journals. From start to end, not just a few words here and there. I figured it was time to give up something to receive something in return. I gave up the possibility of losing my mom to receive her words of wisdom and the power they held. I couldn't have chosen a better time.

At first, I thought it was going to be her life dictated on paper. In some ways, it was, in other ways, it was more than that. Her thoughts, feelings, perception of life, and everything combined was there for me to dissect. It helped me understand that the world is a cruel place, even though I already knew. But it also provided me with optimism, for now, and for the future.

Her words gave me a reason to continue pursuing more. Always more—some pages resonated with me more than anything.

Nothing can stay the same. We're all part of a changing power that twists and turns us in unconceivable ways until we experience it for ourselves. There may be harsh and eccentric lessons to learn, but they are all a reminder that nothing stays the same—not even when you want it to. Every so often, that can be something to look forward to, and other times, it's something we shy away from. Nevertheless, take everything as it comes, for it's a gift to be able to move through time and experience what the universe offers you—no matter how forbidding it may seem.

In some ways, it seems like my mom wrote the journals for me. It's like she knew this moment would come when she wasn't here to provide me with motherly guidance. And yet, I can't help but imagine the struggles that she went through herself to have the need to write that.

I step out outside and inhale the crisp, cool air. I glance up at the sky, and snowflakes fall on my face, melting when they meet my warm skin. The blanket of snow that surrounds the streets is soothing. I stand for a moment with my boots squeaking beneath me at every slight movement.

A blue butterfly catches my attention. I stare at it in amazement and reach toward it. It lands on me. Where could it have possibly come from in the middle of winter? I glance behind me. Perhaps it was stuck in Brody's house, and I let it out?

I blink. Once, twice—and it's gone. The only reminder of it is in my mind. Am I genuinely going insane?

Maybe I don't believe in omens, or fate, or any of that nonsense. But at this moment, it truly does feel like my mom is watching over me.

The memories flood through me when I walk into the old bedroom that I spent only a few months in. My hands tremble as I frantically pack all my stuff into the suitcase that I brought with me at the start of the semester. I can't fathom an extra second in here. The memories, the smell, the small reminders. It's all too much—too much of him.

My books, my clothes, everything I can find, I throw it all into the suitcase vigorously. For a moment, my eyes flicker toward the bedside table, and I make my way to it.

On top lies a pink sticky note. I squeeze my eyes shut, afraid to read what is scribbled on it. Taking a deep, shaky breath, I open my eyes and let myself skim the words that will be entrenched in my mind for the rest of eternity.

Maybe we'll meet again in another life. When the stars align.

ACKNOWLEDGEMENTS

It's impossible to sum up in one paragraph how many people I would like to thank. So, I want to start off by acknowledging my amazing partner for putting up with me while I wrote this book. Thank you for listening to me, even though I sounded like a broken record. Thank you for brainstorming ideas with me when I experienced writer's block.

Thank you for always believing in me.

I also want to acknowledge all my online readers for making this happen. Thank you for pushing me to finish Ace and Calla's story. Thank you for adoring them as much as I do. Without all of you, there would be no book.